# You Make
# Me Feel

# You Make
# Me Feel

*Monica Walters*

www.urbanbooks.net

Urban Books, LLC
300 Farmingdale Road, N.Y.-Route 109
Farmingdale, NY 11735

You Make Me Feel

ISBN 13: 978-1-64556-588-8
EBOOK ISBN: 978-1-64556-589-5

First Trade Paperback Printing March 2024
Printed in the United States of America

10 9 8 7 6 5 4 3 2 1

*This is a work of fiction. Any references or similarities
to actual events, real people, living or dead, or to real
locales are intended to give the novel a sense of reality.
Any similarity in other names, characters, places, and
incidents is entirely coincidental.*

Distributed by Kensington Publishing Corp.
Submit Orders to:
Customer Service
400 Hahn Road
Westminster, MD 21157-4627
Phone: 1-800-733-3000
Fax: 1-800-659-2436

# You Make Me Feel

*Monica Walters*

*Hello, Readers,*

Thank you for purchasing and/or downloading this book. This work of art contains explicit language, lewd sex scenes, moments of grief/depression, and other topics that may be sensitive to some readers.

This book is also a spin-off of *Stuck On You* by Monica Walters. While it isn't necessary to read that book before reading this one, it will flow a lot better if you do by clarifying certain situations mentioned in this book that I don't go into great detail about.

Also, please remember that your reality isn't everyone's reality. What may seem unrealistic or unrelatable to you could be very real and relatable to someone else. But also keep in mind that, despite the previous statement, this is a fictional story.

Kinisha and Oliver's story is beautiful, no matter how it starts. LOL. So, I hope you enjoy the ride this story will take you on.


Monica

# Chapter 1

## *Kinisha*

*That man knows he is too fucking fine.*

"Sorry, Lord," I whispered.

We were in church, and I could never stop my mind from drifting. Jarod was sitting his fine ass over to the side, near the deacons, while his father delivered the sermon. Our pastor had gone out of town, so the assistant pastor was preaching. He wasn't as great a preacher as Pastor Adolph, but he was still good. I suppose it didn't matter how good he was if I wasn't listening.

I closed my eyes for a moment and took a deep breath. The devil was busy. This was probably a sermon I needed to hear. However, that Godiva chocolate had me so damn distracted. I loved a medium- to dark-complexioned man. I wasn't too fond of yellows, but he could get my attention if he were fine enough. I was trying not to discriminate since my internal clock had started ticking.

I was only twenty-four, but by my age, my sister, Kiana, had found her forever. They'd gotten married, and now, she was pregnant. Although I knew I shouldn't be comparing my journey to hers, I couldn't help it, especially since my mama brought up my single status every chance she got. *When are you going to settle down? The constant dating has to be tiring.*

How in the hell did she think I would find my forever if I weren't dating? Secondly, they were totally against who Kiana had chosen to settle down with because he was twelve years older than her. They'd resorted to kicking her out of the house to get her to do things their way. My sister stood up for herself and didn't let them deter her future with Lazarus. I loved and admired how strong she was, although I also had doubts in the beginning.

I wasn't as strong. I moved out of my parents' house when I started working as an accountant for Mr. Taylor at Taylor, Wesin, and Sylvesters Accounting Firm. He paid his employees well, and I could move out within three months of working for him. I did my best to respect my parents' home. However, what they didn't know didn't hurt them. I never fucked in their house, but I surely fucked everywhere else.

We were a Christian family, and when my mama found out Kiana and I were no longer virgins, she nearly lost her mind. At the time, Ki was twenty-four, and I was almost twenty-two. She should have been happy that we were educated young women who loved God and had never given them any problems. We always did what they told us to do, but the minute Ki decided to do what she wanted, there was a problem.

Lazarus was very respectful, and he loved Ki. While even I was hesitant about their relationship, Kiana was sure. She knew he was the man for her, and, eventually, we didn't have a choice but to respect it, or we would have lost her forever. I would have never let my doubts about them come between us, though. My sister was my best friend. I was concerned about Lazarus's intentions, and as her friend and sister, I felt I could voice those concerns. After she assured me she knew what she was doing, I backed off and supported her decision.

My parents fought her tooth and nail. My mom broke first. After so much time passed without even talking to Ki, it took a toll on her. She was trying to keep a united front with my dad, but it had become increasingly difficult. When she folded, so did my dad. They had no choice if they wanted a relationship with their oldest daughter.

So it turned out that Kiana was right. She knew who and what was best for her life, but here I was, still struggling. I wanted Jarod to be that man. He had to know I was flirting with him. Whenever possible, I walked right in front of him, being sure to sway my hips just right. He was a few years older than me, so we didn't grow up together. When he was a senior in high school, I was barely in middle school.

However, I was grown as hell now. His being thirty didn't mean shit. That was only a six-year difference. As I stared at him, his eyes met mine. Since I didn't have a shy bone in my body, I didn't look away. His ass wasn't as holy as he pretended to be, but I didn't know if he knew I was well aware of that fact. He continued to stare back at me, probably thinking I would look away first.

When I didn't, he licked his thick lips . . . slowly. *Mm. He wants this sex appeal I'm serving.* He'd finally noticed . . . or at least shown *me* that he'd seen my subtle flirting. He was the deepest shade of medium chocolate a man could get before being dark chocolate. I was so damn thirsty as I got lost in his gaze. He licked his thick lips again, and I knew I would have to go to the bathroom to clean myself up.

I was so happy Ki wasn't here today. She would have distracted me. Her morning sickness was about to take her out. Laz stayed home with her and catered to her needs. He'd finished school and was working for an investment firm. He only worked weekends when there was some special event. My mother had retired, so if Ki needed help tomorrow, she would probably be there for her.

When I stood from my seat, I lifted the Baptist finger, which expressed my apologies for walking, and made my way to the restroom. I was sure to strut like I was on the runway because I knew he was watching all this ass. It was rare that I wore loose clothing. If I did, it was somewhat revealing. It would either show off my legs or my cleavage. Today, I wore a bodycon dress. It covered all my skin but exposed every curve.

I wasn't a skinny chick by far. I was thick and had ass for days. The older traditional women in the church probably rolled their eyes every time they saw me, but I didn't give a damn. Surprisingly, neither of my parents had a thing to say either. They must have learned their lesson after the fiasco with Ki. They gave me a hard-ass time when Ki first moved out, but they got over themselves after a couple of months.

I thought I was gonna succumb to the pressure, though. They were literally going through all my things like I was a teenager. When I got home one day and saw my mama going through my underwear drawer, I nearly came unglued. I had to walk back out and cool off. Kiana walked away from my parents, but she had Lazarus. I didn't have anyone to have my back . . . just a bunch of random fuck buddies, except Braylon and his sister, Ramsey. They'd moved out of their parents' house and had offered me a place to go, but I couldn't find a job in time.

As I went inside the bathroom, I nearly ran into Ramsey. My mind was still on Jarod's fine ass, and I didn't even see her coming out. "Girl, who got yo' attention? Because watching where you're walking doesn't seem to be a priority."

I chuckled. She and I used to go out together sometimes. She'd settled down, though. Her boyfriend, who'd recently become her fiancé, seemed perfect . . . in the beginning. They'd been together almost a year now, and she always bragged about the romantic things he did. I was happy for her, but I kept my eyes open. I had to look out for my girl. She was so in love with Robert's ass that she wouldn't notice the small signs saying something was up. That was okay, though. That was what she had me for, and I definitely saw some questionable shit. But until I had solid proof, I would keep my mouth shut.

"I was too busy daydreaming about Jarod. I had to come in here to get myself together."

She rolled her eyes. "I don't know why. You know what he does. He's the male version of Jezebel around here."

I took a deep breath. "I guess I'm the modern version of her then. It ain't like I'm celibate."

"Naw. He's a player. Y'all ain't the same. He sells promises of love and devotion only to get what he really wants. Be careful with him."

I nodded. I knew what Jarod was about, but I was practically about the same thing. Maybe he wasn't boyfriend material, but I wasn't innocent either. I needed to experience him for myself. I needed to experience him sexually. If that was all that came out of it, then so be it. My curiosity would be satisfied.

She left the restroom, and I went to a stall to mop up the spill between my legs. After washing my hands, I walked out and ran right into someone. I swore I needed to pay attention to where I was going. When I looked up, I smiled politely. It was a man I'd seen in church a few times. Our church was rather large, so I didn't always see him. He put his hands at my waist to steady me so I didn't bust my ass on the floor.

"I'm so sorry, sir."

"Oliver. No problem, ma'am."

"Kinisha."

He removed his hands and extended one for me to shake. I did so and offered him another smile, then walked away. He was okay looking. His dark skin was a plus, but he had a somewhat funny-shaped, bald head. His eyes had stayed on mine the entire time. It made me a little uneasy. Usually, I didn't mind attention from guys, but there was something kind of innocent about him. I could see it in his big, expressive eyes, even through the black-framed lenses he wore. Maybe it was the fact that he looked sort of like a computer geek. He had the look perfectly. The glasses and plaid shirt really set it off.

Before returning to the sanctuary, I looked back and found him still standing there, watching me walk away. There was something slightly intriguing about him. I couldn't put my finger on it, though. I would have never paid attention to him before I ran into him. He just didn't have the looks that would grab me. He wasn't ugly by any means, but he was extremely low-key.

When I returned to the sanctuary, Rev. Speights was wrapping up his sermon. As I sat, I noticed Jarod's eyes on me. *Mm-hmm.* He wanted me just like I wanted him. Since he knew of my interest, I would let him make the first move. Giving my attention to Rev. Speights seemed to be the best thing to do because if I didn't, I would be making another trip back to the restroom. That man was my undoing. If I wasn't careful, he could be my downfall too.

Once service was over, I grabbed my things and immediately headed to my car. I'd gotten a message from Ki asking me to come by before I went home. My apartment was on the other side of town, and she lived along my route. Just as I was about to open my door, I heard my mother's voice.

"So you were just gonna leave without speaking to me?"

I turned to her. "Hey, Mama. Sorry. Ki texted, asking me to stop by before I went home, so that was where my mind was."

"It's not anything serious, is it?"

"I don't think so. At least, that wasn't the vibe I got from her text."

"Okay. Well, we're about to head to Longhorn."

"Okay. I'll call you later."

She kissed my cheek as she hugged me, then said, "Okay, baby."

After she walked away and I got into my car, I saw Jarod. His eyes were on me, and his gaze nearly took my breath away. I thought he would approach me, but he turned in the opposite direction and walked away. I supposed he wanted to take his time. I didn't know why. It wasn't like he wasn't familiar with who I was. We'd been members of Antioch for forever. While we'd never had a conversation, we knew the particulars, or at least I did.

Since I was obsessed with his sexiness, I expected him to think the same of me. I could be very wrong about that. He could be showing me attention now because he knew I was feeling him, and he was planning to take advantage of that. Whatever the reason, I had a feeling I would soon find out.

When I got to Ki's house, Lazarus was outside with grocery bags in his hands. I smiled as I exited the car and approached him to help.

"Hey, Nisha. If you could grab the keys and unlock the door, I can handle the rest."

"Hey, brother-in-law. Are you about to cook?"

"Yep. Your sister wanted meat loaf."

I rolled my eyes. Kiana loved meat loaf. I believed she was starting to love it more than she enjoyed a good steak.

Lazarus chuckled at my verbally silent but very loud response to what he said. "Hey, na. Watch it. That's my baby, and she can have whatever she wants, especially since she's carrying my child."

I chuckled as I unlocked the door. If I had a man that loved me as much as Laz loved Ki, I'd be doing well. That was all I wanted. While I was in school, I wasn't looking for anything serious. Unlike Ki, I wouldn't have been able to concentrate on school while being in a serious relationship. I would want to spend all my free time with my man. Now that I was ready, it seemed love wasn't ready for me.

When I walked to the front room, Ki was on the couch, wrapped in a blanket, watching TV. "Hey, sis. How are you feeling?"

She looked up at me and smiled. "Hey, girl. I'm feeling okay now. I can't wait until this morning sickness is over. Next week, we will find out if we're having a boy or a girl. I'm way too excited about that."

"Aww, yay! I hope it's a girl. What are you hoping for?"

"Same. I wouldn't know what to do with a little boy."

"And that's when his father would step in," Lazarus interjected. "I'll be happy with either. I'm just happy to be able to experience fatherhood. I'm damn near forty."

"You still have a couple of years, baby," Ki said.

"Whew. You getting up there, old man." I giggled as he side-eyed me. "I'm just picking, Laz." Turning back to Ki, I asked, "Why did you want me to stop by?"

"Ramsey texted me. She said you were talking about Jarod's ho ass. Leave that nigga where he is."

"Aww, shit. I think he's fine as hell. I just wanna find out for myself what he's working with."

Even with two warnings from people I trusted, my curiosity was beyond piqued, and there was no turning back. Jarod would get all this curiosity wrapped up in a huge, hot-pink bow. Ki rolled her eyes. "Suit yourself. Can't say you weren't warned. Warning comes before destruction."

"Or sometimes, love comes from it," I responded as I glanced at Lazarus.

Her gaze softened as she followed where my eyes had gone. "You're right, but Lazarus didn't have a bad reputation. He was just older and more experienced than me. Totally different, Nisha. But I'm not here to judge you or beat you up. Do you, and I'll still be here for you if you need me. You know that."

"I do. Thanks, Ki."

She and Ramsey had always been my ride-or-die friends. I appreciated them more than either of them knew. Their support meant the world to me. I sat beside her, lifted her feet onto my lap, and massaged them. Her eyes rolled to the back of her head as I chuckled. She was so overdramatic. I loved the hell out of my big sister, but I couldn't heed her advice. Jarod was going to get all this size-sixteen body—every inch of it.

# Chapter 2

## *Oliver*

My mind was all over the place when I got to my cousin's house for Sunday dinner. Kinisha Jordan had slightly been in my arms for a couple of seconds. That woman was the entire reason for sitting where I sat in church. Besides going to hear the word, having her in my view was the best thing going. She was so damn beautiful. When she bumped into me, it afforded me the opportunity to feel just how soft her body was.

She stared at me like she was trying to read me, but her taking a final glance at me before going back into the sanctuary gave me hope that she saw something memorable in me. I'd been watching her for a while, long enough to know she was feeling one of the ministers' sons. Jarod Speights was one of the biggest hoes our church had to offer. It was like he came to church strictly to prey on vulnerable women.

I'd been a member for nearly five years and had immediately noticed Kinisha. She seemed kind of young, though, so I kept my distance, watching her mature. She used to appear to be playful, and she laughed a lot. I knew she wasn't in high school, but she didn't seem too far removed from it. It wasn't that I was super old. I'd just turned thirty but was far older mentally than physically.

I graduated from high school at sixteen from North Shore High School in Houston and got my bachelor's degree in computer science at nineteen from TSU. I also obtained degrees in computer information systems and business management. I was hella smart, and it was a turnoff for some women. That just meant I was pursuing the wrong women.

In high school, I barely got any play. Being the valedictorian didn't help. Girls in my grade were older than me as well. My thick Coke-bottle glasses back then were a nuisance that my mama couldn't seem to understand. So, I tended to stay out of people's way so I wouldn't be noticed. When I *was* noticed, it wasn't good attention. It was so that I could be bullied or talked about.

After getting to TSU and getting turned out by a girl wanting help with a paper, I hit the gym hard. That shit was a confidence booster like no other. Now, women said I was cocky. *Go figure.* My body was sculpted like God had taken the time to mold it himself, but it couldn't be seen most times. I rarely wore short-sleeved shirts, unless I was at the gym. For work, I wore long-sleeved dress shirts.

I owned an information technology company. Different businesses contracted us to handle their computer systems. We maintained the hardware and software, and my company built a reputable reputation in Beaumont and the surrounding areas as it had in Houston. I wanted to relocate to a less busy area. While I still had the office in Houston, I moved here five years ago to start another office.

My parents were instrumental in my success. They'd been saving money for me since I was a baby, and the day I turned twenty-three, they handed me over a hundred grand. That was how I started my office in Houston. The success of the company had made me a rich man. Most people didn't notice that at first sight. I dressed modestly, but I was anything *but* modest. When asked, I wasn't bashful about boasting about my accolades.

I worked hard to get to where I was, and I'd be damned if I were going to let anyone make light of the time and effort I'd put in over the years. People seemed to think that this shit was easy. Getting my name out there and convincing people to trust me took a lot of free labor. I had plenty of sleepless nights trying to find new ways to market myself to a market that was oversaturated in the first place.

As I sucked the meat off these tender-ass ribs, my cousin's friend said, "Shit. Some lucky woman would be extremely happy."

I closed my eyes and slowly shook my head. I swore Shannon was a handful. She was in her late forties or early fifties and married but never hesitated to flirt. Instead of responding verbally, I stared at her and sucked the barbeque sauce from my fingers.

When she started fanning, my cousin, Anise, said, "I wish you would quit teasing her ass. You about to give her heart palpitations. Second, I don't like the picture you're painting. Eww. You're my cousin, and I don't wanna see that shit."

I chuckled. "I couldn't help it. Shannon, if you were younger, I'd give your husband a run for his money."

"Shiiiid, I can outrun these younger women. Don't fuck with me, boy. I ain't took my medicine today. I'll have you screaming in that bathroom."

I laughed so hard I nearly choked. Every time I was around Shannon, it was the same shit. She had some type of mental disorder because of the abuse she suffered as a kid, and Anise told me that she was a handful when she didn't take her meds. She was introduced to sex at a young age and had become an addict. I wasn't sure what medication they had her on to tame it, but she often joked about not taking it.

I hoped I never had to be around her when she hadn't because I wouldn't be able to fight her off for long. She was beautiful, and her husband had to be extremely trusting or understanding of her illness. I'd fuck her for sure, but I did my best to abstain from casual sex with women I saw no future with. Now, Kinisha's ass, I'd rub that shit just right. I could imagine a future with her, but I would settle for casual sex until she saw what I saw.

As I ate my food, Anise and Shannon continued discussing some interior design Shannon was working on. When I finished my greens, I brought my plate to the sink, rinsed it off, and then loaded it in the dishwasher. "And he cleans up. Can you cook, baby?" Shannon asked sweetly.

"Shannon, focus," Anise yelled.

I laughed, thanked my cousin for the food, and then went to the other room to turn on the basketball game. It was getting close to All-Star Weekend, and I planned to be there. It was in Houston this year, so I would be near an office if I had to work. I owned a loft in Houston just in case I ever had a long day. I could just stay the night. I wished my parents were still alive. They were up in age when my mother got pregnant. My dad was in his late forties when I was born, and my mama was forty-two.

They called me their miracle baby. My mother was told she couldn't conceive for reasons I didn't remember, but according to her, God had other plans. They spoiled me rotten, but they also made sure that I was afforded the best education I could get. I got to high school when I was twelve. They decided to keep me there for four years so I could mature a little more before going to college. Otherwise, I could have graduated at fourteen or fifteen.

My mama had said that God had given me the gift of knowledge. Some things that I knew, I didn't even know how I knew it. I just did. Things I thought were common sense were difficult for most people. It wasn't until I was a college sophomore that I realized my mother was right.

However, there were some things that intelligence couldn't quite help with—matters of the heart. It couldn't make a woman love me. It helped me notice quickly when a woman I thought I was compatible with wasn't interested. I'd given up on love for a while. It seemed to be eluding me anyway. However, I'd been craving it for the past couple of years. I think it started when my mother died.

She was one of the only women in my life who genuinely loved me. Many of my family members, except Anise, only wanted what they could get out of me. I discovered just how lonely I was without her. My mama was my best friend. My dad was too. He died seven years ago of a massive heart attack. My mama died of a broken heart. Now, I was in this world, navigating it alone.

Anise had a boyfriend, so most of the time, she was busy. The only reason I was chilling here today was because he was out of town on a business trip. He wouldn't be back until Wednesday. I honestly thought he was a fuckboy, but she loved his crusty ass. Judging her personality and demeanor, I knew she would defend him at all costs until she caught him for herself, so I kept my analysis to myself.

As I watched the game, I couldn't stop my mind from going back to Kinisha. I didn't know how to ask her out, but I had to shoot my shot. I had to see if she was semi-interested. That was if Jarod didn't make a move first. I wanted to roll my eyes at the thought. Her milk chocolate skin tone spoke to me. It constantly said, *"Oliver, come eat me."*

To say she was young, she had a few gray strands in her hair, and that shit was sexy as hell. The small gap between her two front teeth added to her personality. She knew she was sexy as hell. I could tell by the way she strutted. Her thick lips were perfect for sucking and getting sucked, and her nose ring added to her sex appeal. Her slanted eyes and high cheekbones gave her exotic features that I could drool over all day, every day.

She looked somewhat lost today without her sister. They always sat together, and her sister seemed to be the more mature one. She was also older. I remembered when she participated in graduate Sunday about two or three years ago. Kinisha graduated the year after her. I wished I had shot my shot then. I didn't know what I was waiting for. I was reserved but never intimidated. While I was a little nervous about how she would respond, I had no problem speaking my mind.

"You're quiet over there. You good?" Anise asked.

"Yeah, I'm cool. I'm probably gonna head out in a few minutes. This game is a blowout, so I already know who will win."

"What are you about to go do?"

"I'm gonna go get ready for my week. I have to make a trip to H-Town to check on the office and make sure everything is running smoothly. What'chu got going on for the week?"

"Well, Shannon has us booked to redesign an entire house. I can't wait to look at it and get started."

"That's what's up. I'm gon' have to get y'all to do my house. I think it's outdated, so it can use a touch-up."

"Oliver, just say you want me in yo' space, baby boy. I'll be in that thang with bells on."

"Don't have WJ knocking your head between the washer and the dryer, ho," Anise yelled, then laughed.

Shannon joined her and said, "You know WJ my baby. I ain't fucking up no more." She turned her attention back to me. "If you're serious, call the receptionist to set up a consultation."

*No more?* So she'd cheated before, I assumed. If he was still fucking with her after that, he was man of the decade as far as I was concerned. "Shit, we consulting now," I said with a frown.

"I know I clown a lot, but I'm a professional when it comes to Jameson Taylor Interior Designs. So handle it like you don't know me. It keeps me organized."

"I guess. I'll call tomorrow."

I stood from my seat, preparing to leave. I walked over to Anise and kissed her cheek. "Thanks for dinner. I won't be good for anything but sleep when I get home. I got too full."

I walked over to Shannon and gave her a side hug as Anise said, "You're welcome. Call me tomorrow because I need help picking out a new computer."

"We could have done that while I was here."

"It's Sunday. We're off. I don't believe in working on my off days. I have plenty of other shit to do to keep me occupied."

I rolled my eyes. "A'ight. I'll holla tomorrow around lunchtime."

"Okay. Be careful going home, Oliver."

I gave them a nod and headed to my car. When my phone rang, I pulled it from my pocket, knowing it was probably Anise. "Hello?"

"I fixed you a to-go plate. I forgot to give it to you."

"Shit, I'm on my way back in."

She knew that I would be hungry later and would end up eating fast food. I knew how to cook, but I hated cooking on Sundays. I wasn't really all that fond of cooking for just me anyway. It took me by spells. My mama had taught me everything she knew about the kitchen. She said I needed to be able to cater to my woman when I got one. Hopefully, those skills would come in handy sooner rather than later.

After getting my food from Anise, I headed back to my car. My house was only about ten minutes from hers. I knew that once I got home, I would end up working. I often found myself doing that because I didn't have shit else to do. Loneliness was a horrible beast to endure. I briefly thought about getting involved in one of the ministries at church to get me out of the house and interact with more people.

My people skills were decent, but I only talked to customers. My only friend in college had moved back home to North Carolina, got married, and started a family. We kind of fell off after that. I was always the one calling, and I didn't want to be that friend who didn't know how to take a hint. So I backed off, thinking he would call me whenever he had time. I guess he never had time. I hadn't spoken to him since my mama died and, before that, since my father passed.

He'd probably seen my status on Facebook to know they'd passed away. To say I wasn't popular in school, many people had shown up to offer their condolences. I was touched by their concern for me. A couple of them had even messaged me on Messenger to see how I was holding up. I appreciated that more than they knew. When my dad died, I still had my mother to lean on. When she died, I had no one.

Anise had been there for me, but I was the type of nigga who held in his emotions until he was alone. I had a bad habit of saying I was okay when I really wasn't. I found that it was typical behavior for men. We were afraid to admit we were weak. My dad did it all the time. I told myself that if I ever got close to anyone else, I would be truthful concerning that, but it would definitely have to be someone I trusted.

When I got home, I set my food on the stove, then went to shower, fantasizing about the beautiful woman I kept from busting her ass on that hard floor. I couldn't get her face out of my mind. It had been a long time since I'd been practically obsessed with a person. I wasn't obsessed to the point where I was stupid over her, though. I had enough sense to know that I needed to take my time with this one.

She seemed more outgoing than me and wouldn't have a problem telling me exactly what she thought of me. I needed to have my ducks in a row and know exactly what I would say to her. My mind was already coming up with possible responses to whatever questions she could ask. The obvious questions would be simple, but other questions, like why I wanted to go out with her, could be asked. I wouldn't hesitate to answer, or she would call bullshit quicker than I could count to five.

Next Sunday, I would make sure to be where I needed to be to talk to her. I couldn't let her escape any longer. She had to be mine.

# Chapter 3

## *Kinisha*

I was in the office reviewing a financial plan for one of our clients. The day went by quickly because we'd been busy the entire time. Mr. Taylor had taken on two more clients, and we were stretched to our limits. However, he knew that we could do it. I loved working for him because he didn't hesitate to get in the trenches with us to ensure we met deadlines and handled our clients' businesses efficiently.

After tweaking some numbers, I set the folder to the side. When the door opened, I looked up to see Mrs. Shannon walk in. She was Mr. Taylor's sister-in-law and was married to his brother, but she was also his wife's sister. She was funny as hell and loved to give Mr. Taylor a hard time. "Hey, Kinisha. How's it going?"

"Hey. It's been busy."

"Devin is a fucking overachiever. He and Sidney married each other for a reason. I always have to tell them I'm not set up like them. They will work themselves to death and think everybody else wants to do that shit too."

I chuckled. Every time she came in here, it was the same shit. Before I could call Mr. Taylor to the front, he came down the hallway. "Hey, Shannon. What'chu doing here?"

"I came to get my statement to pay these damn taxes. I wish I could tell Uncle Sam to kiss my fat ass."

"Uh-huh. You do that, and Big Bertha gon' be kissing your fat ass too. Keep it up," Mr. Taylor said.

She cut her eyes and playfully pushed him. I was twice her size, so I didn't know why she always said her "fat ass." She had a nice shape, and her butt was slightly bigger than proportionate. I wouldn't say it was fat, though. I could clearly tell she worked out by the definition in her arms. I went to the filing cabinet to get her folder and handed it to Mr. Taylor.

"Thank you, Nisha."

I nodded and returned to what I was doing while they talked about their weekend. I didn't want to come to this job this morning, so I was grateful the time was flying by. Last night, I'd tossed and turned nearly all night, trying to get comfortable and get my mind to stop racing. All I could think about was sliding down Jarod's dick. I swore I was a fiend and hadn't even had him yet.

*Yet* being the key word. I would have him eventually, even if I had to resort to bending over in his face. That shit wasn't beneath me one bit because I knew he wanted it. He just needed a little persuading to take advantage of the opportunity in front of him. While Ramsey and Ki had warned me about him, I still had hope that maybe he'd changed. There was such a thing as a reformed ho. I'd changed and wanted things I didn't want a few years ago. Why couldn't he?

As my thoughts got away from me, my cell phone rang, bringing me back to the present. I silenced it and noticed it was my mother. She probably wanted to go to lunch. I checked the time to see it was only thirty minutes before my lunch break. As I returned to what I was doing, it chimed with a text.

Hey, baby. Do you want to go to Richard's for lunch?
Ki will meet us there.

It was probably Kiana's ass that wanted Richard's. We
rarely frequented soul food restaurants simply because
we cooked it at home. However, that type of meal was
reserved for Sundays. Here it was, a big Monday. Nobody
had time. Well, my mom probably did. That wasn't the
point, though. It just didn't sound right to cook that
much food on a big Monday. I chuckled to myself at the
thought.

I typed out my response. Hey. That's fine. See y'all in
about thirty minutes.

As soon as I put my phone down, it chimed again.
"Damn. You got a hotline today," Mr. Taylor said.

"It seems so. All the times have been my mother. So,
I'm not popping like you think I am," I responded with a
chuckle.

Mr. Taylor was so laid-back. I loved this job. He didn't
micromanage. He had nothing to say about what I did as
long as I got my work done in the allotted amount of time.
I took pride in my job, so he knew I would be efficient
and accurate.

I checked my phone again, expecting confirmation
about lunch from my mother, but it was a text from a
number I didn't recognize. I frowned slightly and opened
the message.

Good morning, Ms. Jordan. This is Jarod Speights. I
got your number from the church directory. I hope you
aren't offended. I would love to call you later this evening
to get to know you better.

The heat settled around my ears. I was shocked because I wasn't expecting him to reach out. I figured he
would wait until the next time he saw me. "Well, clearly,
yo' mama ain't got your ass blushing like that," Shannon
said.

She and Mr. Taylor laughed at my expense and embarrassment as he walked her out of the building. My gaze returned to my phone, and I typed out my response. Good morning, almost afternoon, Mr. Speights. I'm not offended; just a little caught off guard. Yes, you can call any time after six.

I set my phone on the desk and returned to work to finish what I was doing before going to lunch. My mind was wearing me out, wondering why he hadn't approached me yesterday. I would much rather have in-person interactions than phone ones. Text messages didn't require much effort. I tried to engage more in person with someone I wanted to get to know so they would see my effort. Maybe he wasn't as forward as I assumed him to be.

My phone chimed again. Talk to you at six thirty. I can't wait to get to know you better, beautiful.

I was too excited for words, so I didn't respond immediately. I could imagine he was sitting at his desk, doing little to nothing. He was an insurance agent, selling car, home, boat, and life insurance. After I calmed down a bit, I responded. I look forward to it.

Once I finished my work and had filed the client's folder, I grabbed my purse to head to Richard's. Since I was a few minutes behind schedule, I sent my mama and Ki a group text, letting them know I was on my way and would be there in ten minutes. As I was about to walk out the door, Mr. Taylor was walking back in.

"I'm going to Richard's. You want something?"

"Naw. I appreciate that, but I'm actually leaving for lunch when you return. I'm meeting Sidney at Bruno's."

That was a shocker. He rarely left for lunch. Just as Shannon had said, he was an overachiever. The man was damn near sixty, possibly over sixty, but worked like the company was just starting out. He'd been in business for over thirty years and had built up quite a rapport with business owners in the area and abroad. We often had to travel out of town for audits at least once a month. This company had to be next to the word "success" in the dictionary, yet he grinded like there were still heights he hadn't reached.

"Okay. Well, I won't be too long. Is Mr. Sylvester coming in today?"

Chance Sylvester was a partner in the firm. Mr. Wesin had also been a partner, but he died several years ago, before I started working here. "He said he might be in a little later. His wife had to go out of town, and he had to get the kids from school. She won't be back until three. I'm glad I'm done with all that. My son is living his best life, so we may never have grandkids unless his ass slips up somewhere."

I chuckled. His son, Graham, was very handsome, but that nigga was an obvious flirt and didn't give a fuck about what he let fall out of his mouth. He was like thirty-two or so now. I remembered one time he came into the office, and that nigga told me how good I looked and that I looked even better from the back. That was only our second encounter. I told him that if he spoke like that to me again, I would inform Mr. Taylor that he was harassing me. He didn't cross me again. Apparently, he *did* respect his dad, if no one else.

I chuckled. "And here I haven't even started yet. Well, I'll be back in a little bit."

He nodded, and I power walked to my car. My mind immediately returned to Jarod and the fact that he contacted me. I would forgive him for not doing this in person and just see what he had to say. If he were tactless, regardless of what he expected to gain from our connection, I would have to burn my hopes and wet dreams until they disintegrated into nothingness.

As I headed to Richard's, I received another text. Allowing my car to read it to me, it said, "I can't wait to talk to you."

I smiled slightly. Since Layna was off today, I knew I needed to get my food and hurry back. She was another CPA who worked with us. The firm didn't have a lot of employees, but it had just enough to keep it moving like a well-oiled machine. However, Mr. Taylor liked three of us to be there at once. One was a receptionist, and two were accountants. He and Mr. Sylvester were the only two who could be there alone, for obvious reasons.

When I got to Richard's, I saw Ki making her way inside. She was running late too. That was probably why she didn't respond to my message. I quickly made my way inside, finding my mom seated at a table with a number positioned on it. She always ordered for us because she knew what we liked. I could only shake my head. We knew if we wanted to try something different, to let her know so she wouldn't order the usual.

Apparently, they must have been out of whatever she ordered and were cooking more. Richard's Café had a setup like a cafeteria line, like Luby's Cafeteria. The only difference was that it was all soul food. I usually ate the smothered beef tips, cabbage, and black-eyed peas. Kiana always went for smothered pork chops, cabbage, and pinto beans.

I kissed my mother's cheek, then Kiana's, and took a seat. They were staring at me like I'd done something wrong. I frowned as I asked, "What?"

"You just look overly happy, so we're on guard for what's going on," my mama said.

"Man, y'all had me thinking something had happened. I'm just having a good day. It's been busy, but that's helping the time pass quicker."

"Oh. Well, I wanted to take the two of you to lunch because I have some news to share with you about your father. He didn't want to be here because he didn't want to see the emotion in your eyes in a public place."

Well, if that didn't put me on edge, I didn't know what would.

"What's going on?" Kiana asked.

"He has a couple of clogged arteries in his chest. They want to try to put in stents first to see if that helps. If it doesn't, they will have to do a triple bypass operation."

I was silent for a moment. While we were both closer to our mother, it wasn't to say that we didn't love our dad. Tears fell down Ki's cheeks. I knew the pregnancy had her overly sensitive because she usually didn't cry that easily. My eyes began to water too. "How will they know if the stents are working?"

"They'll do an ultrasound or something to check the blood flow," Mama said as Ki shook her head.

"I hate that for him," Ki said.

"Me too," I added. "I'm coming over when I get off."

"Me too," Ki said.

My mama nodded and swallowed hard. This was the first time I'd heard of my dad having any health issues. As far as I knew, he was healthy. "So when did they find out about the blockage?"

"He complained of chest pains, so they did some testing to check. He's at ninety percent blocked in one of his arteries. The doctor said that because the percentage of blockage is so high, they will most likely have to do a bypass operation."

"Mama, get a second opinion. These Beaumont doctors don't have the latest equipment and surely don't educate themselves on the best treatments. Medicine is constantly evolving, and we can't afford to have a doctor who doesn't study. They could kill him here in Beaumont. Take him to Houston. Does he have to have a referral?"

"No, he doesn't."

"Okay. Let me do some research on cardiologists in Houston. While the Bible says not to put your trust in any man, I have a little more trust in doctors and hospitals out there than here. Plus, we're Black, and excuse my language, but they factor in shit based on race that is totally stereotypical and not what's always best for the patient."

"Thank you, Ki," Mama said.

Kiana was a part-time pharmacist and was aware of the shit doctors prescribed for their patients and the complications some had because their doctors didn't conduct enough research. She told me that one patient had two prescriptions that weren't compatible, and it nearly killed her. She realized it when the woman got refills on both of them at the same time. Her husband had gone to pick them up for her and said his wife had been sick as a dog for a week. Ki advised him to take her to the emergency room because her symptoms indicated her liver was about to shut down.

I was grateful that Ki had medical training. She was smart as hell, and she educated herself constantly on the effects of different drugs. She also did her best to educate the students she taught at Lamar. When our food arrived, all conversation ceased, but we were all sort of picking over it, thinking about Dad. I knew that was what they were doing because it was surely where my mind was.

When I got home, I was completely drained. I went straight to the kitchen, grabbed a bottle of wine, and then went to the bathroom to run a hot bath. I sprinkled the water with lavender oil and crystals. I'd gone to my parents' house when I got off work and cried myself into a headache. My daddy held me in his arms, assuring me everything would be fine.

Sometimes, we suffered through things because of what happened in our past. My dad treated Lazarus and Ki like shit simply because he thought Kiana was making a mistake by being with him. He'd put her out of the house during her last semester of school, took her car and phone, and refused to speak to her. I didn't understand why he needed so much control over what we did. Ki's decision to be with the man she loved wasn't hurting anyone. It wasn't even like Lazarus was a thug. He was very intelligent, and his mama was crazy as hell. I loved them both.

So, my mind took this as punishment for the hardship he put on them. However, I also realized that this didn't happen overnight. It came from years of eating unhealthily, stress, and lack of exercise. I was sure his genetics also played a role in it. His parents were deceased, and his father died of a massive heart attack. It was just the spiritual side of me that wanted to call it karma.

I left work a little after four instead of five because it got slow. Once Mr. Sylvester arrived, he told me there was no sense in both of us being there with nothing to do. Since I was on salary, I didn't care. It made up for the times I had to work long days. After staying at my parents' house for over an hour, I decided to come home and get my relaxation on.

I slid into the hot water after disrobing and turning off the faucet. I started some music by V. Cartier and opened the bottle of Stella Black. I didn't bother getting a glass. I drank straight from the bottle. As I did, my mind went back to my dad's condition. Despite his evil tendencies when he couldn't get his way, he'd done his best to make things right with us. For the most part, he was a great dad, and I hated he was having to go through this. It was tearing me apart.

Ki and Lazarus had gotten there as I was leaving, and she didn't seem to be taking the news any better since I'd seen her at lunch. I was sure seeing my dad had caused her emotions to resurface like mine. She was on the verge of crying before seeing him, so the sight of him had tipped her over.

I took a big gulp of my wine. To hell with sipping. If I could handle the hard stuff and still be able to function at work tomorrow, that would have been what I would have had. That Hennessy bottle would have gotten the business. I lay back on my tub cushion and inhaled the scent of lavender as I closed my eyes.

When my phone started to ring, I automatically rolled my eyes. Then I remembered Jarod was suppose to call me. This situation with my dad made me completely forget about him. That should have been a sign, but it wasn't flashing bright enough. I answered anyway. "Hello?"

"May I speak to Kinisha, please?"

"You're speaking to her. Hello, Jarod."

"Hey. How was your day?"

I could hear the smile in his voice, and the tone of it had increased my body temperature. This water would be boiling in a minute if he kept that up. "It was good. How about yours?"

"It was cool. What do you do for a living?"

"I'm a CPA. I work at Taylor, Wesin, and Sylvester Accounting Firm."

"Oh, that's cool. How long have you been there?"

"Almost two years. I got on as soon as I graduated."

"Remind me of your age. I know we haven't really talked because we are a few years apart. It was significant when we were younger, but now it doesn't matter."

I chuckled. "I'm twenty-four."

"Okay. That's about what I thought. I'm thirty. I'll be thirty-one next month. So tell me, why were you staring at me like that?"

"I thought you were intelligent enough to figure that out. I've been watching you for the past year or so."

"Mm. I am, but I also like directness."

"Directness, huh?" I shifted in the water so that he could hear that I was in the bathtub. "I want to feel your dick slide between my walls. Is that direct enough for you?"

"Hell yeah. Damn. I honestly wasn't expecting you to be *that* direct, but I like that shit. You got me bricked up over here. I can only imagine what you look like in that bathtub right now."

I smiled slightly. My pussy had to be gurgling under this damn water. "So you know you don't have to imagine."

"Mm. What you got going this weekend? We can go to dinner and have dessert at your place."

"I don't have any plans. So it sounds good to me."

"Damn, girl. You a freak. I can already tell. So is that all you want from me?"

"I don't know yet. If we aren't compatible sexually, I won't want anything more—no need to set us up for failure before we even get started. However, if we vibe, then, of course, I would like to explore more with you. How do you feel about that?"

"Sounds good to me, but I can guarantee that sex will be off the charts."

"Mm. You've had that much practice, huh?"

He laughed and said, "Man, you wild. But I'm thirty and single. I'm sure you have had a lot of practice too with as open as you were just now."

I giggled. "Probably not as much as you, but I'm no amateur."

"So I've gathered. I can come through tonight if you want."

Did I want him to come through now? I'd already told him in so many words what this was all I was about. After a brief pause, I reasoned with myself. If tonight were trash, there would be no need for dinner this weekend. "I suppose you can since I'm already naked."

He chuckled. "Send me your address, and after I shower, I'll make my way to you."

"Okay. Sending it now. I'm assuming you won't have a problem being discreet."

"My father is the assistant pastor. What you think?" He chuckled. "See you in an hour."

"Okay."

I ended the call, hoping I wasn't making a mistake by letting him come over so soon. If I was, I expected I'd find out soon enough.

# Chapter 4

## *Oliver*

When I got to Houston, I went straight to the office. I was running a little behind schedule because I overslept. I wanted to be back on the road to Beaumont before the lunch rush, and it was already nine. People usually started really moving around by ten thirty or eleven. Checking in on the technicians was a common occurrence, but I had a new hire I wanted to see about. He was fresh out of school and practically begged me for a job.

I felt sorry for him because I knew what it was like trying to find a job and being rejected by employers because I had "no experience." It was like, *How the hell am I supposed to get experience if no one will hire me because of my lack of it?* I was grateful that I was able to start my own company. However, some people weren't as blessed as I was. So, when he applied, I kept that in mind.

He trained with me for a week, then another technician for two or three weeks. This was his second week on his own. I needed to know if he was getting the hang of things or needed more training. The worst thing a company could do was have a poorly trained employee interacting with clients. It could cause severe problems. It wasn't that he would be poorly trained, though, but everyone's attention and retention spans were different. He may have heard every word said to him and saw every action performed, but it didn't mean he could retain everything.

Mya walked through the door as I looked over reviews and tickets for the past week. "Good morning, Mr. Andrews. I brought donuts if you'd like some."

"Good morning. You must have known that I hadn't eaten breakfast. I could use a pick-me-up," I said, then took a sip of the coffee I'd made when I first arrived.

She smiled, and her cheeks reddened slightly. While she was trying to be discreet, I knew she had a thing for me. I didn't believe in mixing business with pleasure. Plus, I didn't feel a connection between us at all. She'd been working here for the past year. She was the first female tech I hired and was doing a great job. However, personally, we had nothing in common besides computers. She was smart as hell and a couple of years older than me.

Mya was also beautiful, but something didn't allow us to connect, and I believed it had everything to do with Kinisha Jordan. That woman consumed my thoughts, even the subconscious ones. She was obviously there too, if I constantly dreamed about her. On my busy days, I didn't think she was on my mind because I was laser-focused on other things, but then I would dream of bouncing her on my dick or just being intimate with her.

I had it bad, and she didn't have a clue. Hopefully, I would get up some nerve soon because that shit was draining me. It was probably why I overslept. I dreamed of her last night. It was nothing sexual, but she'd started dating someone. I didn't know if the Lord was shooting me a warning or if he was giving me insight into what had already happened.

I could almost tell she was a sexual being by the way she walked and the clothes she wore. I once saw her in the grocery store, and her short shorts had my dick's attention. The way her ass jiggled when she walked had me on pause, every part of me, including my breathing.

She hadn't seen me that day, and I was glad she hadn't. She would have seen how she stole my breath away. It was rare that she even looked at me. It seemed like she was looking through me until last Sunday when she fell in my arms. Seeing her notice me in that instance had my body temperature rising. For some reason, with her, my cockiness took a backseat. She was so beautiful her ass made me nervous.

I licked my lips when I got to the front of the office and saw the plethora of donuts Mya had brought. There was an excellent variety to choose from, and I went straight to the glazed and old-fashioned ones. When I took four donuts, Mya chuckled. A smirk made its way to my lips as I turned to her. She bit her bottom lip to restrain her laugh, then asked, "You hungry?"

I chuckled, then took a huge bite of the glazed donut. "Mm-hmm." Once I swallowed, I said, "Thanks."

She winked at me, then smiled. I turned to head back to the office without responding to that. The minute I sat, the office phone began ringing. Since Mya was just getting settled, I answered. "Andrews Technologics. This is Oliver. How may I help you?"

"Hello, Oliver. My name is Devin Taylor. I own Taylor, Wesin, and Sylvester Accounting Firm in Beaumont. We could use an IT company on board. While I'm decent at doing these things myself, I no longer feel like doing it. My brother said I needed to quit being cheap and hire someone to do it for me."

He chuckled, as did I. "Okay, Mr. Taylor. When will you be available for a consult for me to look at your system and set up?"

"I'm available today and tomorrow this week, and then I'm free all next week."

"Okay. I'm at the Houston office today, but I can come tomorrow around ten. Is that a good time?"

"Yes, sir. See you then. Do you know where we're located?"

"I do. I pass it almost every day on my way home."

"Okay, good. I'll see you tomorrow."

"Thanks for your inquiry, Mr. Taylor, and hopefully, your business."

"Oh, if you can do it, the contract will be yours. You came highly recommended."

I smiled, thankful for the word-of-mouth recommendation. "That's great to hear. Who recommended me?"

"My friend, Corey Sheffield, at Sheffield Infinity."

"Oh yeah. He's one of my best customers. I'll have to give him a discount."

"You ain't gotta give him shit . . . just a thank-you. He won't take the discount anyway."

I chuckled again. He sounded like he would be cool to work for, just like Corey was. The dealership was so busy that two of my techs reported there and had their own office. When Corey's IT guy quit, instead of hiring another individual, he decided to go with a Black-owned business and outsource it. He said there hadn't been a Black IT company in Beaumont before me, not a professional one, anyway. I had a great working relationship with him and his son, Nicholas.

"Well, it's worth a shot. I have to try to show him my appreciation."

"Okay, but don't say I didn't warn you when you waste your time. He loves supporting Black businesses. White folks don't give discounts when you refer them."

"I guess. I don't give discounts to everybody, but Corey is my biggest client."

"Well, go ahead and waste your time," he said, then chuckled. "I won't take up any more of your time. See you tomorrow, Oliver."

"Thank you, Mr. Taylor."

"Devin."

"Okay. Enjoy the rest of your day, Devin."

"You too."

When I ended the call, I was excited as hell. That accounting firm worked for nearly every large company in Beaumont. If he passed my name around, I knew my business would reach the next level. I couldn't wait to see what I could do for him. As I looked through the tickets Ronnie had done, I could only nod my head. There were no complaints, and all seemed to be well. I tried to go with my gut when hiring people, and my gut told me that he was a good hire. Hopefully, he wouldn't prove me wrong.

When I got to Mr. Taylor's accounting firm, I was anxious to see what work he needed. I was excited to work for him and know he was so cool. After getting my bag from the backseat, I went inside. As soon as I opened the door, I saw him standing there talking to Corey. They smiled when they turned to me, and Corey extended his hand. I shook it and said, "Thank you so much for the recommendation. I got'chu next month."

He frowned. "What'chu mean?"

"I'm going to cut your invoice in half next month."

"Naw," he said as he pulled his hand away. "I don't expect shit in return for a recommendation. People that expect that shit doing it for the wrong reasons. If you give everyone a discount that recommends you, how you gon' make money? Keep that."

I glanced at Devin as he shrugged. "Told you."

I chuckled as I heard a woman talking as she came down the hallway. When she entered where we were, and I saw it was Kinisha, I damn near stopped breathing.

Seeing her in her business attire wasn't too much different from her church attire. "Kinisha, I'd like you to come
and meet our new IT guy. This is Oliver Andrews. He
owns Andrews Technologies."

She smiled brightly. "Hi, Oliver."

I couldn't help but smile in return. "Hey. Small world,
huh?"

"Absolutely. Welcome to the team."

Her smile never faded as she extended her hand. I
shook it and could feel sparks from her touch. Pulling
away, I tried to keep my professional demeanor at all
costs. While Devin seemed cool, I couldn't get too relaxed
and fuck up.

"Y'all know each other?" he asked.

"We go to church together."

"Really? My wife and I go to Antioch. My whole family,
actually. Corey too."

"The world just got even smaller," I responded and
chuckled.

"Why you had to say Corey too, like I'm not part of the
family? Keep on, nigga. You gon' get fucked up."

I chuckled as they clowned around. I was happy that
they felt comfortable enough around me to be themselves. They were both in the elite of Beaumont.

"My wife consulted with Kinisha's brother-in-law a
couple of years ago, I believe. She's an attorney. Sidney
Taylor," Devin added.

"Oh yeah, I know who she is. I remember seeing her at
church when she was speaking about being registered to
vote."

*Even more prestige.*

"Yeah. She likes telling people what to do."

"Especially *his* ass," Corey added.

They laughed, and Devin playfully punched Corey
in the arm. "Shut up, fool. Oliver, let me show you
around the office."

I nodded as I glanced at Kinisha. She wasn't paying me the slightest bit of attention. She was at the front desk, seeming to be looking for something. When she found it, she stood up, and her eyes met mine. She gave me a soft smile and then went to her office. As I followed Devin around, and he showed me all the offices, along with their systems closet, he said, "She's single."

I frowned slightly. He looked back at me with a smirk on his lips. I supposed I was being more obvious than I thought. "Yeah, I know. I see her every Sunday."

"So when you gon' shoot your shot?"

"I don't know. Soon, though."

"I wouldn't wait too long. She's a beautiful woman." He glanced around me, looking to see if anyone was listening. I did the same. "She has a date this weekend. I overheard her on the phone. Apparently, it isn't their first date either. So you better get a move on before that shit turns serious."

I nodded repeatedly. "I'll say something before I leave, if that's okay."

He frowned slightly. "Why wouldn't it be?"

"I'm working, and so is she."

"Loosen up, man," he responded with a chuckle.

I let out one as well, then began looking at their network and how everything was set up. They seemed to have a great system. "Who did this?"

"Umm . . ." he said in a singsong manner as his gaze went up and to the right. "Galaxy upgraded everything about five years ago, and I've been maintaining it myself."

"You've done well."

I closed the closet door, and he led me to an empty office to look at their software. After he logged me in, I created myself a personal login, giving me full control to maintain their systems as he watched. "Damn," he voiced.

I glanced up at him as he watched me work. I was very familiar with their setup because I had the same thing at my offices. *How convenient is that?* They had more accounting software I wasn't as familiar with, but I knew I could figure it out quickly. After I adjusted some things to my liking, I looked up at him. "Are there any ongoing issues I should know about?"

"Kinisha has been having a few glitches in her system where it's not adding numbers like it should, but that should be an easy fix. I'm unsure why it keeps deprogramming itself."

I nodded and logged out. Although I could have sent a remote access code to her computer from the computer I was on, I wanted to be in her space. Standing from my seat, I made my way to her office. Devin's smirk didn't get by me. He went back up front with Corey. I was more than sure Kinisha and I would be a topic of conversation.

When I got to her office, I knocked on her door frame since the door was open. She looked up at me and smiled. "Come in."

I walked inside and tucked my hands in my pockets. "Mr. Taylor said you were having some issues with one of the programs you use."

"Yes. Computers aren't necessarily my thing. I can figure out some things, but most of this stuff baffles me. I hate calling him all the time to fix it, so I just handle things manually when I have to."

*Mm.* "So you don't like asking for help?"

"Only when necessary."

"Why?"

She turned away from me and stood from her seat so I could sit at her computer. I didn't press her to answer the question, but I knew a time would come that she would feel compelled to answer it, especially since I felt like her date was probably with that Jarod nigga from church.

Changing the subject, I asked, "How long have you been a member of Antioch?"

"My family joined when I was four. So, practically my entire life. I'm twenty-four. I'll be twenty-five in a hot minute."

I gave her a slight smile. "What's a hot minute?"

"Two months."

I glanced up at her, and she smiled at me. "You have any extravagant plans?"

"Not yet. I kind of wanna turn up in Houston. Nothing extravagant about that, but fun."

I nodded. "What exact day is it?"

She smiled slightly. "May thirtieth. I probably won't celebrate until the weekend after, though."

"My birthday isn't until October."

"Are you a Scorpio?"

"Yeah. You got something against us?"

"Not at all. I actually have a slight affection for them."

I licked my lips, knowing she was probably trying to assess my sexuality. Scorpios were known for their freakiness and sexual prowess. I fit the stereotype perfectly, but I didn't know if I wanted to go there with her just yet. Sex was definitely something I wanted from her, but I wanted more than that. I wanted to establish something more meaningful.

I nodded repeatedly. She was a Gemini and people with those signs tended to like spontaneity and new experiences. That could be a major clash in a relationship if we didn't agree and accept our differences. Whatever, though. I took that shit with a grain of salt. I remained quiet as I adjusted her settings. I wanted to show her what I was doing, but at the same time, I didn't want to.

I didn't want to eliminate myself. If I didn't show her, she would need me. After I finished, I said, "You shouldn't have that problem again. The formula was off.

So whenever you fixed it in whatever you worked on, it would work, but as soon as you went to another client, it would return to the original formula."

"Sounds difficult."

"It's not, and I don't have a problem fixing it. It's my job." I stood from her chair and stared down at her. "Call me if anything is wrong with it. I will be in and out to check on things. So don't have a problem asking me for help. It's my job, okay?"

She stared directly into my eyes. "Oliver?"

"What's up?"

"Are you flirting with me?"

My eyebrows lifted slightly. "Mm. What made you ask that question, beautiful?" I asked as I grabbed her hand.

She smiled, let out a slight chuckle, and then pulled her hand away from mine. "Yellow is your color," she said, glancing at my shirt. After clearing her throat when I didn't respond, she continued. "I'm seeing someone."

"So you shooting me down?"

I bit my bottom lip as I stared at her. My body temperature was going haywire as I glanced down at her tight slacks. Her hips were out of this world, and her titties weren't far behind. She only had slight cleavage showing, but it was enough to make me want to see more.

"Unfortunately, I am, Oliver."

"You know that means nothing to me, right? I'm gon' keep shooting my shot until it goes through the hoop. I don't give up on what I want, and I want to get to know you. Just so you know, I usually get what I want."

"Cocky much?" she asked with a lifted eyebrow.

"Extremely. So, sit back and enjoy the chase. I *will* eventually catch you."

I grabbed her hand again and brought it to my lips. After kissing it softly, I released her hand and dropped a business card on her desk. "If you need me, and I'm not already here, call me."

She nodded. I could tell she was slightly flustered. I could see that I would have to be aggressive to get her attention. That was something I didn't have a problem with. I just knew how to gauge who that would be necessary with. I left her office and immediately got on ProFlowers dot com to order her a bouquet. She had art on her walls, and all of it had some type of flower in it. She also had a nice glass table with nothing on it in front of her window. Sunflowers would look beautiful on that table.

Devin and Corey were standing there watching me as I approached. "She's all fixed up."

They started laughing as I frowned. I slowly shook my head when I realized where they had taken that statement. I swore it was like we had been friends for years. Devin patted my back. "So, you think you can handle being our IT person?"

"Easily."

I shook his hand and told him I would draw up a contract and email it to him. I shook Corey's hand, and as I headed out of the office, I could see Kinisha from my peripheral, watching me walk out the door. She didn't know it yet, but she was *definitely* going to be mine.

# Chapter 5

## *Kinisha*

As I got dressed, my mind was wearing me out. One part of me wanted just to stay home and watch movies, and the other part of me wanted to be wined, dined, and fucked. My romp in the sheets with Jarod Monday night was everything I thought it would be. So much so he came back Wednesday night and fucked me senseless. My body was contorting and doing all sorts of acrobatics, trying to deal with the amount of pleasure I was receiving.

Had I known he was that skilled, I would have flirted way sooner. However, I did want to see if we were compatible in other ways. I wanted more than just sex—mind-blowing sex. Hopefully, our chemistry would be as strong in other aspects than just sexual because I would hate to let go of that demon dick. I truly believed after experiencing him that the devil went to church too. I heard old people say that all the time and would roll my eyes. Hell, they were right.

Jarod's dick held the power to have me losing my damn mind. I swore I was addicted already, so I couldn't give Oliver the attention he sought. Although Jarod and I weren't a couple, I was so fucking sprung already that I wouldn't have room for Oliver. He'd crossed my mind more than once, though, since Tuesday, and I couldn't figure out why. At first, I thought it was his boldness, but I'd been around aggressive niggas before.

With what he wore to the office Tuesday and Thursday, I could clearly see his physique and how fine he was, but again, there was something more that had me intrigued. I wasn't intrigued enough to kick Jarod to the side, though. As I finished getting dressed, I got a phone call. I ran to my dresser to retrieve it. When I saw Ramsey's name, I slightly rolled my eyes. She'd been on my ass about Jarod. She needed to be on her fiancé's ass.

"Hello?"

"Hey. What'chu doing?"

"Getting dressed for a date. What about you?"

"Oh. I wanted to see if you wanted to hit the scene. I'm going to the hip-hop club downtown. I haven't been in years, and I have an urge to go tonight."

Something didn't sound right about that. Her voice sounded shaky. "What time are you going?"

"About eleven."

I checked the time to see it was only five thirty. Jarod would be picking me up in an hour. "Can I let you know? My date will be here in an hour, but we could be done with each other by then. You okay? You don't sound like yourself."

"I'm finna stalk a nigga because I can feel some shit in my bones."

"Shit. I'll be done. I'll meet you at your house at ten."

"Thanks, Kinisha."

"You ain't gotta thank me. I'm your girl. I'll call you before I head your way."

"Okay."

When I ended the call, I was fuming. She'd finally gotten sick of his excuses and sudden changes of plans. He was fucking with the right one, though. I'd put my foot up his ass, and once I got amped up, she would be amped up too. I wouldn't be surprised if Braylon were going with us. That was her brother, and he played no games when it came to his little sister. I didn't play any games about her either because, besides my sister, Ramsey was my best friend. She worked my nerves at times, but so did Kiana. That didn't make me love them any less.

Going back to my mirror, I looked at my reflection. The dress I wore hugged my most valuable assets. Well, my most visible assets. My mind was valuable as well. Just as I was about to start my makeup, the doorbell rang. I frowned as I made my way to it. Jarod was an hour early, so that couldn't be him. However, when I looked through the peephole, it was indeed Jarod.

I opened the door with my hair in a messy bun and my face sans makeup, but my frown was ever present. "Why are you here so early?"

"I have to cancel our outing, but I still wanted to see you."

I stepped aside to let him in. I was confused about why he had to cancel, but I was glad since I needed to be there for Ramsey. Once I closed the door and turned to him, he pulled me into his arms. "You look amazing. I hate I have to cancel."

He didn't explain, and I didn't ask for an explanation. If he had a legitimate reason, I felt like he would have said so. This alone proved that he was full of shit, but his dick wasn't. His hands slid to my ass, just as I figured they would. He had time for sex but not to take me out. This would be a goodbye fuck. I wanted to throw a whole-ass tantrum, though.

I needed to attach his dick to someone else because my body didn't want to let him go simply for having to live without it. I moaned softly, letting him know that I was with what he was trying to do, and he immediately pulled at my dress, bringing it over my head. I wasn't wearing undergarments, and he took full advantage of that shit. He pulled a condom from his pocket, then dropped his pants. I unbuttoned his shirt and rubbed his bare chest as he strapped up.

He quickly picked up my thick ass and practically slammed me against the door as his dick penetrated my folds. "Oh fuck," I yelled.

"Damn, girl. This pussy always ready, huh?" he said, then lowered his mouth to my nipple.

"Shit . . . always."

He was stroking me so good I could barely breathe. My eyes had rolled to the back of my head, and I felt like I was about to pass out from the overload of pleasure. The tremble in my legs alerted him of my pending orgasm, so he said, "Spray me with that good shit, girl."

Within a minute or two, I did as he requested, screaming while my flood overtook him. "Hell fucking yeah. This some good-ass pussy."

He slowed his pace as he watched the action. The minute I stopped, he pulled me away from the door and went to my couch, dropping me on it. Pushing my feet to my head, he entered me again and fucked up my cervix while playing with my clit. I was so damn satisfied that I wanted to cry. It felt like his dick was pushing my ovaries around like hockey pucks, but I wouldn't dare tell him to stop.

When the frown appeared on his face, I knew he was about to nut. I pulled my legs from his grasp and wrapped them around his waist as he dug deep, sending me into another orgasm. The second mine started, he fired off into the condom and yelled, "Fuck."

The sound of our panting filled the air as he rested his forehead on mine. However, when he gathered the strength to pull out of me, he said, "Oh shit."

I frowned and sat up. "Oh shit, what?"

My gaze went to his dick, and there was nothing on it but the top ring of the condom. It had completely detached and was inside of me. I started panicking as he said, "Let me get it. My cum could still be in it."

I widened my legs as he slid his fingers inside my drenched tavern. "I got it."

He pulled it out of me . . . and there wasn't a drop of nut in it. My eyes widened, as did his. "You on the pill?"

"No. I rely on condoms."

"You may need to get a morning-after pill."

"Haven't they pulled them from the shelves?"

"I don't think so. Let me go to Walgreens right quick."

I nodded as I sat here, staring at my naked body with my heart racing. The minute he left, I hopped up from the couch and showered. Suddenly, I didn't feel so good. It was like this shit scared me straight. I couldn't get an incurable STD or get pregnant right now. I knew Jarod slept around. I couldn't do this shit. My parents would be so embarrassed if I got pregnant without even a boyfriend in sight. I was pretty sure they would have plenty to say. Thankfully, I didn't live with them anymore.

Furthermore, *I* would be embarrassed. It was never my intention to raise a baby alone. I didn't feel Jarod would be ready to be a father for some reason. That would leave me on my own. Kiana was pregnant. There was no way I would take away from her joy of motherhood because of my dilemma. She was married, and they were ready to be parents. It wasn't her fault that I fucked up.

I got out of the shower, dried off, then moisturized my skin. I was worrying myself to death about the unknown. This was so stupid. Nothing would probably come of this, even though it was like playing Russian roulette.

By the time I slid on some leggings and put on a bra, Jarod was knocking at the door. I quickly went to it and opened it to find him empty-handed.

"They were out. I don't have time to go anywhere else because I have somewhere to be in the next twenty minutes."

I slightly rolled my eyes. "Okay. I'll go look."

He brought his hand to my cheek, then kissed my lips. "Talk to you later?" he asked as if he wasn't sure I would want to.

"Yeah. Talk to you later."

I was irritated that he flaked on me for probably someone else, but whatever. The only reason he probably wanted to talk later was to see if he could come by whenever he was done with whomever. He kissed my lips again and left. I closed the door and returned to my room to find a shirt. As I searched my closet, I called Ramsey.

"Hello?"

"Hey. Change of plans. I'm headed to your place."

"I'm sorry you canceled your plans, Kinisha. I'm just tired of keeping up the façade. I've been feeling that something wasn't right. So if I felt it, I know you did."

"I did, but I didn't want to have you doubting your relationship on a suspicion. I'll be there in about thirty minutes."

"Okay."

I could hear the sorrow in her voice. It was probably best that Jarod canceled our plans. Ramsey needed me, and I was glad I could go see about her and have her back.


As I parked across the street from the club, I checked my makeup and the tube top I wore. These niggas in here were gonna get all these rolls tonight. I didn't give a fuck. I was fine, and I knew that shit, regardless of what their definition of fine was. Most of them liked all this body anyway. I glanced over at Ramsey, and she looked nervous as hell. I grabbed her hand and said, "If we see something he shouldn't be doing, it's his loss, not yours. You are *more* than enough. You hear me?"

She nodded, but I wasn't convinced that she believed me. "We will definitely bust his ass. I know he's in there doing something he has no business."

With that, she flung open the door and got out. Shit, she was already on one, and I was right behind her ass. I was beyond ready to punch that nigga in the mouth, especially after she said he told her he didn't care much for her hanging with me because I had no morals. *Fuck him and his fucked-up morals clause.* Apparently, that was only a form of control he'd tried to implement in their relationship.

Aaron stood there, shaking his head when we got to the door. "Where the hell y'all been? I ain't seen y'all in a hot minute."

"We ain't had time. Our careers needed us more. You been good, handsome?" I asked him.

Aaron knew I didn't want his ass, but I always flirted. I'd been knowing him awhile. He was friends with Lazarus. This was the same club Lazarus was working at when he met my sister. "I got'chu, handsome."

He grabbed my hand and kissed it, then said, "Y'all go on in, gorgeous. Shit popping tonight."

I smiled at him, winked, then walked through, holding Ramsey's hand. Our eyes scanned the crowd, trying to see if we could see him. We wanted to spot him before he spotted us. "His punk ass is upstairs," she said.

She pulled me toward the stairs. I wasn't sure how we would get in since that was VIP, but maybe she had a plan she hadn't made me aware of.

When we got to the staircase, the nigga that had been trying to get with Ramsey was standing there. He scanned her curves and licked his lips. "Ramsey, when you gon' give me a shot to make you happy, baby?" he asked when she stepped closer.

She pressed her body against his, pulling his head down to her mouth. "As soon as I handle this business that you about to let me in VIP to do."

He lifted his head with a frown, then twisted his lips to the side.

"Give me your phone, Blaze," she said as she glanced behind him.

He did as she requested and bit his bottom lip. I didn't know if she was playing him or if she was serious. He liked her, so I hoped she wasn't playing with his emotions. She called herself from his phone, then handed it back to him. "Lock me in, and I'll do the same with your number."

"That's what's up, baby. Finally."

He smiled at her and stepped aside to let us handle business. She placed her hand on his cheek as she stepped up, causing her to be closer to his height. That nigga was tall as hell. He had to be every bit of six-five. Ramsey wasn't even my height of five-seven, so he had to be at least a foot taller than her.

After we passed him, she glanced back and winked at him. "Ramsey, please tell me you're not fucking with him."

The smile fell from her lips. "No. I'm gon' fuck him. I've been wanting him, but this muthafucka got to me first," she said as we reached the landing.

My eyes immediately landed on her nigga. There was a bitch sitting on his lap, and his hand was resting on her ass. They kissed on the lips as we approached, causing Ramsey to halt her forward progress. That shit wasn't a peck, either. They were tonguing each other down as he groped her. My heart was broken for her, but at the same time, the pieces of it were burning in anger.

My face had begun twitching. I was trying to wait for her to make the first move, but she seemed frozen in fucking time, watching him slob this bitch down. I gently nudged her. She turned to me, so I asked, "What we doing? 'Cause I'm ready to bust all this shit apart."

She frowned hard and walked away from me toward him. *Hell yeah.* We were about to get kicked out of this bitch tonight. She pulled that bitch to the floor right off Robert's lap by her hair. He looked stunned to see us standing there. What was crazy about that was he knew this was a club we used to frequent. Why did he expect Ramsey to stay home like a devoted housewife or some shit while he was out on the damn town?

"Ramsey, what are you doing here?"

She popped him right in the mouth. "Why the fuck are *you* here?"

He stood like he wanted to get at her. I could see the bouncers running over to us, so I punched him in the jaw before they could get to us. I had to get my lick in. "How *dare* you, nigga?" I yelled.

Blaze grabbed Ramsey as she kicked her leg out and caught Robert right in the shin. I knew she was aiming for his nuts. Thanks to Blaze, Robert lucked up on that. Another bouncer grabbed me, and they escorted us out as Robert helped that pathetic-looking ho from the floor. When we got outside, Ramsey fell against Blaze and cried. He wrapped his arms around her. "Come on, ma. Don't worry about that muthafucka. He ain't worth it."

She lifted her head and said, "I'm sorry. Come on, Nisha. Let's go."

As she tried to walk off, Blaze grabbed her hand and kissed it. "I get off in a couple of hours. I'ma call you. Okay?"

She nodded, and we headed to her car. I put my arm around her as we walked and kissed her forehead. I knew she didn't need me to speak at the moment, nor did I want to. Frankly, I didn't know what to say. I was angry, and no encouraging words were coming to mind.

However, what *did* come to mind was that the couple of stores I went to didn't have that morning-after pill. What in the fuck was going on? I knew the longer I waited, the lesser my chances of preventing a pregnancy.

Once we got to the car, I walked Ramsey to her passenger seat. "I'll drive, boo."

She gave me a slight smile as she unlocked the doors. I walked around to the driver's side and got in, immediately pushing the button to start the car. Finally finding the words, I said, "Everything will be okay. I promise."

She squeezed my hand as I secretly prayed that same prayer for myself.

# Chapter 6

## *Oliver*

"I don't know how you keep deprogramming this computer."

"Me? Why it gotta be me and not the computer?"

I slowly shook my head as I worked on Kinisha's computer. I wanted to laugh because I was the one fucking with her computer to have a reason to be in her space. I'd been on board for three weeks already, and we hadn't gone beyond casual conversation. I'd sent flowers several times, but it seemed like she was trying to friendzone me. We'd even gone to lunch once.

I thought she was feeling me as much as I was feeling her, and maybe she was, but she was clearly occupied with someone else. We had the most conversation when I was fixing the shit I'd messed up on her computer. "Kinisha, you are the only person sitting at this computer. Who else could be messing it up? Maybe you're doing something that you don't realize is deprogramming it."

She shrugged. "Maybe I need a new computer," she mumbled.

I chuckled slightly as I reprogrammed her computer. "You wanna go to lunch today?" I asked.

She narrowed her eyes for a second, then said, "Yeah. I wonder if my computer is getting help from someone."

I frowned as I stared at her like I didn't know what she was talking about. We'd gotten somewhat cool in the past three weeks, so it was never strained or forced when we did talk. "Someone like who?"

"Humph," she said and looked away.

"Girl, if you insinuating me, you can pipe that shit down. Why would I put more work on myself? I ain't getting paid extra. No matter how little or how much work there is, I'm on contract."

She shifted her weight as I turned my head to continue reprogramming her spreadsheet. I wanted to laugh so badly. She was smart and had figured me out. This was the third time I'd done this shit. I'd have to slow down, though. She huffed for a moment, then said, "I'm sorry. I'm a little stressed out, and this isn't helping."

I glanced up at her. "Work related?"

"No."

"You wanna talk about it?"

We'd never really talked about anything personal. It was always about her job or mine. The most personal we'd gotten was that she had a nephew on the way and had a sister, along with other things I already knew. She knew that I was a loner and that my parents were deceased. There were other minor things we learned about each other, like our tastes in music. Other than that, we were practically strangers still.

"No. I'm cool."

"Okay. Well, for future reference, I'm a good listener."

"Thanks."

"You're all fixed up. You wanna ride with me, or do you want to meet up?"

"We can meet up. Same spot as last time?"

"That's fine with me."

I walked out of her office and headed to mine. We were about to go to Chuck's Sandwich Shop downtown. She loved their baked potatoes, and I loved their burgers. I could already taste it. I took a deep breath as I grabbed my keys and phone from the desk. Kinisha didn't seem to trust me, but she should have been questioning that nigga she was seeing. Surely, she had to know he was a ho, but I suppose that wasn't my business.

When I got to the parking lot, she got in her ride. I gave her a head nod, and she rolled her eyes playfully. The more I was around her, the more I wanted to know, but it didn't seem she would be too forthcoming with any personal information. I turned up my radio to hear Silk Sonic's rendition of "Love's Train," originally done by Con Funk Shun. I had to say, they'd done it justice. Remakes were hit and miss, especially the classics. In my opinion, they had to be just as good or better.

Lucky Daye had done a good job with Earth, Wind & Fire on the remake of one of their songs, so it went over well. However, I wasn't too fond of the Isley Brothers remake that included Beyoncé. "Make Me Say It Again, Girl" was one of my favorites by them, but that remake didn't hit home for me. I was an old soul. I loved seventies, eighties, and nineties music, particularly R&B and soul. Some of this new shit was lacking big time.

After parking, I saw Kinisha walking toward the entrance. I quickly got out of my car and made my way to her. It looked somewhat crowded. Sure enough, there was nowhere to sit when I stepped inside. She turned to me and said, "Looks like we'll be taking this to go."

"Yeah. You wanna go to a park or go back to the office?"

"The office. I hate eating outside. I don't want nothing flying near my food."

*Well, picnics are out of the question.* "Noted. Well, can we at least eat in the lounge together?"

She frowned slightly. "Yeah . . . sure," she said hesitantly.

I knew if I didn't ask, she would go straight to her office with it. The whole point of us going to lunch together was so I could spend time getting to know her more. She faced the front for a moment, then turned back to me. "Oliver—"

I shook my head as I stared down at her. "We'll talk about it later."

I already knew she was about to try to shoot me down. She wasn't about to do that in a restaurant full of patrons. She wasn't about to do that, period. When we got to the counter and she ordered her potato, I immediately ordered my burger and paid for everything. "Oliver, I could have paid for my own food."

I just stared at her. She eventually looked away but remained silent. This woman didn't know how to let a man do things for her, and I planned to change that. Obviously, Jarod hadn't done shit for her, but she was still giving him her time. That could be for one thing, and one thing only. They didn't sit together at church, and I saw them speak only once or twice. I assumed he was her sneaky link. While I wanted her to know she wasn't being as discreet as she thought, I chose to leave it alone.

She would swear I was stalking her if I told her that I saw how she stared at him or put an extra sway in her hips when she thought he was looking. That nigga only wanted what was between her legs, and maybe that was all she wanted too. I needed to mind the business that paid me until I no longer could. I could only sit idly by for so long, watching her make a fool of herself. I truly believed her stress involved him in some way.

While waiting for our food, she said, "Thank you, Oliver."

I simply nodded, not offering her any words. Honestly, I was slightly irritated that she couldn't see the good man standing before her. I wasn't pressuring her to be mine. I was just trying to do something nice for her. However, I could feel that she would push me past the point of aggression I wanted to go. It wasn't that I would do anything she didn't want me to do. I could tell that she was interested. She was trying to convince herself that she wasn't.

Once our food was ready, I grabbed the bag and headed out of the restaurant as she followed me through the crowd. I held the door open for her. She smiled politely, thanked me, and then headed to her car. When she got to it, I was right behind her to open the door. Her gaze softened as she stared at me. It was like she was trying to figure me out. There was nothing about me that she needed to figure out. I'd told her that I went after what I wanted. Plain and simple. I was pursuing my future.

When we returned to the office, Devin was up front, looking like he was about to come unglued.

Kinisha frowned slightly. "You okay, Mr. Taylor?"

"Yeah. Just some personal stuff. I'll be back, y'all."

I nodded as he grabbed his keys and headed out the door. I didn't know what was happening, but it must have been serious. Kinisha glanced at me, and I shrugged my shoulders, indicating I didn't have a clue about what it could have been either. We made our way to the lounge area and had a seat. I unbagged our food and handed her container to her first, then took out mine. The smell of that burger had my stomach growling.

"Dang. You hungry?"

"Yep."

"Oliver."

I looked up at her. "I'm sorry, but I was trying to tell you in the restaurant that I'm involved with someone. I can't be trying to get to know someone else when I'm not sure where the relationship I'm pursuing is going."

"I can promise you that if you don't know after three weeks, then it ain't going nowhere. I make my intentions known from the beginning. When I pursue a woman, she will definitely know exactly what I expect to gain from being with her. Regardless of whether men express that, after three weeks, they know, especially if y'all are spending a lot of time together."

She looked down at her potato and played in it with her fork. I took a bite of my burger as I stared at her. When she didn't say anything, after swallowing what was in my mouth, I said, "I didn't say that to make you feel bad. I said that to put you up on game. If you were mine, I would tell you that I want to know everything about you, from what side of the bed you wake up on to if you wear a bonnet on your head at night. I would be interested in every detail about you, Kinisha. But I mean, that's just me."

She stared at me momentarily, then said, "Neither of us have questioned anything about each other. While I want to speak freely, I don't know you well enough yet. You seem trustworthy, but I don't typically trust people with my personal issues so soon."

"It's cool. I'm gon' still be here until you do."

"Why?"

"Because I want you." I grabbed her hand and held it in mine. "I want you to be mine. I pay attention to you when we're around each other, and I can tell you're a good person. A li'l nasty, but you have a good heart."

I cracked a slight smile to lighten the mood, and she shoved my hand and smiled back. "Thank you, Oliver. You really are a good guy. I'm only nasty when coaxed, for your information."

I chuckled. "I wanna get to know you, Kinisha—all of you. You have my number. Just call me when you feel the same. Just so you know, friendly talk here at work is cool, but outside of work, it is totally different. I don't need a female friend. I need a woman I can share my life and create a future with. If you call me outside of work hours, I will assume you ready for all I have to offer."

Her cheeks were slightly pink as she brought her fork to her mouth. Those lips had me wanting to lick the potato residue from them. As she licked them, I bricked up something fierce. I had to look away from her so I could calm the fuck down. It was quiet between us for a couple of minutes until she asked, "What is it about me that makes you want all that with me?"

I swallowed my food and wiped my mouth with my napkin. "You're beautiful. Gorgeous. That was what first attracted me. Being around you at church without you even noticing me gave me further insight into who you were. You love God. You seem lighthearted and outgoing. Everyone seems to know you, and when they come in contact with you, they can't help but smile."

"You've been that close to me at church?"

"Mm-hmm. I don't mind not being noticed. You didn't have a choice but to notice me when you almost busted your ass, though."

She laughed loudly. "You damn right. I could have messed up my whole left side on that tile floor."

I laughed. "See? You're funny too. Working here has helped me get to know you a little more, and it only makes me want to know everything."

"No man has ever spoken that way to me. If my mind changes, I'll let you know. Honestly, I don't see what you see. You're cool and seem to be a good man, but I don't think I'm as attracted to you as you are to me."

"I know, but I'm working on that. The more of me I let you see, the more you'll feel me. I like talking to you this way too. It helps me know how to approach you."

She frowned slightly. "What do you mean?"

"You like aggression. I saw that in Chuck's today. You seem to like a good dude with a bad boy swag. Plenty of BDE. So I'm gon' have to show you the depths to which my shit swing."

She cleared her throat, and I swore I saw a tremble go through her. Suddenly, the door chimed, alerting us that someone had entered the office. She was saved by the bell. After closing her box, she patted her thick-ass lips and fixed her nose ring, then made her way up front. I finished off my burger as I heard another woman talking. Throwing away my leftovers, I walked up front to see Devin's wife. I'd never met her in person, but I recognized her from the pictures.

"Mrs. Taylor, this is our IT guy, Oliver. Oliver, this is Mrs. Taylor."

"Nice to meet you," I said, extending my hand for a handshake.

She was a beautiful chocolate-complexioned woman. She nodded, then turned her attention back to Kinisha, clearly focused on something else. "He didn't say where he was going?"

"No, ma'am. Just that it was a personal matter. He was moving rather fast, so I thought it was an emergency of some kind."

She frowned, and right after, her phone rang. She huffed and answered, "Devin, what's going on?"

Her eyes widened, and she turned her back to us. "He done lost his fucking mind," she said as she left the office.

Kinisha looked over at me. "It has to be Graham. That's their son. He's a couple of years older than you, but he sometimes acts immaturely. I'm more mature than he is."

"Humph. Hopefully, it's nothing too bad."

"Right. Thanks for the talk today. I'm gonna get back to work. I enjoyed lunch."

I gave her a slight smile. "So did I."

I watched her walk to her office in her tight skirt, wishing I could grab her ass just one time. However, something told me that despite her words, my time was coming, and I'd be ready.

# Chapter 7

## *Kinisha*

*Pregnant.* I could scream right now. How could I have done this shit to myself? No one had the morning-after pill, so I had to order the shit. It took two days to get to me, making it nearly a seventy-two-hour wait since the incident. It was obviously not effective. I'd gone to my doctor to have blood work done to make sure I had no STDs, and he walked back in to tell me I was pregnant.

I hadn't talked to Jarod in a week. It was like he was trying to disappear on me. We'd still been fucking, against my better judgment, until a week ago when he went MIA. Here I was, walking to my car with a bag of "goodies" to welcome my pregnancy and baby, and I was feeling everything but welcoming. I didn't know how I would go back to work like this. The tears had been falling from my eyes since he revealed that shit.

Once I got inside my car, I felt like I would throw up. It had been a month since that encounter with Jarod, and I wished I would have kept my fucking legs closed. My worst fears had come true. I couldn't tell anyone right now because I didn't know what I would do. I, for sure, had to tell Jarod. That thought only made me feel sicker. I cranked the engine and pointed the A/C vents to my face to calm the nausea.

Before I could pull off, I received a text from my mother. Hey, baby. You wanna go to lunch together today?

I closed my eyes, concentrating on keeping the bile from my throat, and then responded. I have to work through lunch since I'm late. I had a doctor's appointment this morning. Before you panic, it was just a routine checkup.

I smiled slightly but immediately started crying because I could only think about how disappointed she would be. I was a grown-ass woman and was still worried about how my parents would perceive me. I engaged in ho activities and suffered the consequences of it. After taking a deep breath, I sucked up my emotions and drove to work.

When I got there, I checked my mom's response to see laughing emojis. A message came through shortly after. Okay. Talk to you later.

My dad's surgery was next week in Houston, and I had this looming over my head. I knew I would have to tell them eventually, but I wasn't sure if I should tell them before or after his surgery. The new doctor had assured us after running more tests that the stents would be sufficient. We thanked God because his recovery time would be far easier with the stents versus them having to do a bypass operation. Kiana was right to suggest he get a second opinion.

I got out of the car and noticed Graham's car was parked out front. I rolled my eyes as I made my way to the door. Maybe his foolishness would keep my mind off my problems. He'd gotten into a wreck last week, and for some reason, he thought it would be okay to come and get his mom's Maserati to drive around until his car was out of the shop. That was what they were so pissed about. Mr. Taylor said he almost reported it stolen when his friend Corey had called to say he saw Graham in their car.

I almost laughed about it until I saw how serious he was. The rest of the week had passed by quickly. We had quite a bit of work to do to get ready for an audit and still had more work to do this week. Oliver stayed out of our way the rest of the week and told us to call if we needed him. Going to lunch with him last Monday was eye-opening. I wished I had talked to him sooner. Coincidently, it was the last day I'd heard from Jarod. It was like he'd heard the game Oliver had let me in on and went ghost.

When I walked inside, Mr. Taylor and Graham stood up front talking. Mr. Taylor didn't look all that happy, but I wouldn't either if I still had to worry about a grown-ass man child. I wanted to walk by them and speak to Mr. Taylor later, but Graham had to speak to me first. "Good morning, Kinisha."

"Good morning, Graham. Good morning, Mr. Taylor."

I quickly went to my office, not bothering to wait for a response. Graham could be so damn obnoxious. I didn't care how fine he was. His attitude and demeanor were a complete turn-off. As I turned on the light in my office, I heard Oliver's voice greeting them. I had to admit, I missed him in the office last week. There was something about him that slowly attracted me to him. I couldn't pinpoint exactly what it was.

It could have been his style. Since I'd told him that yellow was his color, he seemed to wear some shade of yellow at least twice a week. He dressed nicely, no matter what color it was. It was business casual but sexy. I could also tell that he had a nice physique. Those shirts he wore didn't hide as much as he probably thought they did. His arms looked strong, and I wouldn't mind being held in them again. However, it could be his smile and wit. He was funny, and his smile could light up a room.

He was somewhat aggressive and expressive. The way he told me how he felt about me without fear of what I would say in return was mesmerizing. His confidence was on overload, and he was somewhat cocky. I suppose if everything he said were true about how he treated his woman, then he had a reason to be cocky. He was the total package. Why would he want me now, though? I was carrying another man's baby. I'd fucked up my life by fucking around with Jarod.

I grabbed my phone as I noticed Oliver glance my way and sent Jarod a text. We need to talk. It's important. I rolled my eyes as I set my phone on the desk. My last few texts had gone unanswered, and he wasn't at church yesterday. As I prepared to work, Oliver knocked on my door frame. I smiled slightly, silently inviting him inside.

"Good morning, beautiful."

"Good morning, Oliver."

I tried to sound as happy as possible, but it just wasn't there. He smiled a bit. "You look tired. You good? Looks like you just got here."

"I'm okay. I had a doctor's appointment this morning, so I did just get here. How's your morning?"

"It's good, especially now."

I glanced up at him to see his gaze on me. It wasn't in an admiration sort of way. It was more like he was analyzing me, trying to see what I wasn't saying. Usually, I would meet his gaze, but I knew if I did that today, I would burst into tears. I shouldn't have come to work. This wasn't a good idea.

"Kinisha?"

"Yeah?"

"I can tell something's wrong, baby." He sat in the seat in front of my desk. "What's up wit'chu?"

I glanced up at him and saw the concern across his face through his slightly raised, scrunched eyebrows. Just the fact that he called me baby had me feeling even more sensitive, especially by how softly he spoke it. "I'm fine, Oliver. Have a great day," I responded, dismissing him.

He nodded repeatedly and stood from his seat, going to his office. I immediately dove into work, trying to get my mind off my dilemma, but that only worsened it. I had to wipe my tears several times. Thankfully, I didn't wear much makeup today, only lipstick and lashes. Since I got those done professionally, I knew they wouldn't come off as easily.

Although I was busy, time seemed to be creeping by at a snail's pace. I was just ready for the day to be over with. I was two hours late, but it felt like I'd worked a full day already. It was lunchtime, and Jarod had yet to respond. The knock on my door frame caused me to look up and see Oliver standing there with a bag from Jason's Deli. I smiled slightly, and he walked in with it.

"I bought you something to eat. Since you were late, I figured you wouldn't be taking a lunch break."

*God, why is he so perfect?* "Thank you so much. What did you get?"

"Well, I noticed the last time you ate from there, you had one of my favorites: the Club Royale. So I got that again with a cup of fruit and Baked Lays."

I couldn't stop the tears that escaped me. He was so attentive. He was providing what I needed without me even saying a word. Pushing him away would be hard as hell, but there was no way I could bring this man in on my drama. He sat at my desk and grabbed my hand, which only caused me to cry more. *Get it together, Nisha. Shit.*

He stood from his seat and came around the desk, then pulled me from my seat and into his warm embrace. I exhaled because it felt just as I remembered, only better. Closing my eyes, I realized what I had to do. "I'm sorry, Oliver," I said, gently pushing him away. "Thank you so much for lunch."

My mind was saying to tell him to get the fuck on, but I couldn't be that cruel to him. It wasn't in my heart. I would reserve that shit for Jarod's pathetic ass. I would just keep rejecting him nicely. He was too good for me, and I didn't deserve someone like him, not now anyway. I stared up at him as he stared at me. His gaze was so powerful. His high cheekbones and dark skin were calling me back to his strong, comforting arms. The glasses he wore only added to his appeal. They were so sexy on him.

After taking a deep breath, I looked away. "I have to get back to work. Thanks again."

He gave me a soft smile as my phone buzzed. When he left, I looked at it to see a message from my mother. They moved your dad's surgery up because he's complaining of chest pains. We're cooking dinner tonight so we can dine together as a family. His surgery is tomorrow. See you when you get off, baby.

I closed my eyes and slowly shook my head. I would tell them about my lack of judgment after the surgery. This was too much to bear. Daddy's surgery and this baby already growing inside me had my nerves frazzled like they'd been electrocuted. Unwrapping my sandwich, I took a bite and moaned softly. I loved the Club Royale. That only brought my thoughts back to Oliver.

After my second bite, a wave of nausea swept over me, causing me to sprint to the bathroom. I threw up the little bit I'd eaten, then rinsed my mouth. If it continued, I didn't know how to hide this from my parents tonight.

When I looked up, Mr. Taylor was standing there watching me. "You okay?"

"Yeah, I'll be okay."

"Stomach bug?"

"I just have a nervous stomach. They moved my father's surgery up to tomorrow, and my nerves are on edge."

"I understand. You know you can take the rest of the day and tomorrow if you want."

"I'm good for today. I may need the morning, though. I can come in later after his surgery."

"You sure?"

"Yes, sir. Thank you, Mr. Taylor."

He gave me a tight smile and gently rubbed my back. I smiled and returned to my office to find a bouquet of pink roses on the glass table near my window. I knew that they were from Oliver without even reading the card. However, I approached them and pulled the card from the stem.

*If no one told you how beautiful you are today, let me be the first. One day, I will wake up to your beautiful face, telling you, "Good morning, gorgeous," every morning. Until then, I'll settle for seeing you in the office and trying to manifest our future. I'll continue to practice loving you until it's a reality. Enjoy your flowers, baby. Have a good day. ~ Oliver*

This man was gonna have me in a pool of tears. *Jesus Christ.* As I felt the waterworks building, I walked over to my desk and gulped some cold water. Grabbing my cell phone, I decided to text him. I glanced at his business card positioned on my desk for his number. The flowers are beautiful, and the message is even more beautiful. Maybe I'll see what you see one day, but I can't see it now, Oliver. Thank you so much. I needed the pick-me-up.

I had to keep reminding him that we would never be a couple because the last thing I wanted to do was hurt him. If he chose to keep trying, that would be totally on him and not because I was leading him on. God had a weird way of doing things. Perhaps that was why the scripture said his ways and thoughts were not ours because I was definitely confused about why he would allow perfection to find me when I was everything but.


My entire body trembled as I walked through the back door of my parents' house. The rest of the workday had been quiet, and, as expected, I didn't get a response from Jarod. I wasn't a worrisome female, but this situation was about to turn me into one. I needed him to know what we created in our lust. There was nothing passionate about it. We were fucking. It was good as hell, but emotionally, there was nothing.

"Kinisha, hey, baby," my dad said excitedly.

I could have sworn that he wasn't having surgery tomorrow. He didn't seem worried in the least bit. "Hey, Daddy. How are you feeling?"

"I'm having some slight pains, but I know God has me. After tomorrow, I will feel much better."

I was glad he was feeling optimistic. His mood was helping mine. I leaned over and kissed his cheek, then sat on the couch as I heard the door open. Kiana and Lazarus entered the family room, where we were seated. Since they found out she was having a little boy, Lazarus's chest had been puffed out whenever I saw them. I chuckled at the sight of him. "Hey, Ki. How are you feeling?"

"Hey, Nisha. I'm good. What about you?"

I stood from my seat and hugged her. She held me a little longer than usual but quickly backed away and grabbed my hand, bringing it to her stomach. The slight flutters I felt made me smile. "The baby is excited to be in your presence."

I chuckled, then hugged Lazarus, realizing I'd gotten away without answering her question. That pregnancy brain was already in full effect. I was happy about that, though, because it kept me from having to lie. I felt shitty, but there was no way I could tell her that without an explanation immediately following that statement. "So, have y'all picked a name yet?" I asked.

"No, not yet. I suggested Lazarus, but my husband adamantly disagreed," Kiana said, then chuckled as Laz eyed her.

I had to say, it was a very different name. I'd never heard anyone naming their child Lazarus until I met him. I laughed, so I was grateful he said no. The kids would tease my poor nephew all through school. "Well, what about just naming him Laz, like Laz Alonso?"

"Laz is his nickname as well. His whole name is Lazaro," Ki said.

I frowned slightly. "Well, dang. You must follow the man heavy to know that."

"If you must know, he was once my celebrity crush. Now, I can only focus on my real-life crush, who became the love of my life."

I rolled my eyes as Mama appeared from the kitchen. I stood from my seat as Daddy chuckled at our antics. "I'm sorry, Mama. Do you need any help?" I asked.

"No, baby. Everything is just about done. Well, maybe when it's time to take everything to the table, I'll need that help."

She smiled and sat next to Daddy. I sat back in my seat and watched their exchange. They were so in love, and so were Ki and Laz. I felt like the fifth wheel, me and my bastard child. I would probably be Hagar in the Bible, and my baby would be treated as Ishmael, banned from the city, and cast out of the lives of the people who were supposed to love him. Abraham's wife suggested he sleep with Hagar to create a son since she couldn't have any. Then she was jealous after he was born.

I must have zoned out because Ki said, "Nisha, snap out of it. Your phone chimed, girl. You good?"

"Yeah. I was just thinking about my schedule tomorrow and what I needed to accomplish at work later."

She twisted her lips slightly, indicating she didn't believe a word I'd said. There was a text from Oliver. He'd never responded to my text earlier, so I figured he wouldn't. As I read it, I felt myself becoming emotional. This man had a way with words that pulled at all my damn feelings.

I have no doubt in my mind that you will eventually see it. That's why I've been persistent. Kinisha, you are meant to be mine. It's God's will. I see it clearly, and one day soon, you will too. I believe that wholeheartedly, beautiful. Sorry I'm just getting back to you. I got busy and didn't look at my phone. I'll be praying that your dad's surgery goes well, and I'm also glad the flowers helped brighten your day.

It wasn't the flowers that picked me up. It was his words on the card. Although I couldn't have a relationship with him, his attention felt good. Hell, I wasn't even sure if I *wanted* a relationship with him. Oliver was a nice guy, somewhat cocky, but I liked that. However, once again, I was sure his perception of me would change when he noticed my stomach was growing.

"So, did the doctor say how long the procedure would take?" Kiana asked Daddy, breaking me away from my thoughts and Oliver's text message.

I wanted to respond, but I remembered what he said about after-hours texts. It meant that I was ready to proceed with him. I wasn't and didn't know if I would ever be. Putting my phone away, I tuned in to the rest of the conversation. "He said maybe only an hour or two, but he'll have a better time frame for us tomorrow before he begins the procedure. He will explain everything in-depth for you guys in the morning," my dad explained.

"I'm just happy to see you're in good spirits. Your attitude toward this has helped me tremendously, Daddy, because I've been so emotional," Ki explained. She turned to me and said, "Shut up, Nisha."

I frowned as my mouth dropped open. "What did I do? I haven't said a word."

"Yeah, but I was waiting for you to say that I'm always emotional because of the pregnancy."

"Well, I mean . . . you are. There was no need to say it since you already know that," I said with a chuckle.

She stood and playfully pushed me on the arm. Had we been alone, she probably would have cursed. Of course, I overexaggerated the strength of her shove and fell over on the couch. That only caused everyone to laugh. My mama stood to go to the kitchen, so I stood as well. Before I could get there, I received another message from Oliver. That was interesting. I opened it and was caught off guard by what he had to say.

I know what I said about you not contacting me after work unless you wanted what I did, but I'm gonna have to renege on that, baby. Any interaction with you is a welcomed distraction. Text me anytime.

I smiled slightly as my mama said, "Who's got that beautiful smile on your face?"

I cleared my throat, slid my phone into my pocket, and told her. "His name is Oliver. He's the IT guy at work and goes to church with us."

"Oliver Andrews? He works on the computers at the church too."

I was beyond shocked that she knew him. "Oh really?"

"Yeah. Kinisha, where have you been? He's been Antioch's IT person for like three years."

*Somewhere with my head stuck up Jarod's ass.* I secretly rolled my eyes at the thought of him. I swore, when I saw that nigga, there wouldn't be anything nice about it. "I don't know, but I ran into him coming out of the restroom about a month ago, and he started working at my accounting firm a week later."

I smiled as I looked away to see what she cooked. "Well, it seems like you like him."

"He's a nice guy, but I'm unsure how I feel about him. He likes me, though. Things he says make me smile."

"And blush. Girl, your face is so red right now."

I chuckled, then had to go to the restroom. I couldn't even respond to my mother. The smell of the food had gotten to me. I ran so none of it would get on the floor and slammed the door, then regurgitated my hopes and dreams into the toilet because I hadn't attempted to eat anything since lunch. I grabbed a towel from the cabinet, wet it with cold water, and held it to my face. That offered so much relief.

Once I rinsed my mouth, I rejoined my mother in the kitchen. "I'm sorry. I suppose my nerves are finally settling about Daddy's surgery, and it made me sick to my stomach."

She frowned slightly and said, "Humph. Maybe so. Your nerves can definitely cause uneasiness and queasiness."

She didn't believe me, but I wouldn't say a word if she didn't say anything. I went back to the stove to help her fix plates and prayed that I wouldn't have to throw up again. As I fixed Ki's plate, Mama said, "Did you hear that Jarod finally decided to settle down?"

I frowned hard. "Settle down?"

"Girl, yes. His mom told me he got engaged over the weekend. That's why he wasn't in church yesterday. He took her to South Padre Island, I think she said."

"Wow. That's good, I guess. I would have never thought I would hear him and the words 'settle down' in the same sentence," I said as I fumed inside.

That low-down muthafucka was *definitely* going to hear from me. I didn't give a fuck about his fake-ass proposal. He and I both knew that was only for appearances, especially since he was deep in my pussy a week ago. My mother chuckled and said, "Chile, me either. He was always trying to talk to somebody's daughter. I saw him watching you a couple of times."

I kept my cool and only rolled my eyes. "Braylon was a saint compared to him," I said.

My mother chuckled once again. "Absolutely. I had no clue about Braylon, so he was at least discreet about his conquests. Jarod doesn't seem to care."

*Nope.* That muthafucka didn't care, but I would blow up his spot Sunday. He'd better hope it would be in private and not where everyone could hear us.

# Chapter 8

## *Oliver*

Something was going on with Kinisha. If it was what I thought it was, this would get bad. She'd been throwing up all week at work. While she'd used her father's surgery as an excuse Monday and Tuesday evening, she couldn't do the same afterward because the surgery had gone well. Her dad was up and moving around the next day. I'd seen him at Bible study Thursday evening. Reverend Adolph had praised God for how well he was doing.

Everything within me was saying that she was pregnant. She wasn't showing, but there was no other logical reason for her throwing up all week at work and refusing to go home. She wouldn't have forced herself to come to work if it were a stomach bug. Today was Sunday, and they had to start an audit at one of the grocery store chains tomorrow, so they wouldn't be in the office at all. Knowing Devin would need her more, she would have taken that time to rest up and get better.

I did my best to stay engaged in Sunday service, but my mind had remained on Kinisha. I had to go to the restroom when Pastor Adolph finished praying and the choir started singing. It had to be all that orange juice I drank this morning. For some reason, I couldn't seem to drink enough of it. All I knew was I couldn't wait to get to my cousin's house this afternoon to eat and clown

with her and Shannon. She said she was cooking smothered turkey wings, and I was all for that. I didn't care
what sides she was cooking to go with it. Turkey legs and
wings were my thing.

After finally relieving myself and heading out, I heard
someone ask, "How do I even know it's mine?"

"Because you're the only one I've been with."

"Shh. You're loud in here. Just like you bust the pussy
wide open for me, you could've been doing that for
someone else."

That was Kinisha's voice. There was no mistaking it.

"You know what? I respect the Lord's house, so I'm not
gonna say what I want to say to you right now. When I
call, you answer, or I will walk to that microphone next
Sunday and let the congregation know precisely what
kind of trash you are."

I couldn't take anymore. I walked out of the bathroom
and saw them standing there. I assumed they thought
they were alone. After looking back and forth between
them, Jarod walked away. Kinisha tried to walk away too,
but I grabbed her arm. "You okay?"

She shook her head rapidly, then disappeared into
the women's restroom. *Damn.* I couldn't believe she
was pregnant from that nigga. However, I felt like
this was what God was preparing me for all this time I'd
been actively pursuing her. There had to be some logical
explanation about how she ended up in this predicament.
She didn't seem like she was irresponsible in any regard.
Instead of returning to church, I decided to wait for her
to come out.

When she did, she stared at me for a moment. After
my head tilted slightly, I saw embarrassment flood her
reddened face.

"You heard everything, didn't you?"

"I heard enough."

"Please don't say anything."

"It's not my business. You wanna talk about it?"

"Since you know, it would probably do me some good. I thought you didn't want female friends."

"I told you almost a week ago to hell with that." I glanced around and said, "Sorry, Lord."

She gave me a slight smile. "Can I call after church?"

"Mm-hmm."

She nodded, then tried to walk away, but I grabbed her hand. I gave it a reassuring squeeze and then released her. I didn't know what the hell I was doing. I still wanted to pursue a relationship with a woman carrying another man's baby. This could come back and bite me in the ass, but I still wanted to do it anyway. Was I obsessed or something? I had to be. I was doing everything I said I wouldn't do. I didn't want to be her friend, but here I was, making myself available in that capacity.

I returned to church and sat back in my spot, not too far away from Kinisha and her family. She always sat with her sister and brother-in-law. Before her sister got married, it would just be the two of them. Just watching their interactions made me wish I had siblings. As I stared at the back of her head, she turned in her seat, and her eyes met mine. She gave me a soft smile, then turned back to face the front.

Everything inside of me wanted to punch Jarod in his mouth. How he spoke to Kinisha had my hands itching to grab him and choke the shit out of him. Had there been enough room on the pew Kinisha had sat on, I would have sat right next to her and mugged the hell out of him. I had a decent working relationship with his father, and he didn't seem to be the type to breed such a nigga. His mother was sweet as pie. She played the piano for the women's choir on fifth Sundays. While I knew I couldn't judge a book by its cover, I just couldn't fathom which one of them had passed down the traits he exhibited a little while ago.

When church was over, I gave Kinisha one last glance and was about to head to my vehicle. However, her eyes met mine, and she called me over to her. I frowned slightly, trying to figure out what she was setting me up for. Then, the more I thought about it, the more I realized she wanted to introduce her coworker to her family. I walked over, and she extended her hand to me. *Hmm.* I grabbed it, and she said, "Kiana and Lazarus, this is Oliver. We work together now, and although he says he doesn't do female friends, I'd like to think that we're friends anyway."

She giggled, and I twisted my lips to the side as Lazarus extended his hand. "I feel you, bruh. I told Kiana the same thing not long after we met."

I nodded. "I must be in good company then."

He chuckled as I turned my attention to her very pregnant sister. I smiled softly and gave her hand a gentle shake. "Nice to meet you."

She smiled big and glanced at Kinisha. I didn't know what that was about, but I turned to Kinisha and said, "I'll talk to you later."

She smiled slightly and nodded as I squeezed her hand, then released her. As I was walking away, she said, "Oliver."

I turned back to her to see she was walking toward me. "What's up?"

"Umm . . ." She turned back to look at her sister, then back to me. "My family wanted me to invite you to Sunday dinner."

"Your family or you?"

"My family."

"I already have other plans. Maybe some other time."

She nodded. I didn't want to be there if she wasn't inviting me. I knew I would be there in a friend capacity. I only wanted to be around her family if I was her man. I already had to be her "friend" at work. I wasn't feeling that shit. When I got to my car and saw Jarod standing there, a deep frown made its way to my face. He stepped away from my vehicle when I unlocked the doors.

"Oliver, I trust you will keep the conversation you overheard to yourself."

"I'm not Kinisha. Unfortunately, I *will* disrespect the Lord's house and ask for forgiveness later. So your best bet is to get the fuck on."

He lifted his hands in surrender. "No need to get all defensive."

"Naw. It was no need to speak to that woman like that. She approached you respectfully and should have been given that same respect in return. I don't have shit for a nigga that can speak to a woman disrespectfully. I hope she blasts your ho ass."

I opened the door to my car, and my pointed glare dared him to say another word. Kinisha wasn't mine, but at this moment, it sure felt like she was. After cranking my engine, I headed to Anise's house. Those turkey wings were the last things on my mind now. I just wanted to hold Kinisha in my arms. I didn't know what the fuck she was thinking, messing around with a nigga like him, but what was done was done.

If she chose to move on from it, I would be there if she decided to move on with me. Obviously, she wouldn't be moving on with him, especially not after his father announced his engagement in church today. I damn near swallowed my fucking tongue when that man said that. That poor woman didn't have a clue what she was getting herself into. I could only pray that she figured it out before it was too late. That was the most drama I'd ever witnessed going down in church. While I'd heard of shit like that, I was caught way off guard today.

When I got to Anise's house, my cell phone chimed with a text. I had a feeling it was from Kinisha. I grabbed my phone to confirm that it was. I can't disappoint my family. I don't know what to do. I wasn't ready. The condom broke, and the morning-after pill didn't work. I feel like such a fool.

An idea hit me, but I didn't know how she would accept it. So, I responded with something that would give me more clarity. Why would your family be disappointed? You're a grown woman.

My parents are old-fashioned. Sleeping around isn't something they would agree with. For their daughter, who they taught well, to be bringing a baby into this world without a husband is bad. However, bringing a baby into this world without a boyfriend is even worse. If they knew he didn't even want to be involved in our child's life, it could make them totally disown me. I saw it when they did it to my sister for something way less serious. This would prove to them that I was just fucking to be fucking. It's eating me alive that I have to tell them this.

I momentarily thought about my plan of action, trying to figure out if I could do what had come to mind. I realized I could, but the real question would be whether *she* could do it. I knew how I felt. I sent her a text. Can we talk in person later? Around four or so?

Yeah. Call me, and we can meet up, or you can come to my place.

Okay.

I stepped out of my car to head inside Anise's house, and I could hear loud laughter coming from inside and noticed more cars than usual. I slightly rolled my eyes to prepare for her and Shannon's foolery and whoever else was there. I wasn't a big fan of eating dinner with people

I didn't know, but it was either that or missing out on those turkey wings. *I'd be damned.* Nothing was gonna keep me from those wings.

I knocked on the door since I noticed Anise's boyfriend's car in the driveway. I only walked in when she was alone and expecting me or if it was just her and Shannon. When Robert opened the door for me, he gave me a head nod, and I did the same. I believed he knew that I could feel the fuckery within him. Our vibe was totally off. I heard a familiar voice as he stepped aside to let me in.

I frowned slightly as I went inside to see Devin and his wife. When he saw me, he stood. "Man, what you doing here?" he asked as he shook my hand.

"Anise is my cousin. What are you doing here?"

"Shannon is my sister-in-law. She and Sidney are sisters, and she's also married to my brother."

He turned as another man stood. To say he was his brother, they were like night and day. Devin was dark complexioned, and this dude was light as the sun with blue eyes. However, Devin had gray-colored eyes, so I assumed that gene came from one parent in particular. "This is William, but everyone calls him WJ. Bruh, this is Oliver. We contracted his IT company about a month ago."

"That's what's up. Nice to meet you," he said.

"Likewise."

I turned my attention to Anise, and she smiled and offered me a hug while Shannon said, "Hey, Oliver."

"What's up?"

She wasn't being her usual flirty self since her husband was here, but I was sure he knew how she was. From our introduction, I could tell he was laid-back and let her be who she was. That was why they worked.

"I'll tell you what's up. Yo' ass ain't scheduled a consultation yet."

I chuckled as I rubbed my bald head. "My bad. I forgot."

"Forgot my ass. Put it on tomorrow's schedule, or I will do it for you. I'm pretty sure Anise knows where you live. We will just show the hell up."

"Shannon, how you gon' bully that man into a consult?" Devin's wife asked.

"I'm not bullying him. I'm just making him stay true to his word. If he had no intention of scheduling one, he shouldn't have said he would. I didn't even ask him to. He volunteered that information."

"Shannon, I forgooooot! I don't say shit I don't mean. I'll schedule it for Tuesday. I have to go to Houston tomorrow to check on my other office."

"Go to the site and do it now before you forget."

I chuckled and did as she asked. I was serious about getting my house's interior upgraded. Once I was done, Anise was placing food on the table. My eyes zeroed in on the spread, and I noticed I wasn't the only one. Devin had done the same thing. We were the first two to start moving. His wife giggled. He turned to her and asked, "What's funny, Sidney?"

"You have a partner in crime."

He looked at me as I frowned playfully, causing the women to laugh more. "That's all right, though. We won't be hungry," Devin said as we sat at the table.

Shannon and Sidney went to the kitchen to help Anise as WJ and Robert joined us at the table. Robert's phone was going off back-to-back, and he was ignoring that shit. I kept glancing at him, and the moment he noticed, he powered down his phone. He was doing exactly what I suspected he was doing. He was fucking around on her.

I could always peep game because I was the type of nigga to lie back in the cut and observe shit. The nigga was rarely here, and when he was, he was quiet and on his phone most of the time. I didn't know why she put up with that shit. He had to have been beating her ass with the dick for her to allow this mediocrity.

I didn't see a woman overlooking shit like this unless she was getting fucked like she liked it. Apparently, Anise didn't have any complaints in that department unless she just wasn't expressing those complaints to me. I couldn't concern myself with that right now because she'd just set those wings right in front of me. I was ready to dig in and apologize to everyone else when I was done.

When the ladies returned carrying drinks, they set them in front of us, and then they all sat. We all grabbed hands, and Devin blessed the food. The moment he finished, I was digging in. "Damn, nigga, you hungry, huh?" Shannon asked as she stared at my mouth.

"Uh-huh."

I was hungry in more ways than one, and I wanted to fulfill that other hunger with Kinisha as soon as possible. If my plan worked, that would happen sooner rather than later.

# Chapter 9

## *Kinisha*

I'd sent Oliver my address, and I was nervous as hell. It wasn't like I hadn't had a man over. I knew Oliver way more than I knew Jarod. I believed it was because he knew what had happened. Besides Kiana and Ramsey, I'd never shared so much with someone. I trusted Oliver, though. It wasn't like he didn't already know the situation. Unfortunately, he was well aware of what was going on. The fact that he still wanted to talk to me had shocked me.

As I waited, I called Jarod. He was a fool if he thought I would let him off the hook that easily. He sent the call to voicemail, then sent a text. *Jackass.* I opened our thread to read, I'm with my fiancée. What do you want?

That only further pissed me off. It was like he wanted to throw into my face that he was engaged. I didn't give a fuck. If I wanted to be a petty bitch, I could get her number. All it would take was one call to Mrs. Speights and me saying I wanted to congratulate her and get to know her. She would give me her number without hesitation. I was tempted to do that shit, and I would if I felt like I had to.

I gathered my thoughts and began typing. You know the only reason that condom broke was because it was too small. Why would you buy condoms that are too small? Second, whether or not you want to admit it, this is your baby. If you want a paternity test, make it happen, but it won't change a thing. Be a man and accept responsibility. My legs were only open for you. Unlike you, I only sleep with one man at a time. I'm far from being in the streets like your community dick having ass.

We need to talk like civilized adults to decide what's best for us and what will work best for this baby. I can't have an abortion since it's now illegal. So either you will step up to the plate and quit being a childish-ass lil boy, or I will make your life miserable. Fuck with that, nigga. You wanna play stupid-ass games, you gon' win stupid-ass prizes. I don't have a problem resorting to being stupid ratchet if I have to be. It takes two to create a baby, so I refuse to take care of this baby by myself. Fuck around if you want to. You gon' fucking find out, bitch.

I stared at the message and was super proud of my pettiness as I hit send. I was fuming on the inside, and nothing could soothe me like some alcohol right now. Sliding my hand over my face, I slowly shook my head. I couldn't believe I'd put myself in this predicament. It felt like a long-ass nightmare. The way I kept zoning out with my family was only bringing attention to me. I still hadn't told them what was happening, but they all seemed to sense that something was wrong.

The knock at the door halted my thoughts. I stared at it for a moment, thinking if I should allow Oliver in my space. I gave him the address, but I was overthinking. I supposed fooling around with Jarod had me questioning stupid shit. Finally, I stood and went to the door. After checking the peephole and seeing him standing there, I opened it. He had on a yellow buttoned-down Polo-style shirt. I gave him a soft smile and invited him inside. When I closed the door and turned to him, he was staring at me.

Closing in the space between us, he came to me and pulled me into his arms. I wrapped my arms around his waist and closed my eyes. "Thank you for coming, Oliver. This has to be awkward for you."

"Why so?"

"The woman you've been chasing is pregnant with someone else's baby."

"The only way it would be awkward was if you were mine first and got pregnant from someone else afterward."

I pulled away from him and grabbed his hand, leading him to the couch. Once we sat, I huffed and fell back onto the couch cushions. "I fucked up my life."

"How? You're already in your career field. It's not like you're in school or something. This baby could be a blessing. Just because it didn't happen how you wanted it to doesn't mean it has to be bad. You're a strong woman. Fuck him."

"My parents—"

"If you're so concerned about what your parents think, do something about it."

"Something like what?" I asked with a frown.

"Be mine. I'll be your boyfriend, and the baby will be mine. Simple fix."

My eyes widened, and I sat straight up. *Be his?* "Oliver, how would that change anything?"

"You'll have a boyfriend and a father for your baby. You'll save face in front of them, and I'll go with you to tell them you're pregnant."

My heart was racing. I brought my hand to my chest as if that would steady it any. "Are you saying what I *think* you're saying?"

"I don't know. What do you think I'm saying?"

"That you would pretend to be my man and father of my child."

"You're only half right. I wouldn't be pretending to be your man. I would be. You wouldn't be able to see anyone else. The buck stops here. You would be mine, and I would pretend to be the biological father of your child. However, I would be a father to them as well. We could raise your baby in love."

"I . . . I need to think about that," I said as I stuttered.

He nodded, then pulled me to him and hugged me. He laid his soft lips on my forehead as my mind traveled rapidly. If I said yes, I would only be pretending to save face. Was my image worth all that? That would mean I could no longer hassle Jarod's ass about being a father. He would get off easy, and I could be miserable in a relationship I didn't want. When his lips touched my forehead again, I looked up at him.

Oliver stared into my eyes as the tears fell from them. I was so stunned by his offer that I was at a loss for words. Why would he want to raise a child that wasn't his? I couldn't understand his reasoning. Finally, finding my voice, I asked, "Why? Why would you settle?"

"Who said I was settling? You aren't the only woman out there, but you are the only woman I want. A baby isn't going to stop me from wanting you. It just gives me one more person to love eventually. The question is, do you want me?"

"I . . ." I looked away from him, but he swiftly grabbed my chin and turned my head back to him. "I don't know. I don't want to say yes because I'm vulnerable and want to pull the wool over my parents' eyes."

"Take time to think about it. Even if you are only with me to pull the wool over your parents' eyes, I can promise you that won't be the reason why you stay. Give me a chance to prove I can be the one for you, baby."

He touched my cheeks and gently caressed them with his thumbs. His gaze was taking me down faster than I could count to five. I closed my eyes for a moment. When I reopened them, his face was closer to mine. His lips lightly grazed mine, and the heat encompassed me. He pulled away, and I was left wanting more. I didn't know how that happened when he was a man I wasn't even sure that I wanted to be with in any capacity.

Oliver was my coworker, and he seemed like he would be an amazing friend. However, I didn't want to set myself up for failure. If I wasn't satisfied, would I be able to be faithful? I stared at him as he mumbled, "You think too much about the wrong things. Don't take too long to decide, or it will no longer be on the table."

"You'll change your mind about wanting me?"

"No. I'll change my mind about taking the heat. You'll be facing your parents and family alone, telling them about the baby a nigga like Jarod wants nothing to do with. Once you start showing, I'm not coming to save the day. I'm going to be there from the beginning. I won't tarnish my reputation because you can't decide."

He released me from his arms, and I immediately felt a chill. Not because I was cold but because he'd taken away his soft words and hit me with the truth. I lowered my head to my hands, wishing I could have a drink. This should be a no-brainer, but for the life of me, I didn't understand why I was having such a hard time with it.

"So, if I say yes, I'm all yours whether or not I want to be, right? No going out or talking to other men."

He side-eyed me as he stood from his seat. "I don't know who you take me for, Kinisha, but whoever that muthafucka is, he ain't me. You a smart woman. You know that shit wouldn't fly. What confusion about the words 'you're mine' is there? That's as straightforward as it can get. Take it or leave it. Your decision. I gotta go."

He walked to the door, and my heart rate picked up speed. "Oliver."

Turning back to me, he held his position until I approached him. He faced me, staring at me, waiting for me to say what I wanted. I grabbed his hands and closed my eyes, silently praying I was making the right decision. "Okay."

"Okay, what?"

"I'm yours. I do have the option to change my mind, though, if you get on my nerves, right?"

He frowned slightly. "You act like I'm holding you prisoner or some shit. There *is* a stipulation, though. If we don't work out, you have to tell your family the truth. They will not be dragging my name through the mud for not taking care of a child that's not biologically mine."

I nodded, and he pulled me in his arms. It was so comfortable here. His arms were unlike anything I'd ever felt. It was like love, adoration, and peace were within them. Oliver made me feel things I didn't expect. Pulling away, he grabbed my hand and led me back to the couch.

"I thought you had to go."

"I did as long as you were in limbo. You're mine now. I never *have* to go."

His words sent a chill through me as he sat and pulled me close to him. I was somewhat tense because I didn't know how quickly he planned to move with us, but I supposed we had to move extremely fast if we had to convince my people that this baby was his. It had to be believable. I didn't think I was ready for sex with him, but at the same time, I didn't think I would be in this predicament either. Anything could happen.

I took a deep breath, trying to release tension, then lay against him.

"I'm going to All-Star Weekend if you wanna ride out with me. It's in H-Town this year."

"Really?" I asked.

"Mm-hmm."

"When are you leaving?"

"It's in a couple of weeks, so you have time. I'm leaving on a Friday morning."

"Let me check with Mr. Taylor. I should be able to go, though. We're supposed to wrap up this audit by Wednesday, then start on the next one. That one should be done before you leave."

"Have you taken a shower yet?"

"Yes."

He stood and pulled me from the couch. "Show me to your room so I can rub you down, baby."

My tension was back until he brought his hands to my shoulders and gently rubbed them. That shit propelled me forward. He was diving all the way in, and, for right now, I was okay with that. Once we got to my bedroom, he looked around and said, "This is nice. I'm gonna take it that blue is your favorite color."

"Yep. All shades."

"A'ight, Ms. Gemini. Get your lotion or whatever you want me to rub you down with."

I swallowed hard, then got the lotion. I wasn't ready to get naked in front of him, so I hoped he wasn't expecting that. "Umm . . . Oliver . . ."

He placed his fingertips on my lips. "Just take off the leggings. After I do your legs, if you feel comfortable enough to take off more, that will be on you."

I nodded, then stepped away from him and slowly pulled them off. It wasn't my intent to tease him, but it seemed that was what I was doing. He licked his lips as he stared at my thick-ass legs. That print appeared out of nowhere, and I instantly got thirsty. It seemed I was struggling to breathe until he made his way to me, reminding me that I had to if I wanted to live. "You okay?"

I nodded quickly as he gently swept the stray strand of hair from my cheek. He kissed my forehead again, causing me to close my eyes. Those were the best. I lifted my hand and stroked his cheek, allowing the hairs of his beard to tickle my palm. When I felt his lips against mine, I didn't pull away. He kissed me softly, and the chemistry I felt between us had to have been imagined. "Lay down, baby, so that I can take care of you."

I lay on my stomach in the bed, feeling my T-shirt hike up a bit on my ass. I'd worn boy shorts, so I knew my cheeks were hanging out of them. I could feel the trembling course through my body when he softly moaned. What was I doing? This wasn't right. Just as I was about to get up, he firmly gripped my leg right at my calf muscle and began kneading it like I'd never experienced. I'd had plenty of massages but by women. None of their hands were as firm but tender at the same time as Oliver's.

"Ooooh, Oliver. That feels good."

It wasn't even sexual, but I knew that was how I sounded. I didn't even care. That was just how good it felt. He didn't say a word . . . just continued rubbing my leg and foot. It made me long for the future with him during my pregnancy. If he was already showing me this kind of care, and I hadn't even had my first doctor's appointment yet, how would he be when I was eight months? I needed to give this a legitimate shot.

"So, when is your first appointment?"

"In two weeks, on the seventeenth . . . at eight. You want to come?"

"Why wouldn't I, baby?"

God, he was saying everything right. "O-okay."

I was tensing up again, and he noticed. "Relax. I got'chu. I won't do anything to hurt you."

I tried to do as he said as he massaged my thigh. The higher he went, the more nervous I got. However, when he began making his way back down, I took a deep breath, exhaling all my tension. He showed my other leg and foot the same attention, then allowed me to get up and put my leggings back on. Once I did, he wrapped his arms around me from behind and laid his hands on my stomach. I closed my eyes and wished things were different. Maybe Oliver and I could have actually gotten to know each other and dated before diving into this foolery.

I turned around in his arms. "Thank you for that. I was slightly uncomfortable, but I know it will become natural with time. Can I offer you the same courtesy? Can I massage your back?"

"I didn't do that for anything in return."

"I know, but I want to give you something in return. Is that a bad thing?"

"No."

I began unbuttoning his shirt as he stared at me. His gaze seemed to be penetrating my soul. I couldn't maintain it. I had to look down at what I was doing. When I finished unbuttoning his shirt, I slid it off his broad shoulders. He wore a wifebeater underneath, but dear Jesus of Nazareth, this man was fine as shit. I didn't know how he hid all this under this long-sleeved shirt, but praise God for His many blessings. I could see the definition with his shirt on, but I had no clue his shit was on this level. *My God today.*

Sliding my hands under his beater on his bare abs, I could see the goose bumps invade his skin. I lifted his shirt and pulled it over his head. After that, I pulled his glasses from his face. I set them on my dresser as he went to the bed and lay on his stomach. My eyes didn't want to part with all that dark chocolate lying on my sheets. Somehow, I accomplished the feat and grabbed the lotion, squirting some in my palm, then rubbing my hands together to heat it.

I placed my hands on his shoulders and rubbed them gently, feeling how tight his muscles were. The desire to get in bed and straddle him had reared its ugly head, and

I almost succumbed to it. It would have made it easier to reach the areas I was trying to get to, but maybe I would do that next time. I rubbed his shoulders, doing my best to make him feel as good as he made me feel. When I heard a soft moan leave him, I was happy. However, it only made me want to work harder to hear those sounds from him again.

When I finished, he turned over on his back and smiled slightly. "Thank you."

"You're welcome. So, are you going to miss me tomorrow? We aren't going to the office for you to jack with my computer."

He chuckled, and my eyes widened. I playfully slapped his chest. "I knew it. I *knew* you were fu . . . I mean messing with it."

"I wanted to be in your space without seeming weird." He stared at me silently for a few seconds, then said, "You don't have to filter yourself. I like that about you. I like everything about you. So when would you like to clue everyone in?"

"After my appointment. That way, they will have all seen us together at least a few times. I'll mention you to my mama again."

"Again?"

"Yeah. She saw me smiling as I texted you Monday before my dad's surgery. When I told her who you were, she already knew you."

"She did?"

"Yeah. She said you handled the church's computers."

"Humph. I guess people do pay attention to me."

"She asked if I liked you because I was blushing."

"Well, I'll be damned." He sat up, grabbed my hand, and pulled me to the bed. "Get in. I don't bite unless you want me to."

I smiled slightly, then crawled over him and lay next to him. He pulled me into his arms and angled his body to where he could stare into my eyes. I stared right back, knowing that I was foolish for doubting this. I should have been doubting Jarod's punk ass. However, my only concern was that Oliver's presence didn't speak to me. Only after I started getting to know him did he become more attractive to me.

He gently caressed my cheek as he stared into my eyes. "I can't wait to openly show you how much I care for you, Kinisha. And for the record, I'm gon' miss the hell out of you tomorrow. I might go by the office and fuck up your computer for the hell of it."

I pushed his shoulder as I laughed, then said honestly, "I'm gonna miss you tomorrow too."

# Chapter 10

## *Oliver*

My time with Kinisha yesterday had wrapped up way too quickly. We lay in bed talking, laughing, and staring at each other for hours. She was the most beautiful woman I'd ever seen, and now, she was all mine. While I know our desires were somewhat one-sided, I also knew with time, they wouldn't be. When the idea hit me to ask her to be mine to help her save face, I thought I was losing my mind. In my mind, it sounded desperate as hell.

However, when it came out, it didn't sound so bad. I wanted Kinisha, and I needed her to *see* how much I wanted her. I was willing to raise another man's child as my own to have her in my life. If I appealed to her good sense, I knew it would buy me time to show her what I already knew. She wouldn't have agreed to it had I not offered to pose as the father of her child. She was already somewhat pushing me away, and we were only friendly at work.

At church, we spoke, but never for too long, just in passing. That woman drove me wild inside, and I knew I wouldn't be able to be with anyone else until we knew whether we were compatible. Judging by how Sunday evening went, I would say we were extremely compatible. She had even gotten more comfortable with me by the time I was about to leave.

She didn't hesitate to slide her fingers through my beard, and I constantly kissed her forehead and stroked her cheeks with my fingertips. The moment seemed surreal because I'd imagined being that way with her for a couple of years. Regardless of whether she wanted to believe it, this baby was definitely a blessing. While I had no doubt that I would eventually get her to see me for who I was as a man, this predicament caused her to jump right in without much thought.

She couldn't have been a good judge of character if she thought Jarod would be the man for her. Ray Charles could see he was a ho, and he was blind and dead. I never asked her if she was even pursuing a relationship with Jarod in the first place. It was like our conversation had unintentionally stayed away from him. Maybe it was intentional on her end, but it surely wasn't that way on mine.

I messaged her this morning to wish her a good day, and she responded immediately. The smile had stayed on my face the entire ride to Houston. Before getting to the office, I'd gotten breakfast. I met with the team, so everyone was in the office this morning. Ronnie had been doing extremely well, making me happy that I took a chance on him. Things were running smoothly, and more business was coming in.

The meeting was to evaluate whether we could even handle another contract right now without getting more people hired and trained. I'd placed an ad online and with a couple of temp agencies. Sometimes, I hired temps to see if they could cut it. One of my best techs had come through a temp agency. The nigga didn't have the first degree but was smart as hell. I put him through school to beef up his résumé. I wasn't naïve to think he would always work for me, but I wanted him to have the tools to get an even better job than with Andrews Technologies. Without a degree, that would be damn near impossible.

After our meeting, I kind of just hung around the office. There wasn't much to do, and it only left time for me to think about Kinisha and how hard she was probably working. I stared at a picture of her on my phone and smiled slightly before closing it out. As I was about to get up for lunch, Mya appeared in the doorway.

"Hey, Mr. Andrews. Did you wanna get lunch?"

I glanced at the time, then smiled slightly. "Why not? Where did you have in mind to go?" I asked as I stood and grabbed my keys.

"Well, I know you're always down for a turkey leg. So you wanna go to the Turkey—"

"Girl, I know you ain't about to say the Turkey Leg Hut. You ain't even have to say the name. Let's roll."

She giggled as I walked past her and opened the door to head to my car. After getting to my ride, I opened the passenger door for her, then walked around to my side. Suddenly my brain started thinking about shit other than those turkey legs. *Why is she always the one left at the office?* She wasn't a receptionist, but she was never in the field when I came to town. I knew the answer to that shit, and I was gonna shut her ass down as soon as I got in the car.

I slid into my seat and started the engine. After my Bluetooth connected, I hit Kinisha's picture. "Hello?"

"Hey, baby. How's your day going?" Without looking at Mya, I could see her eyes were as wide as saucers.

"Hey, handsome. Devin Taylor is working me to death, but he's buying lunch, so I guess I can chill."

I chuckled as I heard Devin say something in the background. "How are you feeling, though?" I asked softly.

"So far so good. We'll see what happens when I try to eat. What are you up to?"

"Mya and I are heading to the Turkey Leg Hut."

"You're gonna turn into a turkey leg," she said and laughed.

"You laughing a li'l too hard at that. If I didn't know any better, I'd think you'd gotten a visual."

She only laughed harder, causing me to laugh too as I left my parking spot. I was surprised she hadn't asked who Mya was. So I asked, "You aren't going to ask who Mya is?"

"I assumed she was one of your employees. You wouldn't have told me her name if she was anything else besides that. Plus, I trust you, Oliver."

"Wait a minute! Y'all a couple?" Devin asked.

I could imagine Kinisha had probably rolled her eyes. "Baby, you're on speaker," Kinisha said as I chuckled.

"What's up, boss man?"

Devin laughed loudly. "You finally wore her down, huh?"

"I'm sitting right here, Mr. Taylor," Kinisha said sarcastically.

I chuckled as I glanced over at Mya. She was extremely quiet and was fidgeting slightly. This entire conversation had made her uneasy. Maybe now, she wouldn't try me with her subtle flirting. "Yeah, she finally gave me a chance to prove myself. I promised her that I wouldn't let her down."

"Oliver, really?" Kinisha said, interrupting my conversation with Devin.

"What?"

"You sent me a Cash App. What for?"

"Lunch, baby."

"It's fifty dollars."

"You have to eat tomorrow too, right?"

She was quiet for a moment, then took a deep breath. "Thank you," she said softly.

I could tell it was hard for her to accept gifts. She had better get used to it because I would be showering her with them often. Besides physical touch and quality time, it was how I showed my affection. Hell, I seemed to be in tune with all the love languages when it came to her. Whatever I could do to keep her happy, I would do. "You're welcome, baby. I'll text you when I hit the road to go home. If you're free, call me."

"Okay. I can't wait to see you."

"Damn. I can't wait to see you either, baby. Talk to you later."

Nothing about our conversation felt put on. I loved that. Maybe she was falling into this like I had. I really hoped that was what she was doing. After ending the call, I glanced at Mya to see her looking at me. "What's up, Mya?"

"I'm sorry. I didn't know you had a girlfriend."

"Yeah. We made it official this weekend, so you didn't miss anything."

"Oh. How did y'all meet?"

"We go to the same church, but recently, we took on Taylor, Wesin, and Sylvester Accounting Firm. She works there."

"She's a CPA?"

"Yeah."

She lowered her head for a moment. "I know you weren't feeling me, but I was hoping I could wear you down, like the man in the background said about you wearing her down. You're a good man, and I really like you, Oliver."

"I'm sorry, Mya. While I'm not in love with Kinisha, my heart belongs to her. She is the only woman I want to fall for. There's a man out there for you, but I'm not him. I'm sorry."

"Yeah, me too."

She remained quiet all the way to the Turkey Leg Hut. I couldn't pry words from her mouth with a crowbar. When I parked, she got out without waiting for me to open her door. "Mya, above all else, I'm still a gentleman. I was coming to open your door."

She glanced at me, something she'd been doing since I called Kinisha. I wasn't sure what that shit was about, but I would have to find out. I'd have to use better judgment whenever I was around her. For some reason, I felt uneasy, like she was gonna try some slick shit. "Mya, you good? What's up?"

She turned to me as we approached the counter, loud as fuck. "I wanted you! *That's* what's wrong with me. But you chose someone else! What about *me?* I love you, Oliver. How could you do this to me?"

I looked around to see all eyes were on us. "Umm . . . Mya, please lower your voice. I never led you on to think we would ever have a relationship of that kind. I'm your boss. That's it."

She stood there and started crying like I'd broken her heart. She said she loved me. This was some weird shit. To hell with lunch. We had to get out of here so I could get her back to the office. I grabbed her hand to lead her out, but she jerked away. "Why were you so nice to me if you weren't feeling me? Why do you smile at me so much? Every time you're here, you're extra friendly. We're even at lunch together."

"Mya, I ain't gon' tell you but one more time to pipe that shit down."

"Or what?"

"I'm gon' leave your crazy ass here, *that's* what."

She was fuming as she crossed her arms over her chest. I didn't know what the fuck had happened to make her snap like that. "You're just like all the rest of them. I thought you were different, Oliver. Fuck you."

"Okay. I tried to reason with you, but that don't seem to be working." I pulled my wallet from my pocket and took out fifty dollars. "This should be enough to get you lunch and get you back to the office. This behavior you're exhibiting right now tells me I don't need to be alone with you."

A man and woman from the restaurant approached us, probably to put us out. Instead, they asked if there was something they could do to help us. I slid my hand down my face and slowly shook my head. "Thank you for your concern. We've had a terrible misunderstanding, and I'm not even sure how. I'm assuming that me being nice has been misconstrued. We need orders, mine to go."

"I'm not staying here. I got here with you, and I'm leaving with you."

I glanced at her from the corner of my eyes, ready to unleash on her ass. Although I was a naturally quiet and laid-back person, I had my breaking points, and she was tiptoeing on the line. I snatched my money back from her and ordered our food to go. After that, I got on my app and requested a Lyft. I turned to her and stared at her for a moment. She stared right back. Her eyes were somewhat shifty, and she looked nervous as hell. Something was surely up with her.

"Look. It's not safe for me to be alone with you. I'm two seconds from snatching you up. The best thing is for you to get a ride with a Lyft. At this point, I don't know what you're capable of, and clearly, you don't know what I'm capable of. I don't wanna be that person with you, Mya. What's going on with you? I'm nice to everybody. I have not shown you any preferential treatment. Whatever I do with you, I'd do with anyone else in the office if they're available. I find it funny, though, that you're always the one available. What's going on?"

"I told you already. I love you! From the first time I saw you when you interviewed me, I made a vow that I would strive to be everything I thought you needed and that you would notice. I thought you did. But today, you broke my heart."

I slid my hand over my bald head as other patrons looked on. I had to get away from her. If she put her hands on me when I left, I wouldn't be able to stop myself from showing her how rough I could be. I led her to a table to sit while we waited for our orders. Hopefully, the Lyft arrived after I left because I knew I would have a time trying to get her ass in that car. How did I miss her crazy? She'd been so mild mannered.

As I sat there, my phone buzzed with a text message. I pulled it from my pocket to see a picture from Kinisha. She was smiling big. Then there was another picture of her eating a big-ass slice of pizza with her eyes closed. I chuckled slightly as I noticed the scowl on Mya's face in my peripheral vision. I responded with a heart face and laughing emojis. Hopefully, she'd be able to keep it down.

The guy who had approached us earlier brought our food to us in to-go containers, and I couldn't be happier. I stood from my seat, and she did so as well. "Mya, I got a Lyft for you. You can't ride with me."

"Why? You've never had a problem with me riding with you."

"You ain't never flipped the script on me, either. I don't trust you. You gon' have to find another job too."

There were clearly some mental issues present because she stood there crying like I'd hurt her feelings. She was mild again, like she hadn't just flipped out a little while ago.

"Okay, Mr. Andrews. I'm so sorry. I really love working for Andrews Technologies."

She sat at the table just as the Lyft arrived. "Your ride is here."

She nodded as she wiped her face, then grabbed her food. "Is it taking me to the office to pack my things?"

"Yes, ma'am."

She walked out without another word, leaving me standing there confused as hell. I walked out to my car and followed them to the office. Thankfully, Ronnie was there so I wouldn't be alone with her. When I walked in after her, Ronnie smiled and said, "Boss man, how you doing today, sir?"

I smiled slightly as his smile dimmed. He frowned when he saw Mya grabbing a box from the back. "We need to have a meeting after the original meeting today if you have time," I told him while sending a text to the other technicians.

That irritated the hell out of me because I wouldn't get to see Kinisha today. The meeting would obviously keep us here a lot later. This shit was frustrating as hell. I'd put out an ad for a new tech, but I'd have to hire at least three now. This was bullshit I didn't need, and I could only hope I wouldn't encounter future problems with Mya because she seemed crazy as hell.

Before Ronnie could respond to me, Mya started screaming. *That bitch is crazy as fuck.* Ronnie and I quickly ran to her office to find her on the floor, pulling her hair. I was about ready to pull hair I didn't fucking have. I was two seconds from calling the nuthouse to come get her ass. When Ronnie walked closer to her, she only started screaming more. "You all hate me! I don't want to leave, Oliver!"

Ronnie looked back at me, his eyes wide. I slightly rolled my eyes and gestured for him to follow me with a tilt of my head.

"What is going on with Mya?" he asked as we stepped out into the hallway.

"We were going to lunch. I called my lady, and when I got off the phone, she admitted that she thought we could be together and how much she loved me. She flipped her fucking lid at the Turkey Leg Hut. I was so damn embarrassed. She was screaming and shit, like she's doing now. I have never insinuated that I wanted a relationship with her, so I don't know what her issue is. The most physical interaction we've had is a handshake, so I'm lost as hell."

"I have a sister with mental issues. She's bipolar, and I swear, Mya seems to be doing some of the same shit she be doing at times. She overexaggerates everything. What do you want to do?"

"I'm going to look at her file to see if there's someone listed I can call to come get her or calm her down."

"Okay. I'm going to go back inside her office to watch her."

"Thanks, Ronnie."

I headed straight to the file cabinet in my office to pull her file. I knew for a fact that she didn't list any illnesses on her application. That was something I wouldn't forget. I sat at my desk and looked through paperwork and evaluations and shit. There was nothing there indicating that she had problems. Slowly shaking my head, I went to her application and saw her mother listed as an emergency contact.

I quickly dialed the number from the phone on my desk, and she answered on the first ring. "Mya, what's wrong?"

"It's her boss, Oliver Andrews."

"Oh no. Something has happened if you're calling me."

"She kind of uhh . . . flipped on me when we went to get lunch. Is there a diagnosis I should be aware of?"

She took a deep breath as Mya started screaming again. "My God. Is that her?"

"Yes."

"She was diagnosed as a manic depressive a year ago. She didn't want to tell you for fear of losing her job," she said as I heard keys jingling.

"That would have been discriminatory. She's a good worker. I wouldn't have fired her, but this wouldn't have caught me off guard. Can you please come to help her? Whenever I try to calm her down, I only make it worse. She said she was in love with me. When she found out I had a lady, she flipped."

"Lord have mercy—my poor baby. I'm on my way, Mr. Andrews. It's gonna take me about thirty minutes to get there, providing there isn't much traffic."

I glanced at the time to see it was twelve thirty. I was more than sure there was plenty of traffic. It was the lunch rush. "Yes, ma'am. Thank you for coming."

"Yes, sir. See you soon."

I wouldn't expect her until an hour from now. Jarvis knocked on my door as I sat at my desk, contemplating what I would do. I gave him a head nod, and he entered. "Yo . . ." he said with his thumb pointed behind him over his shoulder toward Mya's office.

I lifted my hand. I couldn't even talk about that shit right now. All I could focus on was that her mama would be here soon to get her out of here.

# Chapter 11

## *Kinisha*

I hadn't seen Oliver since Sunday, and surprisingly, I missed him more than I thought I would. I'd been throwing up like crazy, so I took off work today. Mr. Taylor had surely peeped game on Monday. After I ate my pizza, I had to run to the restroom immediately and regurgitate my stomach's contents. I couldn't wait until this phase of my pregnancy was over. Not having Oliver to baby me only made it worse.

I'd talked to him over the phone every evening and night. This situationship with him was progressing easier than I thought it would. He wasn't overbearing or clingy like I thought he would be. I actually found myself wanting to call him more than he called me. I wanted to believe he was restraining himself, so I didn't change my mind.

What he didn't know was that I liked attention . . . plenty of it. His massage from Sunday was still fresh on my mind, and I couldn't wait to experience it again. As I snuggled under my covers, someone knocked at my door. I wanted to roll my eyes, but I somehow managed to get out of bed and trudge to the door.

After checking the peephole and seeing Oliver, I got so excited. However, that excitement produced bile in my throat. I opened the door and ran to the bathroom.

This shit was getting old, and it had just started. Before I could get up from the floor, Oliver rubbed my back in a soothing motion. The tears were already streaming down my face from gagging so much, but the cries left my lips as he helped me from the floor to the sink.

I rinsed my mouth, then closed my eyes and just stood there, trying to breathe deeply. When he placed the cold towel on the back of my neck, I silently thanked God. I grabbed my toothbrush, squeezed a bit of toothpaste on it, and began brushing my teeth. As I did so, Oliver gently rubbed my stomach and kissed the side of my head.

He was so tender with me, and I loved that. I needed every bit of it. Tears continued falling down my cheeks as I rinsed my mouth and toothbrush again. When I finished, I turned to him and hugged him. "I'm sorry. Hi, Oliver."

"What are you apologizing for? I hate that I haven't been here for you this week. I'm here to make up for it."

When I pulled away from his embrace, he picked me up, cradled me like a baby, and went to my bedroom. I lay against his chest until he lowered me to the bed. I watched him take off his shoes and shirt. Then he got in bed with me and held me in his arms. I remained quiet as I listened to him breathe. "I missed you, Kinisha."

I tilted my head back to stare into his eyes. "I missed you too."

He lowered his face to mine and softly kissed my lips. The stirring I felt down below had caught me by surprise. Here I was, just throwing up a few minutes ago, feeling queasy and undesirable, but now feeling horny. He stroked my cheek with the backs of his fingers as he stared into my face. This man had to be an angel because there wasn't a man alive walking this earth that was as perfect. Jesus had already been crucified and had risen and gone to glory.

"So, how are you recouping after losing Mya?" I asked.

He took a deep breath and blew it out slowly. "It's been a little tough. I had to ensure all the jobs were covered on Tuesday and today. She was scheduled for an appointment yesterday, so I had to pick up the slack on that. I have to go back to that residence tomorrow to resolve their issue. Thankfully, it should be just a one-day thing and only take a couple of hours."

"Have you heard from her?"

"No, and honestly, I hope I don't. She was a great employee until Monday. What I saw from her Monday, I don't ever want to see again. I ain't never had anybody go crazy on me like that. Had them people at the Turkey Leg Hut looking at me like I had fucked her over or something."

I stared at him, noticing he was getting worked up by how he slightly bounced his leg. Bringing my hand to his chest, I began rubbing it, similar to how he rubbed my back when he was trying to soothe me. He closed his eyes, then said, "You make everything better, though. Being in your presence gives me a peace I didn't have before. I can only hope my presence will do that for you one day."

"Wow. I believe it's starting to Oliver."

He kissed my forehead, and I closed my eyes, thankful he was here with me.

"Do you mind if I stay the night? Are you working tomorrow?"

"Not at all. I plan to work, but it depends on how I feel. I'm going to have to tell Mr. Taylor something, though. I believe he knows."

"Devin is a smart man. I'm sure he does. What are you going to tell him?"

"I haven't decided yet. He knows how long we've been around each other and how we didn't hang out after work hours. He would never believe that the baby is from you.

I'll probably tell him the truth and swear him to secrecy. He's very attentive and will ask questions if he wants to know something."

"Yeah. I figured that out about him."

He chuckled, and I relaxed in his arms once again and stroked his hairless chest. I closed my eyes and hoped that things continued going well between us. That situation at his job with Mya made me nervous. That woman seemed like she could be fatal attraction crazy. I didn't want her stalking him, appearing in places, freaking him out. These women were something else, and I didn't put anything past them.

I'd told him Monday to be careful, and I seriously meant that. The behavior he described was scary. He said when her mom had come to pick her up, she threw an entire fit. Her mom had said that she would calm down on her own, and once she did, she got her out of there, vowing to take her to see her doctor the following day.

Seemed like we both had issues with crazy, ignorant people. I hadn't heard from Jarod's ho ass, but I was more than sure I would before Sunday rolled around again. Unbeknownst to Oliver, I still wanted to make him suffer. He shouldn't get off scot-free. It wasn't fair or right. He needed to man up and do what he should as a father. The problem was that I'd agreed Oliver would be my baby's father. There was no way I could have both. Oliver would walk away from me so quickly if he knew I was still fucking around, trying to get Jarod to accept his responsibilities.

"What are you thinking about, baby?"

"How I love lying in your arms this way."

I stared up at him and gently pulled his face to mine by putting my hand on the back of his neck. There was no resistance as he pressed his lips against mine. Despite my mind telling me not to, I slid my tongue to his and kissed him passionately, causing my body to heat up with desire. When his hands slid to my ass, I knew this was going too far. I wanted to have sex with him, but at the same time, I didn't. My body craved him, but I didn't want him to think I had fallen all in yet. My mind was in such turmoil, and I didn't want to cloud it even more with sex. That was what got me into the predicament I was in now.

I slowly pulled away as he stared at me. He didn't say a word; he only pulled me even closer to him and kissed my forehead. I felt like crying, but I knew I would surely throw up again if I did. Doing my best to change the direction things were going, I asked, "Did you have your consultation yesterday?"

"Naw. I had to cancel it. I'll never hear the end of it, either. Shannon gon' put her foot in my ass. I can already taste the leather."

"Shannon? Mr. Taylor's sister-in-law?"

"Yeah. I met her at my cousin's house. They're best friends, and my cousin works for her."

"Oh, that's cool. Shannon is crazy as hell. When she comes in the office, she and Mr. Taylor go back and forth like they are real-life sister and brother."

I giggled as I thought about the instances. Those two could go back and forth with the best of them. However, Mr. Taylor said Shannon was mild compared to his other sister-in-law, Sonya. I slowly shook my head as I thought about them. Tilting my head back, I stared at Oliver, then asked, "Are you hungry? I have some leftovers in the fridge."

"Naw. I'm good. I ate not long before I came over. Let me know if you wanna try to eat something. Maybe I can go get you some soup or something. You probably need something light on your stomach."

"Yeah. Maybe later. Are you only staying tonight?"

"I don't know. You want me to stay longer?"

"Yeah, I do. This is nice."

"If I don't have to return to Houston Friday, I'll stay. I just couldn't go another day without seeing you."

"That's sweet, Oliver."

"Mm," he hummed as he nuzzled his nose to my neck. "You smell good, baby."

"Thank you. So do you."

I closed my eyes and rested in his arms, totally relaxed, knowing he had my best interest at heart. This was the first time I thanked God for my pregnancy. It forced me to see him, the *real* him, and not just my perception of him. I would be a fool ever to let him go. I made a vow, at that very moment, to let shit go. That included Jarod. If he didn't want to experience the joys of being a father, that was on him. I had a man lying next to me who wanted to experience everything I had to offer him: all of me.

"Are you nervous?" Oliver asked me.

"Extremely. I just want everything to be okay."

He kissed my forehead, grabbed my hand, and led me inside the doctor's office. It had been over a week, and it was time for my first appointment. I was able to keep Mr. Taylor at bay. I didn't want to tell him before I told my family. However, he would know the truth. My family would only know what Oliver and I had discussed. This was his baby, and honestly, it was. I still hadn't heard from Jarod's ass. He didn't show up to church Sunday, like he dared me to out him.

To hell with him. I refused to allow my pettiness to rule over me at this moment, especially since I was partly to blame. I had a baby to think about now. Having Jarod in the picture would only keep me stressed out. Oliver brought peace to my life, and every day I was with him convinced me of that. We sat together at church Sunday, and Kiana and my mom had a field day grilling me about him and asking why I didn't ask him to join us for dinner.

That would be what happened this Sunday. I wanted to tell them at Sunday dinner, but something in me told me to tell them today. After I got checked in and we sat in the waiting area, I turned to Oliver. "What do you think about talking to my parents today?"

His eyebrows lifted. "Really? I mean, we can do it whenever you want to, but you said you weren't in a hurry to have the conversation."

"I know, but for some reason, I just feel the urge to do it now."

"Okay. Well, let's go with that urge. After we get something to eat, we can relax for a little bit, maybe shop a little, then go to your parents' house."

"Shopping?"

"Yeah. I figured after this, we would both be excited and want to buy some neutral baby stuff."

I giggled. Knowing he was just as excited as I was had caught me by surprise. "You never cease to amaze me," I said, gently caressing his cheek.

The way he stared at me always spoke volumes. It was like he loved me. We hadn't had sex yet, but I knew it wouldn't be long. We'd spent the weekend together, and feeling his dick against me was like holding a crack rock in front of a fiend. I almost attacked him in that bed. However, I already knew since he was staying with me tonight, I wouldn't be able to resist his tenderness.

He leaned over and kissed my lips, and I felt like I wanted to melt in my seat. As I sat staring at him, something I found myself doing often, the nurse called me to the back. It was like my soul was in disbelief that he was actually going through with this. I had to make sure that I wasn't dreaming. How could I be so blessed in my foolishness? God really loved me to send this amazing man to me.

We walked through the door, and the nurse weighed me, then took my blood pressure. It was slightly elevated, but that was to be expected since my nerves were heightened. Oliver grabbed my hand and gently rubbed it. "Everything's gonna be okay. I need you to calm down and trust that they will."

I nodded and smiled tightly at him, trying to take his advice. Once I gave a urine sample, the nurse led us to an examination room and told me to undress and put on a gown. They would be doing a vaginal ultrasound. When she left, Oliver asked, "Do you want me to step out?"

He'd never seen me naked. He was a complete gentleman at all times. I shook my head as I pulled my dress over my head. Biting his bottom lip, he grabbed my dress from me as he unashamedly scanned my thickness. He folded it neatly and set it in a vacant chair. When he turned back to me, I was handing him my bra. It was like he was stuck as he stared at my breasts. He licked his lips as he took my bra and set it on my dress.

I put the gown on before taking off my underwear. I didn't need to be turned on when they were about to insert that damn wand in me. It had been weeks since I'd had sex. That shit would probably feel good and make me feel sexual as desperate as I was for some dick right now. The last thing I needed to do was moan. I walked over to place my underwear between my dress, but Oliver took them from me.

He stared into my eyes and brought them to his face. I nearly squirted all over this damn floor. When he moaned and allowed his eyes to roll to the back of his head, I knew we would be fucking later. There was no way around it. "Oliver," I said softly.

"Mm-hmm," he responded, dropping my panties to the chair with my clothes.

"Why did you do that?"

"I've been dying to taste you. I'm sorry if I offended you, baby."

I closed my eyes and licked my lips. Slowly shaking my head, I said, "The last thing I feel is offended. Maybe I should tap into that feeling so I can calm down."

He chuckled softly as someone knocked on the door. I sat on the examination table as the doctor walked in. "Hello, Mom. You are indeed pregnant. When was the first day of your last cycle?"

I searched the sky, expecting the answer to fall on me somehow. "Umm . . . probably the first week of last month. My period varies and never comes at the same time every month."

"I understand. Is this the father?"

I glanced over at Oliver and said, "Yes. He's my boyfriend, Oliver Andrews."

The doctor shook his hand as Oliver smiled big. He was so happy. While I knew that he was excited about hearing the baby's heartbeat, I could imagine that he was just as happy with the scent of my pussy on his face. I smiled at the thought as the doctor turned back to me. He asked me a few more questions, then told me the ultrasound tech would be in shortly.

I lay on the table and found myself staring at Oliver. He stood and came closer to me. When he grabbed my hand, he brought it to his lips and kissed it. "You're so beautiful, and I know you'll be a wonderful mother."

I smiled at his words. That was something that had plagued me. I didn't have a clue of how I would mother this baby, but I could only hope that I wouldn't fuck it up. While I knew I would have help from Ramsey, Kiana, and Oliver, I was responsible for caring for my child. I truly believed that my nerves about that would never go away. I was going to be responsible for a whole-ass life. Instead of spilling my deepest thoughts and concerns in this doctor's office, I said, "Thank you, Oliver."

When the tech came in, she spoke to Oliver and me and got right to business. I was grateful for that. Oliver came to my other side and held my hand as I spread my legs. His eyes stayed fixed on the screen, waiting to see what we knew to be true. I also averted my attention to the screen when the tech inserted the wand. My thoughts from earlier were so damn skewed. The last thing on my mind right now was sex.

Tears immediately fell from my eyes as my butter bean came into view. She turned up the volume, and we heard a strong heartbeat. "You look to be about ten weeks, honey."

Oliver kissed my hand repeatedly, then gently wiped my tears. After taking some pictures, she removed the wand, letting me know I could get dressed. After she left, I sat up, and Oliver hugged me tightly. "Are these happy tears?"

I bit my bottom lip as I nodded. "I'm gonna bring a life into this world. I'm in love already. Hearing the heartbeat of a life growing inside of me is overwhelming. When I heard it, every regret I had dissipated. This baby is all that matters. Whoever doesn't like it doesn't matter. As long as I'm happy and . . ."

I paused, trying to figure out how to word what I wanted to say. I looked up at him. "As long as you're happy, I don't care about anyone else."

His lips parted. "What are you saying, Kinisha?"

I swallowed hard, trying to figure out if I meant what I was saying. "I'm saying that your happiness is important to me. I want this between us to be real. I know it's *been* real for you, and I'm ready to be for real too."

He scooped me up from the examining table and kissed me deeply before setting me on my feet. My heart felt light. I could only pray that I felt this way after leaving my parents' house. While what they thought shouldn't make me feel any different, I knew it could dampen my spirits for a bit. I would still do what I had to for my baby and Oliver, but their acceptance would mean a lot to me. I didn't want to go through what Kiana went through with them.

I wanted to believe they'd learned from that situation, though. They didn't have nearly as much control over me as they did back then. So, prayerfully, everything would be okay because regardless of whether they liked it or not, my baby would be here in a little over seven months, showing me what true joy felt like.

# Chapter 12

## *Oliver*

We'd eaten lunch at the Olive Garden, and Kinisha was able to hold that down. I knew we would be frequenting it a lot more because of that. Hearing the baby's heartbeat was like music to my soul. No one could tell me at that moment that the baby wasn't mine. It sure in the hell felt like it was. My chest had puffed out like a proud father's would.

We went to Target and racked up on white, green, and yellow onesies, Pampers, and baby wipes. I had to ask her what she would do if someone we knew saw us, and she looked me in the eyes and said, "So what? They'll just see us."

I swore that moment made me want to lower her on my dick right there in the store. When I slid her panties over my face at the doctor's office, I knew I would be applying pressure sometime today. Her scent was enticing, and I wanted that shit on my tongue so bad. After shopping, we went to her place to put down all the bags. Then I held her while we took a nap. She was exhausted.

Once we awakened, we got in my car and headed to her parents' house. The ride was pretty quiet, as I knew it would be. I didn't know her parents, but surely this couldn't be as bad as she thought it would be. She was a grown woman, living independently and paying her bills.

I could see them cutting up a li'l bit if they would have to take care of the baby. But that would be my responsibility. I would be signing the birth certificate.

I knew that shit was risky, but I promised myself that Kinisha would be mine. I'd do whatever she needed me to do within reason. For me, this was within reason, especially since Jarod was a jackass to her. Under her direction, we reached the Jordans' house within fifteen minutes. They had a nice brick home in Beaumont's Pear Orchard area.

I grabbed Kinisha's hand, and I could feel it trembling. "Baby, look at me." When she did, I continued. "No matter what happens in there, you aren't alone. I got'chu. Before we go inside, there are some things I need to say to you, so it won't be a surprise if I have to say it in there."

That statement only heightened her nerves, so I got right to the point. "I'm going to marry you one day, and I plan to move you into my home . . . our home. We're going to be a family. Okay?"

She swallowed hard, looking to be trying to restrain her tears. "Kinisha, I'm falling for you, baby. Hard as shit. You complete me, and I knew you would that day you fell into my arms. So you have nothing to worry about. I will be there to sign the birth certificate." I put my hand on her stomach. "This is *my* baby, regardless of blood. Baby Andrews is in my heart already. The questions they could possibly ask I have answers for. So don't be nervous."

She leaned over and kissed my lips as her tears made their way to our shared affection. Once she pulled away, I wiped her tears, got out of the car, and walked around to help her. As I opened her door, I saw her mother smiling on the porch. When Kinisha saw her, she trembled. "Remember what I said, baby. I got'chu. Okay?"

She nodded and kissed my lips as her dad joined her mother on the porch. I grabbed her hand and allowed her to lead me to them. The closer we got, the bigger her mom's smile became. She already knew we were dating and was all for it, so, hopefully, things would be cool.

"Hey, Nisha!" her mom said, pulling her in her arms.

Her dad hugged her next as her mother stood smiling at me, waiting for an introduction. "Mom, Dad, this is my boyfriend, Oliver Andrews."

Mrs. Jordan stuck her hand out first. "It's nice to meet you officially, Oliver. I've seen you around church."

I nodded. "Nice to meet you as well, Mrs. Jordan."

Mr. Jordan shook my hand but didn't offer any words. I could understand. Kinisha was his baby girl, and he needed to size me up. "Y'all come on in. Kinisha, what are you doing off so early?"

Kinisha walked in without a word, and I followed her as she led me to their front room. She sat on the couch, but I remained standing until her mom sat. Once her dad sat, she didn't beat around the bush. I grabbed her hand as she said, "I have something to tell you. I didn't work today because of a doctor's appointment. I'm pregnant."

Her parents were quiet for a moment. Her mother smiled slightly. "Okay. Congratulations, baby."

She didn't sound too enthused, but at least she was somewhat accepting. Her dad, not so much. He glanced at me, then asked Kinisha, "How will you take care of a baby on your salary?"

"Daddy, Oliver works. He owns his own IT company."

He turned his attention to me. "What are your plans? You couldn't wait and marry her first? Or is she not good enough for you?"

"She's too good for me, but I plan to marry Kinisha without a doubt. I would never leave her and our baby without. That's not the type of man I am."

"That has yet to be seen, Mr. Andrews. How old are you?"

"Daddy, come on. Don't go there. You didn't learn anything from the last time?" Kinisha asked.

His face was like stone, so I answered. "I'm thirty."

He nodded as Kinisha frowned. "His age shouldn't matter. He came here with me like the good man he is to let you know that you would be having a second grandbaby."

Mrs. Jordan nudged her husband.

"You're right, Kinisha. You and Kiana are my babies, though. I need to be sure that the men y'all choose measure up. Mr. Andrews, have you ever been married or have any other children?"

"No, sir, neither. I'm originally from Houston, but I've been in Beaumont for about five years. Both my parents are deceased. They were up in age when they had me, so they didn't die young. I want to believe my mother died of a broken heart. She grieved for my dad every day he wasn't here. I'm somewhat of a loner. I have a cousin here and a few friends, one of them being Kinisha's boss, Devin Taylor."

Mr. Jordan nodded and slid his hand down his face. "While I wish you two would have waited, I'm still happy for you, Kinisha."

Kinisha's frown dropped from her face, and the tremble in her hand ceased. "Thank you, Daddy."

He stood from his seat and pulled her up into his arms. "My girls are women. I can't believe it happened right before my eyes. I love you, baby."

"I love you too, Daddy."

The minute he released her, her mother hugged her tightly. He came to me, so I stood from the couch. He extended his hand and said, "I hope you weren't offended by my questions. That's my baby girl. Thank you for stepping up and being a man. We seem to be running short on that these days."

*Shiiid, if he only knew.* "I wasn't offended, sir. I totally get it. If we have a daughter, I'm sure I will be the same way."

"I'm glad you understand."

I gave him a tight smile and nodded as Kinisha made her way back to me. I pulled her into my arms and kissed her head as her parents smiled at us.

"Well, we're going to go. I'm so happy that y'all understood. I was so nervous."

"Kinisha, you're our baby, but you're a grown woman. Kiana's situation was a hard lesson in that area. I think I learned it, though. It helps that you aren't living here anymore," her dad said with a chuckle. "Keep us updated." He turned to his wife and wrapped his arm around her waist. "Can you believe we're about to have two grandbabies?"

She giggled, and Kinisha stared up at me with the biggest smile.

"Now that your nerves are calm, you want to get ice cream before I take you home?"

"Yeeeesss. Chocolate."

I chuckled as she practically drooled at the mention of it. I looked at her parents and said, "It was so nice meeting you. Hopefully, I'll see you Sunday after church."

"We'd like that, Oliver," Mrs. Jordan said as Kinisha approached the door.

She had her sights set on that chocolate ice cream, but I had my sights and taste buds set on *her* chocolate ice cream.


We returned to her place, and I ran her bathwater. I knew she loved bathing in lavender, so I found her crystals and put them in the water. I'd rub her down with oil after she got out. She hated putting the oil in her water because she said it made it hard to clean the tub. When I left the bathroom and joined her in the bedroom, she was taking off her clothes. My dick sprang into action instantly.

He'd done so at the doctor's office too, but thankfully, I could contain him then. There was no reason to have to contain him now. When she looked up at me, her eyes scanned my body, her gaze resting on my erection. That nigga was showing out too. I swore he was leaking. The way he was throbbing, I knew I would need relief tonight, whether from her or my hand.

I made my way to her as she stared at me while unfastening her bra. By the time that shit dropped to the floor, I was standing in front of her. My hands instinctively went to her hard nipples. The moment I touched them, Kinisha's eyes rolled to the back of her head, then closed. When her head fell back, it left her neck wide open for my affection. After kissing her there, I slowly licked and sucked all over it. As badly as I wanted to rush, I knew I had to savor everything about this moment.

Pulling away from her momentarily, I pulled my shirt over my head. She slid her hands up my abs to my chest, then glided her fingertips back down, lightly scratching me with her nails. *Jesus Christ in the morning*. My dick felt like it had doubled in size and was on the verge of bursting right through the skin containing him. The head throbbed, begging me to put him out of his misery.

Kinisha dipped her fingers into my waistband, then pulled them out and unbuckled my belt. Next, she unbuttoned my pants. I remained still and silent as she worked my pants over my erection, biting the fuck out of my bottom lip. After getting my pants to my ankles, I stepped out of them, went to her waistband, and pulled off her pants. Knowing she was wearing a thong, I grabbed her hand and slowly spun her around. I'd fucking drooled on myself staring at her perfection.

"Damn, baby. You are so fucking gorgeous."

Her face reddened as she licked her red lips. I swept her hair away from her face, but my knees nearly buckled when she grabbed my dick through my drawers. "Oh fuck," I whispered.

I slid my hands to her ass and gripped it as she stretched my drawers over my dick. She licked her lips and was about to descend to her knees, but I quickly grabbed her, keeping her from doing so. She brought her fingers to my lips and traced them with her fingertips. "Oliver, you don't want me to suck this big-ass dick?"

"Mm. Hell yeah, I do, but not right now. I need to cater to you first, baby. You in a hurry?"

"Not at all."

"Good."

I tucked my fingers in the sides of her thong, and she widened her stance so I could pull them down. Those thick-ass thighs had to be saving lives. I was just glad to know that my life would be the only one it was saving from now on. I rested my forehead on her stomach and inhaled her scent. I wanted to slide in her shit so bad. Instead, I stood and led her to the bathroom. After turning off the water, I lit her candles, then turned back to her to help her in the tub.

"Oliver," she called out as she stepped in. "Are you getting in with me?"

"No. I want you to relax and soak for a minute. I'm gonna take a shower."

She poked her lips out dramatically, and I knew she would get whatever she wanted from me whenever she made that face. I smiled slightly as I grabbed my phone from the countertop and switched the song to "40 Shades of Choke" by Ari Lennox. I couldn't wait to choke her while stroking her phat pussy. Slowly shaking my head at my thoughts, I turned back to her, seeing she was still just standing in the tub like she knew I would give in.

When I got to the tub, I got in behind her and sat down, then helped her ease down in the hot water. She checked behind her before she sat and said, "I didn't want to sit on that snake in the water."

I bit my bottom lip to keep from laughing. She was serious as hell. Scooting back into me, she pinned my dick between her back and my abs. That nigga was mad as hell that he was touching her, but not the parts of her he really wanted to feel.

"Are you sending subliminal messages, Oliver?"

I frowned slightly as she rested against me. "What do you mean?"

"You wanna choke me? You want me to say that I want you to choke me? That's why you put that song on?"

"I just like Ari Lennox, baby. She's one of the few new-school singers I like. I don't do subliminals. I just come out and say what I want. If you wanna be choked, I got'chu. I'm more than sure my hand will gravitate there when I'm hitting your pussy from the back, though."

She tilted her head to look up at me, so I lowered my face to hers and softly kissed her lips. When she pulled away, she said, "Oliver, I've never experienced this level of intimacy."

"Me either, baby. So, it's a first for both of us."

"If you've never experienced it, how can you execute it so well?"

"My dad always told me that when I found the right woman, I wouldn't need instructions on how to love her and show her how much I need her. Catering to her wouldn't be a mystery. I would know just what to do to please and satisfy her beyond anything she's ever known if I paid attention to her. He was right. You need to feel love just like I do. I can see that plain as day."

"Wow. That was profound."

"Mm-hmm."

I began rubbing her shoulders, then allowed my hands to go on their personal excursion over her body. My lips got jealous, so I brought them to her neck. My hands gripped her thighs as she moaned slightly. "Oh, Oliver, I don't know how much of this I'll be able to take before I erupt."

"Well, let me get us cleaned up. I can't have you erupting but in two places: on my tongue or my dick. I can't let that nectar go to waste."

"You keep talking to me like that, you won't have a choice but to let it waste where it may. My body is so sensitive to you right now that I don't know what to do with myself."

"Mm. Well, turn around and get a taste of this dick, baby."

She turned to me, and I helped her lift her body to straddle me. I positioned my dick just right, and she slid down on my shit, taking my damn breath away. "Oh fuck," she screamed.

That shit was so sexy I wanted to fire off that quickly. I closed my eyes as she rested her forehead against mine, letting my dick marinate in that hot-ass Crock-Pot of hers. I bit my bottom lip, trying to contain myself. I swore I wanted to scream just as she had done. Wrapping my arms around her, I held her soft-ass body tight as a soft moan escaped me. I opened my eyes to see the goose bumps all over her flesh. Her eyes were on me, and I couldn't look away when I noticed the tear that fell from her eye.

I slowly lifted and lowered her on my dick, careful not to splash water everywhere. This was just supposed to be her getting a taste, but fuck if I didn't want the entire meal.

"Say something, Oliver. Talk to me, baby," she said as her head fell back.

"This pussy got me fucking speechless, baby. Fuuuck."

I lowered my head and pulled her erect nipple into my mouth as I squeezed her soft ass. Damn, this was like a dream come true. I'd fantasized about her for a while, so to have her now seemed unreal. She began rolling her hips, causing water to slosh a bit, and she caught my dick just right. The head of my dick was rubbing against her G-spot every time she rolled backward. My eyes literally rolled to the back of my head, and I leaned back against the tub.

"Oh fuck, Kinisha. That's it, baby."

I released a deep moan, then bit my bottom lip as I felt her pussy squeeze me in a tight embrace.

"Oliver, I'm about to cum."

"Naw, not like this. Stand up."

She gave me one more stroke before doing what I said, and that shit turned me on even more. I pulled her to me, and I lowered in the tub some, making my face level where she could sit that phat pussy on me. "Give it to me, Kinisha. Let me taste that shit," I said before her pussy submerged me.

She began rolling her hips against my face as I sucked her pussy for everything it was worth. Going to her clit, I lightly sucked it at first, feeling her legs tremble on my ears. She brought her hands to my head and gripped it as she released screams of passion. When her juices flooded my mouth, I damn near got a sugar rush trying to ingest it all. Before she could finish, I lowered her back on my dick and began fucking her, no longer caring about the water hitting the floor.

"Fuuuuck! Yes, Oliver! Fuck me, baby."

"Aww shit . . ."

Her titties were bouncing in my face as I did my best to fuck her world up in this tub. Before long, more water would be on the floor than in the tub. My dick was the happiest he'd been in a long time, and I knew after this, she would have to kill me to get rid of me. I already had it bad. She had to have voodoo in her pussy, because I felt like I had no control, like she put a spell on me.

"Kinisha, this *my* pussy. You hear me? This *my* shit!"

"Yes, baby. All yours. Fuck, I'm about to cum again, Oliver."

Oh, I loved that shit. She orgasmed freely and easily. *Voodoo and crack.* That was what her pussy held in its confines. I was addicted, and there was no going back from this. "Give it to me, Nisha. Let my dick feel your excitement and passion for him."

I lifted my hips and began thrusting into her as her mouth formed an O. I wanted to fuck the sound out of her. This tasting had turned into dinner, and I knew it would the minute she slid that good shit on my dick. Her body began trembling, and her levy broke, saturating me in her passion. I couldn't take it any longer. My nut was about to take me out. I'd been holding it almost since we'd started.

"Baby, I'm about to nut too."

My thrusts became stronger, but when she squeezed my dick, I fired off in her depths. It felt like every vein in my body was about to burst. "Oh fuuuck!" I yelled as I emptied my soul inside of her.

I held her tightly around her waist, and she held me just as tightly, squeezing my head to her chest. We remained still, I supposed, thinking about how explosive that was. My dick was still resting inside of her, but he was starting to get amped up for more. "Let's get you cleaned up, baby."

She slowly slid backward off my dick, and we both moaned. "Your moans are so sexy, Oliver. I love that you don't mind showing your vulnerability."

I leaned forward and kissed her lips. That quickly became more, and I knew if I didn't put a stop to it, we'd be fucking in this tub all over again. I pulled away, taking her bottom lip part of the way with me. "I love your screams, baby. I knew sex with you would be explosive simply because of how badly I wanted you, but that shit was an atomic bomb."

"Mm. You fucking right about that," she responded.

She stood from my lap and lathered her loofah. I took it from her after standing and began washing her beautiful body. I loved every roll, mole, stretch mark, and discoloration. Kinisha's body was gorgeous. There was no way I would be able to resist it. I pulled the sprayer from the side of the tub and began rinsing her as she stared at me in complete adoration . . . or it could have been lust. Whatever it was, I liked it.

I kissed her in various places as I went to my knees to wash her prized treasure. I grabbed the towel from the side of the tub and put very little Ivory soap to clean what now belonged to me. As I slowly slid the towel between her legs, applying a little pressure, I felt the towel heat up. I glanced up at her to see her pinching her nipples. Her eyes were closed, and her head was tilted back. She was so sexy.

Seeing her enjoy the sensual way I washed her body gave me joy. I slid my other hand up her leg to her thigh and continued rubbing her. Just as I was about to kiss her FUPA, her pussy unleashed on my ass and almost dropped her to the tub. She sprayed me with that good shit. It almost distracted me to where I couldn't catch her. Her knees had given out on her. I wanted to lay her down and make love to her so badly.

After her moment had passed, I kissed her lips. "Come on, baby, so I can get you dried off and into the bed."

"I need to wash you, Oliver," she said lazily.

I chuckled. "I got it this time. You need rest."

After helping her out and drying her off, I led her to the bed. "After I clean up, I'll rub you down. Okay?"

"You're so good to me. I'm glad I came to my senses."

"Mm. Me too. Shit, me too."

I covered her with the blanket, returned to the bathroom to clean up all the water from the floor, and picked up the wet rugs. We were going to be just fine. This relationship would be even more than I imagined, and I couldn't wait to get further in our journey.

# Chapter 13

## *Kinisha*

When I woke up, Oliver was between my legs, eating me out of house and home. *Jesus!* I brought my hands to his bald head and pushed him in farther as I arched my back. How he cared for me in that bathtub had blown my mind. I came three times, once on his face, and the man was still on a mission to ensure I was completely satiated. I almost passed him by. What a fool I would have been.

He moaned against my clit, and I unleashed my affection for him. He lapped every bit of it up, then went to his knees and pushed that monstrosity he called a dick inside of me. That shit stretched me to my limits and turned me on so much until I was cumming every five minutes it seemed. His touch alone had my libido through the damn roof.

When I released his head and he grabbed my breasts, I realized he'd oiled me down without me even waking up. *How in the hell did he have me in a comatose sleep like that?* "Oliver, baby, damn."

I was falling for him . . . fast. He was making it extremely easy to do so. He was everything I ever wanted in a boyfriend and future husband. He said he wanted to marry me. That statement alone had me eating out of the palms of his hands. I'd never been the submissive type, but Oliver was proving that I could be and would be. I knew he had my best interest at heart and that I could trust him. He hadn't given me a reason to question his intentions. He wanted me and my unborn baby without a shadow of a doubt.

My legs began trembling, and before I could cum, he stopped and slid his dick into my paradise. His hovering over me was a totally different experience. Seeing the power in his shoulders and arms as he stroked me to ecstasy was overwhelming. Tears filled my eyes, and the longer he tenderly loved me, the more they fell. He gently swiped them away with his thumb, then kissed where they'd fallen.

Hooking his arm beneath my leg, he lifted it to my shoulder and dug into me like he was searching for something valuable. His dick felt like it was piercing my damn heart, literally and figuratively. "Oliver! Oh my God!"

"Am I hurting you, baby?" he asked as he eased up.

"No, baby. You're taking my soul from me. Jesus . . . Don't stop."

I thought I heard him chuckle as he resumed this massacre he was exacting on my pussy, like he was trying to seek revenge for how she took him out in the bathtub. I had no complaints whatsoever. He could live here if he chose to. He leaned over to my ear and said in a deeper voice, "I love this pussy, baby. I'll never get enough."

His words had me cumming like the Nile. As my body practically convulsed beneath him, he bit my earlobe, then my shoulder, sending me into orbit. "Fuck," I screamed.

This shit was so powerful I didn't know how I would handle it. Our being together had to be ordained by God. I knew the devil was a great deceiver, but there was no way he had a hand in this. God had shown me his mercy, and I was so grateful. When my tremors died down, he pulled out of me, turned me over to my stomach, and reentered me slowly. He stroked me expertly as he placed soft kisses on my back.

My heart was wide open, and so was my pussy. He had them both in his hands, doing with them as he pleased. Thankfully, "as he pleased" also pleased me. He laid his body flat on mine and slowly made love to me. My love was juicing so much for him that I could hear the sloshing noises. Oliver was by far the best I'd ever been with, and a sista wasn't an amateur by any means. He kissed my shoulder and slid his hand to my neck, gripping it slightly as his pace and force became deadlier.

"Kinisha, I wanna fuck this shit up before you get further in your pregnancy and I can't. Can I fuck the shit out of you, baby?"

I hesitated because I was scared as hell. His big-ass dick could mess around and give me a hysterectomy. As I adjusted, I said, "Yes, baby."

"I'm going to do my best to aim for that fine line between fucking up how you walk and hurting you for real. If it becomes unbearable, let me know."

"Cocky ass," I mumbled.

"I ain't being cocky. I'm being factual. This lethal weapon can take you out of the game. I wanna dig in yo' shit tomorrow and the day after that through the rest of my life. I can't be fucking up your spine."

My body trembled once again as he gradually started giving me more power. *Lord, have mercy on my kitty.* "I can handle it, Oliver . . . shit."

That permitted him to lose control on my ass. As soon as the last word left my mouth, he hit me with a one-two punch as he lifted my ass, arching me to his desired preference. I gripped the sheets as he gave me the business while grunting. He thought I was screaming before, but shit, I was doing the most now. I was trying to get away from him and telling him to fuck me harder simultaneously.

The tears left me uncontrollably as I absorbed the power he was hitting me with. I knew I was in trouble when he pushed my face in the bed. There was nowhere for me to run. I had to take it just like he was giving it. My screams were uncontained, and I just knew one of my neighbors would come knocking or call the police, thinking I was being attacked. I *was* being attacked. Downright assaulted in the best way possible.

"Oliver, shit, I love your dick!"

"Mm. Cum on that shit then."

He sounded so fucking calm, like he wasn't rearranging my insides. It was like he was in attack mode and wouldn't let up until he got what he came for. My entire body trembled as I felt his thumb penetrate my asshole. That did it. I came all over the damn place.

"Oh, you like your asshole being fucked with, Kinisha?"

I couldn't even answer him. My orgasm had rendered me dumb, blind, and damn near deaf. His thumb went deeper, and I had no choice but to take it just like I was taking the deep well digging he was doing to my pussy. I fully understood what the saying, *Be careful what you wish for,* meant now. There was no way I should have released him into the wild like that. Oliver needed to stay on the leash. He'd fucked up my mind and my life.

"Kinisha, I'm about to cum, baby."

He was so fucking calm sounding, and that shit was affecting me as much as what his dick was doing to me. "Give it to me!" I screamed. "Cum in your pussy, baby."

The growl that left him as he gripped my ass excited me right into euphoria. I came right along with him. He released my hips, and I collapsed to the bed as he pulled out of me. He fell next to me as I panted, desperately trying to gather my feelings and my next breath. I turned to look at him, and he stared at me as if he were admiring his work. There wasn't a drop of sweat on him. "Was I . . . light work . . . for you?"

He smiled slightly. "I work out a lot, so I'm used to exerting energy like that, but believe me, I am beyond satisfied with you, baby."

I lifted myself from the bed and went to him. He pulled me in his arms and kissed my head. We remained quiet as I stared at his dick. That muthafucka still had some spunk to him. He wasn't rock hard like before we started, but he wasn't completely soft either. After a few more minutes of quietness and catching my breath, I went to it and pulled him into my mouth. I positioned myself between his legs and stared at him as I took as much of him as possible, letting him tickle my tonsils.

He went up on his elbow and brought the other hand to my cheek as he watched me suck the joy of my strength from his dick. My juices had totally covered him, so all I could taste was me. That wasn't a bad thing, though. I was thoroughly impressed with my flavor. He lifted his hips slightly, forcing me to take more of him. I began gagging and releasing my throat's affections all over him. "Shit! Damn, Nisha. I'm about to cum down your throat. You want this shit?"

Apparently, by my silence, he accepted that as confirmation. He began thrusting more, producing tears and causing snot to run out of my nose. This nigga was so much more than I expected. He gripped my hair and fucked my mouth for three or four more strokes, then released his load in the back of my throat. I quickly swallowed, doing my best not to throw up.

When he withdrew from my mouth, he immediately stood and went to the bathroom, returning with a wet towel. Once he laid it on my face and I felt the coolness, I could calm down more. He tenderly wiped my nose, mouth, and eyes, then spread the cold towel on my throat. I held it there as he sat next to me. "I'm sorry, baby. I got carried away. Your head game is insane. Sex with you is off the charts. I never wanna hurt you or make you feel uncomfortable."

He stood from the bed before I could respond and left the room. I was momentarily confused until he returned with a bottle of water. He had absolutely nothing to apologize for. After gulping the bottle he gave me, I dropped the towel to the floor and turned to him. "You have nothing to apologize for. Are you pleased?"

His eyebrows lifted. I assumed he was in shock with my response. "Baby, I'm beyond pleased."

He gently caressed my cheek, and I closed my eyes. I wasn't the least bit upset with the way he handled me. With what he was doing for me and my unborn child, I'd sacrifice my throat repeatedly if that was what he wanted. I opened my eyes, and he leaned in and kissed my lips. "That won't happen again, baby."

"Don't stifle or restrain your desires, Oliver. I'm here for you just like you're here for me. You're falling for me, and I feel like it's only a matter of time before I fall for you too."

"Damn, baby. Don't ever sacrifice your desires for me, either. Honestly, I didn't expect us to get so serious so soon, but I'm not upset about it. Now, I know you're hungry. We've worked up quite an appetite."

"Yes. I'm starving. Then I need to rest up for work in the morning. I need to call my sister before she calls me like I intentionally left her out. Ramsey too."

"Well, definitely clue sister-in-law in."

I smiled hard. Oliver had won the fucking prize. This man was everything I wanted and needed, plus some. I just hoped nothing between us changed.


Life couldn't get any better. I was packing a bag to go to Houston with Oliver for All-Star Weekend. It had been a week since we told my family about the pregnancy, and they were all accepting. Kiana had screamed so loud she had to have burst my eardrum. She was planning pregnancy massages, stomach paintings, and all kinds of bullshit for pregnant women. I told her I wasn't even showing to be doing all that, but she wouldn't hear it.

She even asked to talk to Oliver. He chuckled nearly the entire time he was on the phone. Ki could be so over the top when it concerned me. She got excited about the littlest things. Just her finding out that Oliver and I were a couple had produced a scream out of her. I could only roll my eyes in response to all that overacting she was doing. When I finally ended the call with her, I wanted a drink to calm my nerves.

However, after we'd eaten, Oliver made love to me again and put me to sleep. I loved it when he spent the night with me. I slept so much better in his arms than alone in the cold bed. Us moving in together was sounding better and better. Most times, he was at my place until I fell asleep anyway. Since he had a house, moving in with him would make more sense.

The people that lived next to me would probably be glad to get rid of my ass. I was extremely vocal during sex. I enjoyed it so much that I needed my man to know how much. Unfortunately for my neighbors, most times, that came out as screams.

My cell phone rang as I put my makeup in my bag with a throwback jersey dress. It was probably Ki. She'd been checking on me every day since I told her of my pregnancy. I picked it up and saw that it was Jarod. While my heart told me to ignore the call, my mind told me to answer and curse him the fuck out. I followed my mind. "Hello?"

"I don't guess you gathered the nerve to out me like you said you would."

"Is that why you didn't go to church last Sunday? You was scared, nigga?"

"Kinisha, I know you're miserable and just trying to make my life as miserable as yours."

"Actually, I'm in a great place, muthafucka. If you haven't noticed, I haven't contacted you in nearly two weeks. You know why? Because I don't have time for weak-ass boys who don't know how to handle their responsibilities. I will raise my baby in love without you. You will be the one missing out on the reward. So don't fucking call me again. Matter of fact, I'm blocking your pathetic ass."

I ended the call before he could respond, then noticed Oliver standing in the doorway. He was staring at me with a deep frown, and for some reason, I got extremely nervous. Just that quickly, I was sweating under my breasts. I cleared my throat and said, "Hey."

He gave me a head nod before asking, "Did you call him?"

"No. He called me. I'm blocking his number so he can no longer contact me."

"I hate hearing how he disrespects you. I'm sorry if my frown made you think I was angry at you. That nigga just ignites my crazy when it concerns you."

"He's a waste of time, energy, and skin. I hate that I fell to my lustful desires concerning him."

"You don't think he'll change his mind about wanting to be in the baby's life?"

"He better not. Can we get him to sign something that terminates his rights? I mean, he says the baby isn't his, so he shouldn't have a problem signing it, right?"

"Right. I believe you can have him sign an affidavit of voluntary relinquishment of parental rights and file it with the court. I won't have to adopt him since I'm signing the birth certificate, and he'll have my last name. At least, I don't think I will."

"Maybe we need to research the issue just in case we need it," I suggested.

"Yeah. You about ready?"

"Almost. I couldn't pass up the opportunity to cuss his ass out."

Oliver slowly shook his head and left the room. I took a deep breath and exhaled slowly. I was hoping he wasn't upset with me for answering the call. We'd been doing so well, without even a minor disagreement. His getting acquainted with my family Sunday was the icing on the cake. He and Lazarus talked quite a bit, and I was happy they seemed to hit it off.

After zipping up my bag, I glanced at myself in the mirror. I'd gotten my locs put in, and it was so much easier to deal with right now. They would last for a month or two. I would have to make sure I had them in my hair when I got closer to my due date. They were hassle free. I grabbed my bag and heard Oliver say, "You know better."

I dropped the handle as I stared at him. He walked closer to me and reached around me to grab the bag. "You need to be reminded of the role I play?"

I shook my head, then frowned slightly and began nodding. He laughed at my foolishness. His lessons were always pleasurable. I'd learn one whenever he felt like teaching. When we stopped laughing, I said, "Thank you, baby. I can't wait to be out on the town with you."

"I can't wait to have a woman as beautiful as you on my arm this weekend."

After kissing my head, he left the room with my duffle bag. I took a deep breath and smiled at my reflection in the mirror. My previous thoughts were correct. *Life couldn't get any better than this.*

# Chapter 14

## *Oliver*

When we got to Houston, I was beyond excited to spend time with Kinisha, away from everything. No jobs, no family, just us. It wasn't that her family was a bother. I just enjoyed our alone time together. It seemed since she'd told them of her pregnancy, that alone time had dwindled some. I knew they were excited and wanted to ensure she was okay. Her support system was intact, though, that was for sure.

I knew if there ever came a time that I couldn't be there for her, she wouldn't be short on people who would be. I just hoped there wouldn't be any problems with Jarod. That nigga didn't know what was good for him. If he did, he wouldn't even think about calling her. He didn't realize that I could make so much shit go wrong in his life without touching him. His best bet was to stay as far away from Kinisha as possible.

We went to my place before heading to the Toyota Center to put our luggage down and ended up getting a quickie in. I swore Kinisha Nicole Jordan was insatiable. That worked out fine since I was that way when it concerned her too. I wasn't sure if she was only that way with me or if she was naturally that way. Whatever the case, I was happy to benefit from it.

After getting to the Toyota Center, she was in awe of everyone in attendance. She'd never been to All-Star Weekend. I had to let her know that she was in for a treat. Watching it on TV didn't compare to witnessing it in person. This would be the fourth time I'd attended. She wasn't really a sports fan, but she watched occasionally, and she said she always watched All-Star Weekend festivities.

When we went inside, we headed straight to the concessions to get something to eat. We hadn't eaten dinner, and my stomach was telling me so. I was pretty sure Kinisha's stomach was ready to fight her as well. As we waited for our hot dogs, I wrapped my arms around her, gently rubbing her pooch. While her stomach wasn't completely flat, I could see it starting to round out a bit. She was twelve weeks now, and although we had a long way to go, I was happy about the small progress.

I'd signed up for a baby app that gave weekly updates on the baby's size and development. I knew that he or she was about the size of a plum and fully formed, having all its muscles, bones, organs, and limbs. Every week was getting more and more exciting. It would fill me with immeasurable joy when I could finally feel the baby kicking.

She rested her head on me . . . until the worker called my name. When I looked up and saw Mya holding our hot dogs, I got nervous as hell. "Hi, Oliver. How are you?"

"I'm good. How are you?" I asked as I glanced over at Kinisha. "This is my girlfriend, Kinisha. Baby, this is Mya."

Kinisha's eyebrows rose slightly, and her lips parted like she was about to have words for Mya. Instead, she smiled slightly and said, "Nice to meet you."

Mya gave her a slight smile and nodded, then handed me our hot dogs. The look she gave me put my nerves on edge. There was no way I would eat that hot dog. When we walked away, I threw that shit in the trash. Kinisha was just about to take a bite of hers, but I took it and threw that shit in the trash too. I swore she was about to swing on me.

"I'm sorry, baby. I don't trust that shit. She looked weird like she looked that day at the Turkey Leg Hut and the office. For all I know, she could have sprinkled poison on that shit."

"Well, you need to find another place to get hot dogs before I take a bite of your arm. I'm hungry as hell, Oliver."

"I know. Come on. Let's get in this line."

"Ugh. It's long. Let's get something else for right now."

I followed Kinisha to another stand to get nachos. We stood in line for about ten minutes before heading inside the arena. She was eating them all the way to our seats. That tray was nearly empty by the time we sat. "Damn, baby. You inhaled that shit."

She gave me the side-eye, then dragged her finger through the excess cheese and brought it to her mouth. "Your li'l ex-employee gon' catch these hands for fucking with my food."

It was my turn to roll my eyes. "I don't know for sure if she did, but I wanted to be safe, just in case. If she hurt you or our baby, I'd take her ass out."

She glanced up at me as I stared at her with a serious expression on my face, letting her know I meant business. Kinisha said something, but I didn't hear a word she said because I noticed Mya heading our way. "Shit," I said.

Kinisha frowned and followed my line of vision. When she saw Mya, she said, "See, this ho gon' be a fucking problem."

When Mya approached, she asked, "Can I speak to you privately?"

"Naw. Say what you have to say."

"She's not as pretty as me. What do you see in her that you couldn't see in me?"

Kinisha rose from her seat, and I immediately stood and maneuvered between them. Her fists were balled up, and the frown on her face said she was about to fuck Mya all the way up. "Listen, Mya. You need to carry your ass on back to your job. I'm tempted to file harassment charges on your ass, along with a restraining order. Go take your meds and find you something safe to play with."

She gave me a cynical-looking smile as her lips twitched. This shit was not gonna be good. "Fine. You want a big bitch like her, that's on you."

As she tried to walk away, Kinisha reached past me, grabbed her by the hair, and pulled her to the floor. "I got yo' big bitch. I will *fuck* you up."

I quickly restrained Kinisha as security approached. A few people seated near us explained what happened, so they escorted Mya away. That didn't stop them from putting us out, though, since Kinisha initiated contact. I was irritated and embarrassed. I grabbed Kinisha's hand and halfway pulled her through the arena.

She jerked her hand away from mine and asked, "So you're upset with *me?*"

"I'm upset about the situation. Could you have handled it better? Absolutely. What if Mya would have hopped up and started fighting you? Did you forget you have another life to protect? How you gon' be out here fighting while you're pregnant, Kinisha? That shit wasn't thought out or even considered."

"So let Mya say whatever the fuck she wants to say, right?"

"Your immaturity is loud. Pipe that shit down. I'm not saying she was right, but neither were you. I was handling the situation."

"Mm-hmm."

I didn't know what that shit meant, but she made me even angrier than I already was. She escalated the situation instead of trying to diffuse it. That could have ended in so many ways. I was thankful that it hadn't gotten more serious. Mya could file assault charges against her for putting her hands on her. Kinisha was hotheaded and failed to see the bigger picture. She knew Mya wasn't wrapped tight.

We walked the rest of the way to the car in silence. Our weekend was ruined. When we got to the car, I opened her door while she stood there huffing. "So, you ain't gon' get in?"

She didn't respond to me as she slid onto the seat. I closed the door and huffed as I walked around to the driver's side. Once I got in, she angled her body to mine. "I'm sorry I lost my temper, but I wasn't letting that bitch get away with the shit she said. You didn't correct her and demand her respect. She needed to know I would fuck her up, mentally impaired or not."

"Once again, you're pregnant. All bullshit needs to slide. Period."

She turned toward the window and stared out that muthafucka like she'd never been in Houston and was taking in the sights. I remained quiet as well. When we got to my place, she exited the car before I did. What she failed to see was that her apology wasn't an apology at all. It was an excuse. I probably would have let her do it if she had not been pregnant. I needed her to be more careful concerning our baby. That was it.

I glanced at her as I unlocked the door. She was angry, but I didn't give a fuck that she was angry. I was right about this, and I refused to bend. She walked in, went straight to my bedroom, and closed the door. Our first argument would be about bullshit that should have been common sense. I went to the kitchen, grabbed the bottle of Crown from the countertop, and took a swig before heading to the bedroom. I wasn't up for the drama or the bullshit. Maybe this was where the age difference would come into play. I didn't think six years was a lot, but clearly, it had to be playing a huge role in tonight's incident.

When I opened the door, she was sitting on the bed, crying her eyes out. My heart softened completely. I didn't expect this. I just knew I was about to have to come in here and be aggressive with her ass. I made my way to her and pulled her hands from her face. "Oliver, I love my baby. I would never want to do anything to put her in danger. I'm so sorry. You were right."

I pulled her in my arms. "Don't worry about it, baby. How do you know the baby is a girl?"

"I'm just guessing."

"Mm. If it's a boy, he gon' be mad as fuck at you for calling him a girl."

She looked up at me with her wet eyes and tear-stained cheeks and gave me a tight smile.

"I forgive you, Kinisha. You'll get better at this motherhood thing. It's still early. Let me have your back, okay? I'm not gonna let you go undefended. I need you to trust that."

I gently stroked her cheeks, then kissed her pouty lips. Hearing her admit that she was wrong was a turn-on. However, I knew I was gonna have to do something about Mya before this shit got out of hand. Kinisha wrapped her arms around my waist as she said, "Thanks for being patient with me."

"You don't have to thank me, baby. I'm going to handle this situation."

She nodded as my doorbell rang. I frowned. I never had visitors because I didn't have friends like that. Kinisha scooted away from me so I could go see who was at the door. When I checked the peephole, my blood started to boil. I opened the door, and the officer said, "Hello, Mr. Andrews. We have an arrest warrant for Kinisha Jordan. Is she here?"

I didn't know how they got that shit so fast. They never moved that quickly for black-on-black offenses. They probably thought Mya was white since she was an albino. Playing ignorant, I asked, "Assault against who?"

"Mya Russell. She's in the hospital as we speak."

"Hospital?"

"Yes, sir. Is Ms. Jordan here?"

"I'm Ms. Jordan. What's this about?"

All the wind left my sail. I was about to lie and say she went home because we got into it. I lowered my head as the officer said, "You are under arrest for assault. You have the right to remain silent . . ."

*Blah, blah, blah.* Kinisha's face was red as hell as she did as she was instructed. They handcuffed her as she stared at me, mouthing the words, "*I'm sorry.*" Then she said aloud, "Call Sidney Taylor for me, Mr. Taylor's wife."

I nodded. After that, I quickly got my keys and wallet from the kitchen countertop to follow them to the police station. It was a Friday night. She probably wouldn't be arraigned until Monday. Knowing my baby would be behind bars until Monday made me sick inside. When I got to my car, I immediately called Devin. I didn't have Sidney's phone number. He answered after one ring. "Hello?"

"Mr. Taylor, this is Oliver. I need your wife's number. Kinisha just got arrested for assault."

"Aww shit. I'm texting it to you now. What did I tell you about that Mr. Taylor shit? What happened?"

"I know. I know. She yanked my ex-employee to the ground by her hair. For whatever reason, Mya is in the hospital. This shit done went from bad to worse."

"Don't worry. We're heading that way. What county?"

"Harris."

"A'ight. We're gonna head that way, but go ahead and call Sidney so she can have all the details."

"Okay."

I ended the call and immediately called her. She answered just as quickly as Devin had. I ran down the entire situation, starting when we purchased the hot dogs. She was fuming but promised to try to get the charges dropped. I didn't know how she would do it, but I had faith in her abilities. She was great at what she did. There had to be something that could be done, though. Kinisha had a temper that I hadn't noticed until now. While that could serve her well, it didn't work to her benefit this time.

Sidney informed me that they would most likely release her, and she would have to return Monday for her arraignment. Hopefully, that would be the case. Although I knew I wasn't to blame, I felt guilty as hell. Mya was after me, and that got Kinisha caught up in this bullshit. I wanted to call Lazarus and tell him what was happening, but I thought better of it. They expected her to be gone all weekend anyway.

If they released her after I met her bail, then she could let them know what was going on if she wanted to. When we got to the police station, I was antsy as hell, not knowing what to expect. I'd never been in trouble or associated with anyone who got into trouble. I hadn't educated myself on protocol for an allegation like this. I just hoped it didn't take Devin and Sidney too long to arrive.

As I exited the car, I watched them lead my baby inside. I was grateful they weren't rough with her. It would be no good if we both ended up in jail. I wouldn't have hesitated to knock a cop on his ass if he'd mishandled her. When I walked in, an officer had me sit in the waiting area while they booked her. I was sure I would know of any bail once they were done. I wasn't certain of Mya's condition, so I could only hope her bail was minimal.

# Chapter 15

## *Kinisha*

That stupid ho had gotten me caught up. I was so disappointed in myself. This one time, it didn't matter what anyone else thought because I was disgusted with myself. I was arraigned Monday, and while I wanted to plead not guilty, my conscience got the best of me, especially because she ended up in the hospital with a concussion. She hit her head on the cement and had to get a few stitches for a minor laceration the blow caused.

I pled guilty and accepted my couple of months of probation and community service. Sidney was prepared to go to bat for me, but I knew I was wrong. Had Mya put her hands on me, I would have fought it to the bitter end. That was on me. I didn't control my impulses; now, I had to suffer the consequences.

Thankfully, I had a very understanding boss. He told me his brother had been in trouble with the law some years back and that their mother was a queenpin. That shit was surprising as hell, especially when he admitted to selling drugs while in college. God had spared me yet again. I knew Oliver was just as disgusted as I was, but he held me in his arms and assured me that everything would be okay.

I didn't bother telling my family. They would only blame Oliver . . . at least my dad would. I knew Kiana wouldn't, but I didn't want to involve her or Ramsey in the shenanigans.

As I sat at my desk, reviewing a client's financial report, my phone rang. I glanced at it and answered when I saw it was Ramsey.

"Hello?"

"Hey. Where the hell you been? I was calling you all weekend."

"You forgot I told you I was going to All-Star Weekend with Oliver?"

"Shit. Yeah. I was calling to tell you about this fuck nigga. So I guess it wasn't important."

"Ramsey, your feelings are valid, boo. What happened?" I asked.

She sounded like she was about to put herself down, and I couldn't have that. Robert had done a number on my girl. Although we'd gone to the club and gave him the business, she loved him. He was her fiancé. He was the man she was suppose to marry, start a family with, and spend the rest of her life with. I felt so sorry for her. I knew what it felt like to be duped and taken advantage of.

Jarod had a whole-ass woman that he was planning to propose to while he was fucking me, leading me on to think we could possibly have more. I hated to see her so broken, though. She'd had a relationship with his ass. I wasn't as involved with Jarod. This man had promised to give her the world, although he was rarely present when she needed his ass. She'd given her all to him, only for him to break her heart.

"Robert called, begging me to take him back."

I rolled my eyes. However, when she didn't say anything else, they widened. "Ramsey? What did you say?"

"I told him to meet me at Sertino's to talk about it."

Sertino's was one of our favorite sandwich cafes to go to. It was so laid-back and comfy. I switched my phone to my other ear and asked, "Are you serious?"

"Kinisha, I love him. I miss him so much. Why can't I forgive him, and we move on from this?"

"You know I love you, Ramsey. I'll support you in whatever you choose, but I don't think that's wise. I know I've made some fucked-up choices, but that's why I can tell you. I have plenty of experience with being a fool. He's playing you for a fool. Don't let him continue to do that."

When I heard her sniffing, I wanted to leave work and go hug her. I knew she was hurting and lonely. Since Oliver and I had gotten to know each other, I'd pushed her and Ki to the back burner. My friend needed me, and I needed to make time for her. "Ramsey, I'm gonna come over when I get off. What do you want to eat?"

"Kinisha . . . That's not necessary. You're pregnant and embarking on a new relationship. I'm okay."

"You said seafood? Okay. I'll go to Boil City and be there right after I get off. I love you, Ramsey. I'm always here. You know that."

"Thank you. I know."

"Okay. I'll call when I'm on my way."

"Okay."

I ended the call and returned to work to make up for missing Monday and part of Tuesday. Oliver had to go into his Houston office Tuesday before we made our way back to Beaumont. While Mr. Taylor suggested that I just take the whole day, I couldn't. I didn't get to the office until three but stayed until ten. Oliver met me here to make sure I got to my car safely. After today, I'd be all caught up.

After I finished the client file, Oliver appeared in my doorway, smiling. I smiled back. "Hey."

"Hey, baby. How are you feeling?"

"Good. What about you, Oliver?"

"I'm good."

"After work, I'm going to Ramsey's. I need to spend time with my girl. She needs me. I'm afraid she's gonna take her fiancé back. I need to go and talk some sense into her. I don't know where I'm gonna find that sense from, though, since I act like I don't have any most of the time."

Oliver chuckled as he slowly shook his head. "I promise, I was thinking that very thing. It might be like the blind leading the blind."

I giggled. "Hush."

He laughed more, then said, "Okay, baby. Will I get to see you later?"

"Can we play it by ear? I don't know how long it will take me to convince her to leave that nigga in the gutter."

"Okay. Hopefully, I get to see you. I wanted to rub you down tonight. If not, I'll do it tomorrow."

"Sounds like a plan, baby. You know I love your rub-downs."

"Yep. You almost done in here? I wanna at least walk you to the car."

"Almost. Give me another ten minutes."

He nodded and walked out with a slight smile on his face. Sunday, we were expected to eat at his cousin's house. I couldn't wait since it would be my first time meeting someone from his family. He'd already met my entire family. Since his parents were deceased and he was an only child, meeting family was difficult for him because it made him long for them. He'd gotten somewhat vulnerable with me while talking about his parents, especially his mother.

Oliver appeared back in my doorway as I finished what I was working on. I smiled at him as I grabbed my things from my desk. He walked closer to me and took them from me. "I got it, baby."

I swore that my insides turned to mush whenever this man spoke to me. He cleared his throat as I stood there in a daze. I blinked rapidly as he chuckled, then followed him out of my office.

Mr. Taylor was standing there at the front and gave us a smile on our way out. "See y'all tomorrow."

"Okay, Mr. Taylor."

Oliver placed his hand on the small of my back as we walked out. When we got to my car and he put my things in the backseat, he turned to me. "I don't care what time you get home, call me. I'll come through. You know you my power source. I need to charge up, beautiful."

He slid his hand over my cheek, then lowered his lips to mine. *Damn. My man, my man, my man. Shit.* When he pulled away, I bit my bottom lip, tempted to get a quickie before I went to Ramsey's place. "Okay. See you later."

"Be careful," he said as he rubbed my belly.

I gave him a bright smile, then got in my car and watched him walk to his. The man exuded swag and BDE. I didn't know how I hadn't seen it before, but I was beyond grateful that I saw it now. Oliver Andrews didn't miss. He was consistent, patient, gentle, and aggressive when he needed to be. I thought he would hem me up with that whole Mya incident. He was a blessing to me, and not just because of the baby situation. He made my life better. He made *me* better.

"See, now I have to stay longer since you brought all this food from Boil City. That's my spot," Braylon said.

I rolled my eyes. Ramsey didn't tell me her nosy-ass brother would be here. Nigga was always in somebody's business, especially mine. He'd informed Kiana about how I got down a few years ago. She knew I was promiscuous, but his ass had told her I was a dick hopper. *Jackass.*

"I'm sorry, Nisha. His ass was supposed to be gone by now."

"I had to come check on her. You know she hasn't been to work this week? Let me find Robert's ass. She won't have to worry about him tryna get back by the time I finish with him."

I nodded in agreement. "We fucked him up a li'l bit in the club when he was there with another woman. She caught a li'l bit of that shit too. There was no telling the lies he was telling her, though. He's just a trifling individual." I turned to Ramsey and continued. "The best way to get over his ass is to get under another nigga. Fuck him. Get revenge on his ass."

Braylon rolled his eyes.

"Kinisha, you know that ain't my style," she said.

"Yeah, but it's healthier than the alternative: you sitting in here stressing and depressed. Get out there and try new things. Don't give him the satisfaction of knowing he broke you, sis. That gives him the upper hand."

Braylon glanced over at me and looked away. I wasn't sure what that look was about, but I was sure I would find out soon. In the meantime, I headed over to my food before it got cold. I could talk while I ate. Ramsey and Braylon traded stares. Then both looked at me. "What? Just say it."

Braylon slid his hand down his face. "You was fucking with Jarod?"

I frowned hard as he held his hands up in surrender. "That nigga running his mouth, and I almost clocked him in it. Saying that you said you were pregnant and it was his baby, trying to trap him."

Now, I was fucking fuming. My face had to be red. I would have spilled the beans first if I wanted anyone to know. I looked away as I tried to gather myself before I went off on people who didn't deserve that shit. When I looked back at them, they were eating, but their eyes kept making their way to me.

"I'll tell you the truth, but I prefer this to stay between us. I haven't told anyone."

They nodded in agreement, so I continued. "I fucked around with him. I only mess with one nigga at a time, so there is no mistaking who my baby is from. The condom broke, and his seed wasn't in it. I positively know this is his baby. He wanted no part of it. Oliver came along, overheard an argument between him and me, and stepped in to save the day. He was trying to holla at me before this, but this situation actually made me pay attention to him. I didn't want to tell my parents I was pregnant without a boyfriend or at least a man who would accept the responsibility of being a father."

I swiped the tear that fell down my cheek. "Oliver stepped up to the plate and said I was his, and so was my baby. If I agreed, he would be the man I was missing. He would be everything I needed him to be. After mulling it over a bit, I accepted. Oliver is the best thing that has ever happened to me. While our relationship didn't start with the best intentions on my end, the only thing I would change is not giving in to him sooner. Now, that's the truth. Jarod is a fucking idiot and will say anything to make himself look good."

"I thought you knew he was a fuckboy and that you wouldn't go there with him?" Ramsey asked.

"I knew he was a fuckboy. I concluded that I was good with just having sex with him . . . the biggest mistake of my fucking life. I didn't set out to get pregnant, just like he didn't set out to impregnate me. I wasn't ready to be a mother, but unlike him, I'm not going to turn my back on my baby that I willingly participated in creating."

Braylon stood from his seat and pulled me from mine, hugging me tightly. The three of us had known one another for a long time, so his actions weren't strange. We were close like siblings, and in this moment, I gladly accepted his comfort. It almost felt good to tell someone besides Oliver the truth. It felt freeing. I knew, eventually, I would have to come clean to my parents about it. I should have just told the truth to begin with.

However, I knew I probably wouldn't be with Oliver if I didn't feel some type of desperation. I wouldn't have experienced just how amazing he was. When Bray released me, I went back to my seat. I looked over at Ramsey as she ate a shrimp. "Don't be like me and give in to Robert's punk ass. With this baby, I'll be tied to Jarod's bitch ass forever. God forbid if he decides he wants to be a father. I want to make him sign something saying that he's relinquishing his rights."

"Do it quickly then. When he sees that you ain't fucking with him no more and that you're with Oliver, I have a feeling he's gonna try to give you a hard time. Has he seen you since the argument at church?"

"No. The other arguments were done by phone. He doesn't have a clue about Oliver."

"He's a shady muthafucka. I know because we used to kick it sometimes. I fucked around, but I was never shady like his ass. I never could understand niggas like that. It's like they can't stand to see a woman move on from them, even when they created the distance. He thrives off making a woman fucking miserable or making her chase his ass."

"He's not going to get either from me. I know it doesn't seem like Oliver is the type, but I truly believe he would kill Jarod without a second thought. That man is so possessive of me and my time, but I love every moment of that shit."

"Yeah, he just seems like a computer geek," Bray chuckled.

"Same thing I thought. When he drops that professional tone, Lord have mercy."

"Man, change the subject. Ain't nobody trying to see you on the road to ecstasy, eyes rolling and shit," he complained.

Ramsey and I laughed. "Nisha, I hear you, but I can't believe Robert would do this to me. We were planning on getting married. I hate that I didn't see this side of him sooner. I feel like I've wasted so much time . . . time I could have used to love on myself instead of his selfish ass."

"It's okay, boo. It's in the past now. All you can do is move forward. Don't let him drag you backward. You deserve better. I hope you know that."

"I do. I just wish I could turn my bleeding heart off. I want it to stop hurting."

Braylon pulled his sister in his arms. "Don't cry. You know I hate to see you and Mama cry."

Ramsey wiped her face and took a deep breath. "Come on, y'all. Let's play Uno before we send Nisha back to her man." She giggled. "I'm happy for you, Nisha."

"Thank you, Ramsey. Your knight in shining armor will appear and sweep you off your feet in due time."

"Yeah. I hope you're right."

"I know I am. God knows how much you desire that. He won't leave you hanging."

*God, please don't leave her hanging.*

# Chapter 16

## *Oliver*

I got out of my car, prepared to go inside the house and take a shower. I anticipated Kinisha's call so much my dick wouldn't go down. I didn't know how I would take a piss if I couldn't even bend that shit. Glancing around to make sure I wasn't being watched, I went to the side of the garage and pulled my dick out to piss in the bushes. That was better than getting piss all over the toilet. That upward curve was a beast.

As I put my dick back in my pants, I heard what I thought was a snicker. When I looked around, I didn't see anybody. I knew I wasn't crazy, though. Kinisha didn't play those sorts of games, not that I'd noticed anyway. I paid very close attention to her and the things she did. She played around sometimes, but she quickly made it known she was playing so there wouldn't be any misunderstandings.

I headed toward my door, glancing over my shoulder. When I needed my gun, I never had it. After unlocking the door and heading inside, just as I was about to close it, a hand stopped it. I could clearly tell it was a woman. If that was Kinisha, I was gon' fuck her against the door as punishment for having me on edge. However, when I opened it and saw Mya, I nearly came unglued. "What the fuck!"

She squeezed herself inside between the door and me. I calmly walked out of that bitch. I wasn't about to be in that house with her. Grabbing my phone from my pocket, I called the police. I'd never filed the restraining order, thinking I had time since she was hospitalized. Obviously, I was wrong. Her injuries must not have been as serious as the district attorney let on. Kinisha should have let Sidney do her job.

After I pretty much threatened her life, the dispatcher said someone was en route. I wouldn't kill that woman unless I felt my life was in danger, but she was getting pretty close. She'd never been to my house, either one of them. She'd followed me all the way to Beaumont. This shit was crazy. She was inside the house screaming at the top of her lungs. When the back door flung open, I wanted to hide. That would have been the smart thing, but at the same time, I couldn't be feeling like a scared bitch over a woman half my size.

When she saw me, she smiled and walked in my direction.

"Mya, you need to get away from me. This shit is mad crazy. Like how you know where I live in Beaumont? You've only been to the Beaumont office once or twice. I've never taken you to either of my homes. Can't you see how weird this shit is?"

"What's weird about me loving you, Oliver? I'll do whatever it takes to help you to see how much you mean to me."

"This is illegal, Mya. You're stalking me. This shit could get you killed. I need you to understand where I'm coming from," I said as I heard sirens in the distance. "This could land you in jail as well. You need to take your medicine. Before all this, you were an amazing employee. Don't let your illness destroy everything you've accomplished."

"You don't know shit about my illness. Nothing's wrong with me. Why don't you and my mom see that? I'm in love with a man who's confused about who he wants to love. You don't love Kinisha. She put a hex on you and took you away from me."

The sirens had gotten louder, and she noticed. She began looking around and fidgeting quite a bit. "You called the police on me? Why would you do that? You're suppose to love me, Oliver."

She lunged at me, and I did my best to restrain her without hurting her. I felt sorry for her, despite the bullshit. She needed professional help. When I heard car doors close, I held her tighter. I didn't need her lunging at the officers and getting killed. That shit would haunt my ass for a while. They came around the corner with their guns drawn because she screamed for me to let her go.

"Let her go, sir!"

"Can you listen for a moment? She's volatile, and she's also mentally ill. Please put your weapons away. I'm the one that called . . . Oliver Andrews. I'm going to loosen my grip slowly."

Surprisingly, they listened well. I think it helped that both officers were Black. They didn't put their weapons away, but they nodded in understanding. As I released her, she gripped me tighter. "Oliver, no! I'm scared."

"Mya, please, let go. They are going to take you to get help. Maybe they can call your mom."

"No!"

I tilted my head, beckoning them to come and get her. One of the officers put his gun away while the other maintained his stance. When he got to us, he positioned himself where she could see him. *Smart move.*

"Ma'am, we just need to get you away from Mr. Andrews. I need to ask you some questions about how he broke your heart," he said, glancing up at me.

*Oh, he's good.*

She loosened her grip on me.

"What kind of questions?"

He slowly reached out and grabbed her hand, and she allowed it. "Just about how he chose someone else. He knows you love him, right?"

She nodded and willingly went with him while I took a deep breath. This could have ended in a totally different way. One or both of us could have been dead. The officer led her to his car while the other officer approached me to find out what happened. I told him all the details of my involvement with her and filed a restraining order. I also made him aware of what happened in Houston. As he took notes, he slowly shook his head.

I felt the exact same way. This shit just came out of nowhere. She could put a stop to it if she would take her meds. I'd often heard that it was hard as hell to get mental patients back on their medication when they'd fallen off it. I hoped they could provide her some help; somewhere she could go where they could practically dupe her into doing what she was supposed to do.

By the time they left with her in the back of their squad car, it had been over an hour since I'd first gotten home. This foolishness had left me tired as hell. Mya had drained every ounce of energy I had left. I went inside and went straight to the shower, hoping I could sleep before Kinisha called.

"Baby, I wanna come through. I can hear you're asleep, so I'm gonna come to you."

I sat up in bed to see it was almost eleven. After wiping my eyes and clearing my throat, I said, "Are you sure? I can get up and get to your place."

"I'm positive. I've already gone home and got clothes for tomorrow."

"Okay. Be careful, Kinisha."

"I will. I should be there in about ten minutes."

"Okay."

I ended the call, then went to the bathroom to brush my teeth. I'd been asleep for nearly three hours, so I knew I needed to freshen up. Then I went to the kitchen and sat at the table to wait for her. After a couple of minutes, I saw her headlights in the driveway. I briefly thought about telling her what had happened today, but when I walked outside to see how tired she looked, I decided against it.

"Hey, baby. You okay?"

"As okay as I can be."

"Let's get inside. Have you eaten?"

"Yes. I'm just ready to lie in your arms right now."

I could tell that something was bothering her, but I would let her work through it in her mind without pressure. I didn't need her stressing out and raising her blood pressure. She had another doctor's appointment at the end of next week. The last thing I wanted was for them to put her on blood pressure medication because she was stressed.

Once we got inside, I went to the bathroom and got her lotion. When I came out, she was taking her clothes off. We always slept naked when we were together. It was the way we liked each other. Clothes were only in the way. If she woke up in the middle of the night and wanted to suck my dick, I didn't need no drawers in the way of that. She'd done it a couple of times already.

As I watched her disrobe, my dick woke up, thinking it was his time to shine, but since she was tired, I would have to restrain myself. "Oliver, can you just do my feet? I'm so tired, I'll probably fall asleep before you finish."

"Of course."

After she got in bed, I grabbed her foot and began kneading it how she liked. Her soft moans weren't doing anything to relieve my dick of his duties. He was so hard it was becoming painful. When I finished one foot and had gone to the other, she asked, "What are your plans after work tomorrow?"

"I don't have any. Is there something you want to do?"

"My friends from church want to meet you officially. Braylon and Ramsey. When I got to Ramsey's, her brother was there. He used to have a thing for Kiana. She used to have to shut his ass down almost every time they saw each other. We all grew up together, though, and he had her back when she needed it most. They've seen you around church, but like me, they've never spoken to you."

"Yeah. I don't really make myself appear friendly. I have to work on that."

"No, you don't. I like the fact that people don't know how to take you. That means they won't try to cross you."

I chuckled. "If you say so."

"I *know* so. Kiana and Lazarus want to join us."

"Sounds like a plan. Is Braylon single too?"

"No. He has a girlfriend, but he's gonna go so Ramsey won't feel awkward being a fifth wheel between us two couples."

I nodded as I finished her other foot. Mya again crossed my mind, but I didn't see a reason to bring that up tonight. I would tell Kinisha about all that tomorrow once we were rested. Again, she seemed burdened down about something. I could be just reading too much into her weary state. I slid her socks on, then got in bed with her.

Once I was settled, I pulled her into my arms and kissed her soft lips. "Good night, Kinisha. Get some rest."

"Good night, Oliver."

Within two minutes, she was knocked the hell out. I stared at the ceiling, thinking about Mya. Hopefully, they were able to get her where she needed to be instead of releasing her so she could end up back here at my house. The thought of that happening while Kinisha was here had my nerves on edge. While I felt Mya was harmless, I couldn't let down my guard. Harmless people could turn dangerous with the flip of a switch.

As I turned my body to pull Kinisha closer, I saw her staring at me. I kissed her forehead. "You were asleep. Get your rest, baby."

"Not until you do. What's wrong?"

I slid my hand over my face and decided just to tell her. If something else were to happen, and Kinisha somehow found out about what happened earlier today, I would be in the doghouse for sure . . . or worse. "When I got home this evening, Mya was here. I had to call the police on her."

Kinisha sat straight up in bed. "She was *here?* Has she ever been here before?"

"She was here, and, no, she's never been here before. I believe she's stalking me. I filed a restraining order, but I know that won't necessarily keep her away. It does give me a leg to stand on, though, if she decides to show back up. I'm almost positive they didn't keep her in jail. I need you to be aware of your surroundings at all times. While I don't believe she would try to hurt anybody, she's mentally unstable right now. She could be capable of things I wouldn't imagine she would do."

"Like showing up at your house. I wish somebody would get ahold of her and shove that medicine down her damn throat."

"I wish it were that simple too, baby. I will do my best to be next to you whenever you're on the move. I don't like this shit at all. I feel responsible in a way because she used to work for me."

"Did she say anything about me?"

"Not really. Just that I'm not supposed to love you, and you must have put a hex on me. I mean, she may be right in that. It definitely feels like you cast a spell on me," I said, trying to lighten the conversation and change the direction of it at the same time.

Kinisha gave me a slight smile, so it must have worked. I kissed her forehead, and when I stared back into her expressive eyes, she asked, "Do you love me, Oliver?"

I closed my eyes and searched my soul. I left myself wide open for that question by reiterating what Mya had said without denying that she was wrong. Without opening my eyes, I took the leap, a leap I'd never really taken before. "I do. I love you, Kinisha, so much so until it's scary."

She brought her hands to my face and pulled me to her, kissing my lips tenderly, then sliding her tongue to mine. I allowed my hands to roam her curves, stopping periodically to take in the scenery. When I got to her ass, I squeezed it before pulling her on top of me. This was why we slept naked. With a little guidance and correct positioning from her, my dick found her opening and dove inside her warmth.

This was heaven, peace, love, joy, and happiness all rolled into one. I slid my hands to her ass and caressed it as I felt her juices leaking on my balls. God had given me heaven on earth with this woman. Her moans were intoxicating, and they caused me to release a few of my own. She'd pulled my feelings right out of me. I'd never told a woman that I loved her first. It was always after she'd said it . . . if I said it at all. After experiencing Kinisha, I didn't believe I'd ever really been in love. She slowed her pace as she slid down my dick with a roll of her hips. I wanted to scream. That shit felt so damn good, but it felt like she was teasing me.

She stared at me as she squeezed my dick while going up again, causing me to bite my bottom lip to contain myself. My toes were curled tight, and I was gripping the hell out of her ass cheeks. She placed her hand on my neck and quickened her pace. When she began bouncing, my heart nearly burst out of my chest. "Aww, fuck, Nisha."

"Yes, Oliver, yes, baby!"

I couldn't take letting her handle it any longer. I lifted my hips and began stroking her. My eyes rolled as she gripped my throat a little tighter. "Oliver . . . Shit, I'm cumming!"

The wetness that engulfed the area was the most satisfying shit. As I stroked her pussy, doing my best to maintain my pace, I said, "I love you, Nisha."

She opened her eyes to stare at me. "I love you too, Oliver."

That did it. I couldn't contain myself any longer. I flipped us over and long stroked her into another orgasm. Her walls were taking my dick hostage, and he was sputtering, trying to persevere through the way she was choking him, but it didn't work. I fired off in her depths just as she squirted all over me. Her screams had my dick erupting forever, it seemed. She would have gotten pregnant with this nut if she wasn't already pregnant.

I placed my forehead against hers and closed my eyes. "You love me. I didn't think I would hear that for a while."

"Why? It was hard *not* to fall in love with you. You're everything I need and want in a man. How could I not fall for a man like that? You're amazing, and I'm happy that you're mine."

"Damn, baby. I'm happy that you're mine too. No matter the situation, I pray we will grow stronger together."

She remained quiet. My mind had gone back to this issue with Mya. For some reason, I knew this shit wasn't over. She wasn't the only one I had to worry about, though. I had a feeling it would only be a matter of time before Jarod had some shit to say about Kinisha dismissing him. Whenever that time came, I would be ready. He would awaken the beast in me, and I would welcome its presence and fuck him up.

# Chapter 17

## *Kinisha*

Church was off the charts today. The praise team seemed to have taken us right to the throne of grace at God's feet. There wasn't a dry eye in the place, and the spirit was extremely high. I had so much to thank God for. Even while praising his name, I could feel Oliver's hand on the small of my back. He was so protective of me, and I loved that. Even with as much dirt as I had done, I could still feel the spirit occasionally. I'd even gotten slain once. So, I was grateful for His presence.

Rev. Adolph did his best to smother it so he could preach, but after ten minutes, he gave up and started shouting with everyone else. Eventually, things died down, and he could give a rough outline of his sermon. As I listened, it was like I kept feeling eyes on me. I glanced up at Oliver, who was tuned in to the pastor. I began scanning the crowd, and the culprit revealed himself. It was Satan himself: Jarod Speights.

I didn't know why he was staring at me like I was the one who had rejected him and done him wrong. He repeatedly nodded his head as I turned away from him. I'd been having too good of a time to be worried about his ass. I slightly rolled my eyes and leaned more into Oliver just to be petty. His bitch ass didn't want me. How dare he get jealous that somebody else did? He could kiss my big ass.

Just that fast, he had my mind on fucking him up with every move I made instead of focusing on the sermon. I shifted in my seat again, and Oliver draped his arm around me, leaned over to my ear, and asked, "You okay, baby?"

"Yes. My tailbone is just a little sore."

That wasn't a lie. It had been sore since yesterday. However, my pettiness had come out to play. I was doing extra shit to make Jarod jealous. This could have been his, but he wasn't half the man Oliver was. He would never reach Oliver's level of manhood, not even if he repented of all his sins, got rebaptized, and anointed with oil daily. He was rotten all the way to his core and was no good for anyone.

I noticed his woman was sitting next to him. She'd picked up on how distracted he was. I was dying inside. He couldn't focus on his fiancée because he was too focused on what I was doing, shit that wasn't even his business. Oliver leaned over and kissed my forehead, then tuned back in to Rev. Adolph. As I stared at him, he glanced over at Jarod. He'd seen him staring at me too. *Shit.* Hopefully, things wouldn't get heated at church. Shit, it was already heated, but it was only simmering. I had to somehow keep it from getting to a full boil.

I slid my hand to Oliver's other hand and held it throughout the rest of the service, doing my best not to give Jarod a slight glance, although I could see in my peripheral vision that his eyes were on me. Apparently, his woman got tired of that shit because she walked out of church. A minute later, he stood and went out after her. When he left, Oliver seemed to exhale and relax a bit more. He leaned over to me. "He's walking a fine line."

I nodded repeatedly. Oliver was gearing up to defend and protect me at all costs, even here at church. I could appreciate that. While I did my best to respect God's house, I would fight Satan. The devil went to church too, and he was here in the body of Jarod Speights.

Once the benediction was given, I noticed Mr. Taylor and his wife heading our way. I smiled big as they greeted us. "Are y'all going to Anise's house for dinner?" Mr. Taylor asked.

"Yep. We're about to head that way now. I'm starving."

"Good. Me too. And Shannon said Anise was cooking a roast today. My mouth is watering just thinking about it. My family is gonna be there because Anise wants to get to know everybody. So y'all will meet my brothers."

"Aww, Lawd. I get to hear Shannon's mouth again about us not starting on my house."

Devin chuckled as I smiled at Oliver. Apparently, Shannon gave him a hard time all the time. "Well, I can't wait to meet everyone," I added.

As we headed outside, I saw Jarod and his fiancée standing at the corner of the building, and they looked to be arguing. *That's what his bitch ass gets.* If he hadn't been so evil and shady, maybe he would have reaped a better harvest. When we got to Oliver's car, he opened the door and helped me inside. I was ready to go to his cousin's house to eat too. The nausea had died down, and now I just wanted to eat everything.

After getting inside, closing the door, and starting the engine, Oliver turned to me. "I promise that man will get what he's asking for. I want to know if he ever says anything out of pocket to you. He gon' get what's coming to him on sight. Wherever he fucks up, he gon' get fucked up." He glanced toward the sky. "Sorry, Lord."

He took off from the parking lot, and I grabbed his hand. It was trembling. He had hidden his anger well. It was shining through like a shiny piece of metal now, though.

"Relax, baby. We're gone now. Hopefully, he'll get over himself by next Sunday."

He lifted my hand to his mouth and kissed it. "I'll pray for that, baby."

I got nervous when we got to his cousin's house and noticed all the cars. However, if Mr. Taylor's family was anything like him and Shannon, I knew we would be in for a crazy time. As Oliver helped me from the vehicle, I noticed a couple of men talking at the back of the house. Mr. Taylor walked over to them and slapped their hands. One of them he hugged tightly.

I held Oliver's hand as he led me toward where the men were. Mr. Taylor turned around and said, "WJ, you already met Oliver, but this is his lady and my employee, Kinisha Jordan. Kinisha, this is my brother WJ, and this is my other brother, Shawn."

We all shook hands. His brothers were light complexioned but had colored eyes just like him. Until I worked for Mr. Taylor, I had never seen a dark-complexioned man with gray eyes. He was fine, for sure, and his brothers were just as fine. They were all old enough to be my father, but damn . . . They definitely kept themselves up. "Nice to meet you, Kinisha. My brother isn't giving you a hard time, is he?" Shawn asked.

"No, sir. He's extremely nice and laid-back."

He nodded. "I'm the older brother, and I can still handle his ass if you need me to."

Mr. Taylor rolled his eyes as I said, "No, Mr. Taylor's cool."

"Okay. Chill on the Mr. Taylor stuff. Away from the job, I'm Devin."

I giggled and said, "Okay. I just don't wanna slip up at work and say it."

"And if you do, so what? It's just weird hearing you say it here."

A lady poked her head out the door and said, "Shawn, do you want the potatoes in the meat since we have sweet potatoes too?"

"Naw, I better chill on that, baby. I'm coming in to help."

Oliver pulled me toward the house. When we walked in, there were only three women I had never seen before, although one looked really familiar. They all smiled at me. Shannon and Sidney came to me and offered hugs, and then Oliver introduced me to his cousin. "Baby, this is my cousin, Anise."

When she turned to me, I nearly swallowed my tongue. She frowned instantly, leaving Oliver confused. "What's up? Y'all know each other?" he asked her.

"Yeah. She and her girl practically attacked me and Robert in the club awhile ago. Robert said he didn't even know them like that, and they had him confused."

Oliver looked over at me as I slowly shook my head. His cousin was a gullible-ass bitch. "He's lying. He was engaged to my friend, Ramsey. I don't think she would mistake what her fiancé looks like. You are not the main chick. I mean, you may be now since she broke it off, but you weren't then."

She frowned harder, and I could see this would not be a great dinner. The other ladies were looking on in confusion. Finally, the one that looked familiar said, "Shiiiid, that sounds like some mess I would have been involved in back in the day."

She chuckled as Sidney nudged her. "Umm . . . Kinisha, this is my sister, Sonya, and my sister-in-law, Ericka."

I smiled at them as I realized that I knew who Sonya was. She used to be a CoverGirl model. She was also a model for Louboutin and a video vixen back in the day.

"Nice to meet both of you," I responded, hating that I wouldn't get to converse more with Sonya, the sister-in-law Mr. Taylor had said was off the chain.

I glanced up at Oliver, and he looked pissed and embarrassed. This was the second time my behavior had embarrassed him. "I'm sorry, Oliver. I'll go outside until you eat. When you finish, you can take me home."

Before he could say a word, I walked out of the door. Devin, Shawn, WJ, and now Corey were looking at me, probably trying to figure out where I was going. I couldn't believe this shit. It was such a small fucking world. I sat on the patio furniture as they continued to stare at me. Mr. Taylor walked over and asked, "Everything okay?"

"No. My girl, Ramsey, and I had a run-in with Anise in the club. She's dating my friend's fiancé . . . well, ex-fiancé now."

Before Mr. Taylor could respond, someone said, "What's up, everybody?"

I almost came unglued when I turned around and saw Robert's ass. He looked like he'd seen a ghost when he looked at me. All eyes were on him to see what he would do. For a minute, he looked like he wanted to jet. Instead, he made his way inside. "He bold as shit," Shawn said.

"Damn right. When I would have seen Kinisha, I would have made a U-turn quick as hell," Corey added.

They started cracking jokes about the situation, but it was far from funny. My friend was still suffering from the effects of his betrayal. There was no loud talking, so I assumed everything was okay inside. Oliver hadn't come out, and I didn't know if he would. I took my phone from my purse and called Kiana.

"Hey. Can you come get me?"

"Why?"

"I'll explain it when you get here."

I gave her the address, and she told me she would arrive in a few minutes. When I ended the call, I huffed. I was suddenly nauseated, so I went to the other side of the garage and regurgitated. I hadn't thrown up in a week, but this situation had my stomach so damn nervous. I didn't know how Oliver and I would go on from here. Anise was the only family he had here in Beaumont. Maybe I wasn't the one for him. It seemed I was always doing something to fuck up.

After I finished throwing up, Devin stood there with a water bottle. I smiled slightly at him, rinsed my mouth out, and then drank some. "Thank you, Mr. Taylor."

He rolled his eyes, but I couldn't even laugh. When I saw Kiana turn in the driveway, I was glad to be leaving. I grabbed my phone and sent Oliver a text. I didn't want to go inside and make even more of a scene than I already had. Kiana is here to pick me up. I hope to talk to you soon.

I smiled slightly at Mr. Taylor and made my way to her car. When I got in, my phone started ringing. I thought it would be Oliver, but it was my mother. "Hey, Ki. Thanks for coming," I said.

I went to my phone and answered. "Hello?"

"Umm . . . Nisha, I think you need to get here now. Jarod is here saying some awful things about you, and I think it would be best if you were here to help us understand what he's talking about."

*Fuck!* "On my way."

I ended the call, and the tears cascaded down my cheeks. Everything seemed to be falling apart. Kiana grabbed my hand and asked, "Nisha, what's going on? You're making me cry."

"Ki, way too much is going on, and I only want to explain it once. However, I'll tell you what happened at Oliver's cousin's house. When we arrived, and he introduced me to everyone, I realized his cousin was the woman Ramsey and I had gotten into an altercation with at the club."

"Y'all were fighting at the club?"

"His cousin was with Ramsey's fiancé. We didn't really fight her. We were trying to fight him. Ramsey grabbed her by her hair and threw her to the floor because she was sitting on his lap, tonguing him down. You know that's our signature move for these bitches."

"Oh my God, Nisha. What did Oliver say?"

"He didn't say a word. Anise is still seeing Robert. He told her we were delusional and that Ramsey was lying. She believed him. So, obviously, she wasn't that happy about seeing me, although I never touched her. I could tell Oliver was angry and probably embarrassed. This is the second time I've embarrassed him. I got in a fight in Houston at All-Star Weekend."

"Kinisha! You're pregnant!"

"It wasn't really a fight. She didn't hit me. I snatched her like Ramsey did Anise."

"Oh my God. So now, Oliver is upset. He didn't come outside."

"Yeah. What am I gonna do if he's done with me?"

"Unfortunately, that will be his loss. As long as he takes care of his child, we won't be able to hold it against him."

I swallowed hard because this shit with Jarod was about to throw them for a loop. I couldn't understand for the life of me why he was over there spilling the tea about me like he wasn't a fucking participant. On top of that, he distanced himself from me, not the other way around. It was like that muthafucka just wanted me to be miserable like his miserable ass, just what Braylon told me he would do.

When she turned in the driveway, my insides started boiling. I had a headache from hell and wanted to go home and crawl under my covers. My phone chimed in my hand as I got out of the car. I looked at the screen to see it was a text message from Oliver. I couldn't bear to see what he had to say right now. I was glad he wasn't here with me. He would probably end up in jail.

Kiana caught up with me when I got to the back door. I hesitated for a minute, closing my eyes and saying a short prayer that God would help me keep my hands to myself and my tongue mild in front of my parents. I wasn't feeling feisty and angry. I felt sad and depressed that this was what my life had come to.

Walking inside the house, I could see Jarod sitting on a chair and my parents sitting across from him on the couch. A tremble went through my body as he looked in my direction with a smirk. As I entered the area they were in, I could see the frown on my dad's face. My mom looked perplexed as well. I only lowered my head and said, "Hey."

"Kinisha, please tell me what he's saying isn't true."

"What is his lying ass saying?" I closed my eyes and took a deep breath. "I'm sorry."

"He said that you were trying to pin a baby on him, and when he wouldn't go for it, you pinned it on Oliver. Were you sleeping around like that?" my mother asked.

"I was only sleeping with Jarod. When I told him I was pregnant, he called me everything but a child of God right there in church. We practiced safe sex, but the condom broke one particular time that I know he remembers. Oliver knows all of this. I didn't 'pin' a baby on him. Oliver loves me and wanted to help me save face in front of y'all and a bunch of people who I don't even care about. Jarod refused to step up to the plate. He knows this is his baby. That's why he's here. He didn't care until he saw me with Oliver today, like he doesn't have a whole fiancée."

Kiana was standing to the side with her mouth open. I didn't realize Lazarus was here, but he stood beside her with his arm around her shoulders. Everyone was extremely quiet until Jarod said, "Kinisha, if you were sleeping with me, how can I be sure you weren't sleeping with someone else?"

"What reason do I have to lie? You ain't got shit, nigga! Having your baby won't benefit me one bit. Why do I need to lie? I *wish* I were having Oliver's baby. He stepped up to the plate to claim a baby that wasn't his simply because of how he felt about me. *He's* going to be my baby's father. What was even your point in coming here with this shit? To make me look bad? So I can be as miserable as you are? Why?"

"So they can know they raised a whore. You aren't innocent."

Before anyone could say another word, Lazarus laid him out. "You will *not* come into this house and insult my sister. You have to be out of your mind to think that was gon' fly here."

"Get your ass out of my house," my dad added.

Jarod stood from the floor with a smirk on his face.

"And wipe that shit off your face before you get knocked down again. I will take this to the pastor. Deacon in training my ass," my mama said.

I was shocked they were cursing. That rarely happened. However, I didn't get my hopes up because I was sure I would suffer their wrath once Jarod left. As soon as he walked out, my dad glared at me. He remained quiet until he heard Jarod's car crank up and drive away. "Kinisha, I don't even know what to say. I thought we raised you to have good morals and standards for yourself. I'm not gonna even ask why you slept with him because I can only imagine."

"That's why I didn't want to tell y'all I was pregnant without having a boyfriend. Jarod doesn't want our baby, but Oliver was willing to raise a baby that wasn't his. Now, I may be raising my baby alone. I have to go. I feel dizzy and just want to go home and lay down."

I walked away while my mama begged me to talk to them. I couldn't stand to see the disappointment on their faces. I squeezed Lazarus's hand as I went outside and down the driveway.

"Kinisha! Where are you going?"

Kiana was running down the driveway to catch up with me.

"Why are you running? Stop before you fall or hurt yourself."

"Nisha, where are you going?"

"Home."

"You live five miles from here. Are you crazy?"

"Yeah. I just wanna be by myself."

"I'll take you home. Come on."

I lowered my head and headed back to her car. I hoped she would remain quiet. I didn't feel like talking about it anymore. I sent Mr. Taylor a message, taking tomorrow and Tuesday off. I didn't want to be around anyone.

I hated what I allowed Jarod to do to me. He made a fool of me, and I didn't know how to recover. It didn't help that I had made horrible decisions contributing to today's fuckery. Hopefully, time to myself would help me reset. I desperately needed a recharge because all this shit had depleted me completely.

# Chapter 18

## *Oliver*

It had been an entire week since I'd seen Kinisha. She didn't go to work Monday and Tuesday, and I had to go to Houston on Wednesday through Friday to conduct interviews. She refused to answer my calls or text messages. I'd even called her office phone, but she had caller ID on it, so she wasn't answering. I wasn't sure what was up with her. I wasn't angry at her. I was angry that Anise was still letting that nigga dupe her into believing he loved her.

When he walked his raggedy ass into the house, I was heading out to see about Kinisha. What he said halted everything. He asked Anise if she invited "that bitch." I made my way back through the house to handle him accordingly. He looked like he wanted to take out his anger on my cousin, so that caused me to stay inside even longer. I felt Kinisha was okay outside since Devin and his brothers were out there.

When I received the text that she was leaving, I nearly knocked Anise down, trying to get out the door before she left. I was still too late. They were driving away when I got to the driveway. I got in the car and went to her place. She didn't answer the door. I was so desperate I almost broke into her apartment on Monday. I assumed she thought I didn't want her anymore because I didn't go outside after her on Sunday. That wasn't the case. Kinisha Jordan was still the woman I loved. She was the woman that held my heart in her hands.

I called Devin yesterday, and he said she'd shown up to work for the rest of the week, so I knew she was ignoring my calls. Just the fact that I was trying so hard to get ahold of her should have let her know that I still wanted her. My message had simply asked her why she left Anise's house, but she never responded.

I refused to lose the woman I loved over a misunderstanding. I loved that feistiness in her. I wasn't angry that she was fighting. The situation with my cousin happened before she got pregnant. Why would I be upset about that? I didn't understand. As I stood in the mirror and tied my tie, I could only mumble a prayer that God would make a way for me to get through to her. I hoped she would be at church today. If not, maybe I could talk to her parents or Kiana to help me get through to her.

After giving myself a once-over in the mirror, I put on my glasses, grabbed my keys, phone, and wallet, and headed out the door. My nerves were all over the place because I needed to see and hear from my baby. I needed to know that she was okay. I didn't even turn on the music in the car. I was laser focused on reconnecting with my baby.

When I got to church, I went to where Kinisha and Kiana sat. They hadn't gotten to church yet. I noticed her parents sitting over where they sat every Sunday with the deacons and deaconesses. Her mom gave me a weak smile, which didn't do anything for my nerves. When Kiana sat beside me, she gave me the same weak smile. I leaned over to her and asked, "Is she coming?"

She shrugged. "I haven't talked to her in a couple of days. She's been shutting us all out."

"I've been trying to call her every day, including last Sunday. Why isn't she answering?"

Before she could respond, the musicians began playing, preparing for praise and worship. I didn't feel right even sitting here without Kinisha. Glancing over to my right, I saw Jarod sitting there. He looked like somebody had knocked his ass out. The discoloration on the side of his face said it all. I smirked, thinking somebody had finally given him what he'd been begging for.

I did my best to participate in the service, but I couldn't stop my mind from going over all the events from last Sunday, trying to see if I missed something. Maybe she thought I was siding with Anise since she was my cousin. She had to know that I wasn't that type of person. Right was right, and wrong was wrong in my book, and it didn't matter who was doing it.

It didn't seem Kiana was paying much attention to what was happening either. She looked to be texting someone, and upon further observation, I saw she was texting Kinisha. I leaned over and asked, "Do you have a key to her place?"

"Yes, but I promised her I would never use it unless it were an emergency."

Her phone vibrated, and she checked it. When I saw the crying face emojis from Kinisha, I knew I had to get to her somehow. This was an emergency for me. I wasn't sure what Kiana considered an emergency, but this was definitely an emergency in my book. "Tell her I miss her."

Kiana gave me a tight smile and sent the message to Kinisha as I tried to tune back into the service. When my phone vibrated, I just knew it was her. I nearly fell off the pew, trying to get my phone from my pocket. When I saw Anise's number, I wanted to throw it across the sanctuary. I opened the message to read, I'm sorry, Oliver. You were right. Robert is a jackass that deserved his walking papers. I gave them to him Friday night. I'm cooking if you and Kinisha wanna come over. I owe her an apology.

I didn't bother responding. She'd told me that she didn't think Kinisha was even the one who pulled her to the floor. She thought it was her friend that did so. Either way, Nisha didn't do anything wrong. Anise was so damned gullible and naïve.

Someone walking by caught my attention, so I looked up to see Ramsey. She had a young man with her. I guess she'd moved on too. Good for her. She probably had a level of naivety as well for her not to catch on to Robert's bullshit sooner.

I'd practically choked Robert's bitch ass last Sunday.

*"Oliver, I don't know about her. She rowdy, and she ghetto. How you go to a club to fight? That was what they were there for . . . to start mess."*

*"Anise, listen to yourself. They had a case of mistaken identity? That shit is an obvious lie. Two grown-ass women would come to a club and intentionally attack him because they thought he was someone else? That shit don't even sound believable. Now, him saying that she was lying could be believable if you had a guy whose word was credible."*

*At that moment, the person in question walked through the door, fuming. I was about to walk out and give them their privacy. The ladies that were in the house had walked out as well. As I headed to the door, that muthafucka had the audacity to ask, "You invited that bitch over here? Why is she here?"*

*I quickly made a U-turn and approached him in the front room to see he was all in Anise's face. "You might wanna back up off my cousin. And you calling my woman a bitch is gon' get you bodied."*

His eyes widened slightly, and he said, "This matter is private. She may be your woman, but you don't know her ass. She stay in people business, and my boy said she was nothing but a ho."

He didn't even see it coming. I crossed the room in record time and grabbed him by his fucking neck, pushing him against the wall. Anise didn't say a word. She didn't even scream to alert anybody that anything was going on in here. She knew my temper and how I could get when protecting someone I loved. It happened often when we were kids because she was so damn green. Couldn't see a lie if the nigga told her he was a fucking giraffe.

I delivered a couple of body shots while I had him against the wall, then squeezed his neck as tightly as possible. "Next time you disrespect either of these women, you won't walk away with your life. It will be self-defense, and I snapped. That's what the cops will know, and that's what everyone will tell them. This is your only warning."

I dropped him to the ground as my phone vibrated. I looked over at Anise, and she was just standing there, watching him on the floor, gasping for air. She looked back at me and remained quiet before stooping to the floor to help him. That was it for me. I walked toward the door and saw Kinisha's message saying she was leaving.

All eyes were on me when I got to the glass door. I hurried out of the house and ran to the driveway to see the car pulling away. "Fuck!"

I slid my hand down my face and turned to the Taylors. The women were seated at a picnic table, talking amongst themselves, but Devin, his brothers, and Corey were all staring at me.

"What'chu gon' do?" Devin asked.

I shrugged my shoulders as I sent her a text asking why she left. When I looked back up, Shawn was standing in front of me. "If she's the woman you love, go after her. Don't give up on her, no matter how long it takes. You see that woman over there?" he asked as he pointed to the woman introduced to me as Sonya. "Over twenty years. We both married other people and had kids, but our hearts never left each other. We've been married for fifteen years now, and it's been the best fifteen years of my life despite the adversity and rough times. Go get your woman."

I nodded and damn near ran to my car, peeling out of the driveway like a bat out of hell. Shawn was right. I needed to get to Kinisha. I felt terrible about her going outside to appease my cousin, but because it was Anise's house, I knew there was nothing I could say about her welcoming Kinisha, given their history. Had Robert's ass not come in the house acting like he wanted to buck, I could have gotten outside before she left.

When I got to Kinisha's apartment, I practically jumped out of the car before I put it in park. Her car was in the same spot as it had been when I had picked her up, so I could only hope that her sister had taken her home. She hadn't eaten, so it was probably unlikely now that I thought about it. I ran to her unit and knocked until my knuckles were sore. She probably wasn't here.

Grudgingly, I walked away with my shoulders slightly slumped and my head lowered. I grabbed my phone and tried to call her, but there was no answer. My heart sank to my feet. I could only hope this wasn't the end of the ride for us. This was all a miscommunication that could be fixed with a simple conversation. I needed her.

***

When church was just about over, I leaned over to Kiana. "I think this serves as an emergency. I haven't seen or talked to her in a week. I'm dying without her. I need to hold her in my arms. Please, don't deny me that."

She looked up at me as I pulled away, the tears building in her eyes. She nodded, grabbed my hand, and squeezed it. Hopefully, Kinisha would be receptive to my presence. How could she not be if she loved me as she said she did? I didn't understand why she was blocking me out, especially if she'd read my messages, pleading with her to talk to me and telling her how much I needed her.

It made me wonder if something more had happened that I didn't know about. Why was she shutting her family out? What happened at Anise's house had nothing to do with them. I needed to get to the root cause of her distancing herself. Just as I thought that, I caught Jarod staring our way. I had a feeling that he was the reason. It was like God was giving me the answer to my question.

We stood for the benediction, and I could honestly say I didn't hear a word of what went on today. If God had a word for me, I missed it altogether. As Kiana and Lazarus headed out, I couldn't help but notice the glare Lazarus shot his way. Once we got outside and had gotten to the parking lot, I asked him, "What was that all about?"

"What?"

"That look you gave Jarod?"

"He showed up at my in-laws' house last Sunday, talking smack about Kinisha. I knocked his a—"

He stopped himself before he cursed and continued. "I knocked him out. He wasn't going to get away with basically calling Kinisha trash."

"I knew something else had gone down for her to be secluded like this. I've been in Houston trying to hire people for my office since I took on a new contract. I couldn't get to her at work. She wasn't answering the door yesterday. I knew she was in there because the lights were on. Kinisha doesn't leave lights on, period."

He smiled slightly. Evidently, he knew that about her too. She wouldn't even leave on the Black person's universal night-light: the light over the stove. Her house was pitch black when she wasn't there. "Are y'all gonna go there now?" I asked.

"Yep. Just follow us."

I nodded, then headed to my car. I was nervous but also excited. Holding Kinisha in my arms was one of the best feelings in the world. I turned on my radio and found "Lovin' You" by The O'Jays playing. That song was a testament to how I felt about Kinisha. Everything was all right when she kissed me. Despite her doubts about us at first, she gave us her all. I was absolutely positive that she was the woman for me. If we didn't make it, I'd be single for the rest of my life. If we didn't make it, it would be because she gave up, not me.

I took Shawn's words to heart last weekend. He seemed wise and like he could help me through this journey. I was grateful for Devin Taylor and Corey Sheffield. They were older men who could help me through life's journey. Now, I had Shawn and WJ Taylor added to that, not to mention my future brother-in-law, Lazarus Mitchell. These men provided sound advice and a good time, whichever I needed at the moment.

Devin had given Shawn my phone number, and he even called Wednesday to see how things had gone. He offered more words of encouragement along with Devin and Corey. I appreciated that more than they could know. I had an awkward way of shutting people out of my personal life, but they didn't allow that. That was why I didn't have friends. People took that as I didn't want to be bothered. I just struggled with getting to know people outside of business.

When we got to Kinisha's apartment complex, my heart sank to my feet. Her car was gone. I rested my head against the steering wheel. I didn't wanna become a fucking stalker, but it seemed that was what I would have to resort to if I wanted to see her. The knock on my window caused me to look up. Kiana was standing there. "She's at the grocery store. I told her you were here to see her."

I licked my lips and lowered my head. "She isn't coming. She doesn't want to see me. Got it."

I lifted my window and burned off while Kiana stood there with her hand on her chest. This shit hurt like hell. She'd allowed Jarod to tear her down but wouldn't allow me to help build her up again. This shit was fucked up. If I had to sleep at that fucking office, she would see me and give me a fucking explanation. I needed to understand why she was doing this. No explanation was good enough. I needed to know what her thought process was.

When I got home, I sent her a text. I'm not giving up on us. Fuck Jarod, fuck Robert, fuck Mya, and even fuck Anise. I love you. You supposed to be my wife, girl. I didn't just say all that shit to your parents to make myself look good. I meant every fucking word of that shit. I need you, Kinisha, and I know you need me. If you don't want me close to you, then file a fucking restraining order. I'm angry that you're shutting me out without an explanation. You at least owe me that. Even with the explanation, nothing can compare to our love. You said I made you feel again . . . things you've never felt. Remember that? Why would you want to let go of that?

I sat in the car as I pressed send, hoping she would respond. Before I realized it, a tear had fallen down my cheek. I angrily swiped at it before leaving the car to go inside. This bullshit was going to come to a head and soon. Tomorrow, she would talk to me whether she wanted to or not, especially since I would be sitting in her desk chair when she got there.

# Chapter 19

## *Kinisha*

"Good morning, gorgeous," I said to myself in the mirror.

I closed my eyes and slowly shook my head. Gorgeous was the last thing I felt, but I continued to say it to myself every morning. Depression was real, and I had never felt it to this magnitude. We had a client who requested an in-person visit, and I volunteered to be the one to fly out to Austin. My flight left last night, and I wouldn't return until tomorrow evening. Mr. Taylor told me to enjoy time to myself because I seemed to need it.

He gave me a phone to contact him and told me to shut off my other one. He would make my family aware of my whereabouts and that I was safe and okay. I nearly passed out when I got Jarod's letter for a DNA test last week. I hated his ass, and he was doing his absolute best to make my life hell. Thinking about how Oliver prayed over my baby and rubbed my stomach made me throw up.

Oliver loved the baby as much as I did. In his mind, he was the father. He didn't deserve the bullshit I was going through. To tell him that Jarod could want to be in the baby's life now would be like stabbing him in his heart.

I needed time to myself without interruption to get my thoughts together. That muthafucka wasn't doing this for the right reasons, and I didn't understand why he needed a DNA test for a child he didn't want.

The only thing I could think of was that he was jealous that Oliver was being the man I needed. Oliver was man enough to step up to the plate and take care of his responsibilities. Oliver Andrews was rare. Unfortunately, I didn't deserve him. He was way too good. My life was a fucking mess right now. Seeing the disappointment on my parents' faces didn't help because I was already disgusted with myself.

I needed to find my purpose in this life. Maybe I wouldn't have been so easily deterred if I had known it. For some reason, God thought I would be a good person to raise a baby. Why would He even allow this? I thought it was so He could bring Oliver into my life, but what was the point of having Jarod as a thorn in my flesh? He said he didn't believe it was his baby, so why was he giving me a hard time?

Oliver needed peace, and I brought everything *but* that to him. I brought drama, destruction, chaos, and stress. My emotions were all over the place, and I was on empty. I had nothing left. I was simply pretending to have it all together, something many people did daily. I hated being fake, though. If I was in a fucked-up mood, usually everyone knew it. I had more than myself to think about. My baby needed to be in a healthy and stable environment, and I would do my best to provide that.

After getting dressed and requesting a Lyft through the app, I prepared to start on my makeup. I needed that shit. I'd had bags under my eyes for the past week. I got a text from the phone Mr. Taylor gave me and saw a message from him. The client canceled. Jackasses. Enjoy your vacation.

I rolled my eyes, but I wasn't mad about that. The only thing I hated was all the effort it took to get out of bed and get dressed, putting on a front like I wanted to be there. I quickly canceled the Lyft, undressed, put on my sweats and T-shirt again, and got in bed. Had I done my makeup, I would have gone somewhere just so it wouldn't have gone to waste.

I texted Mr. Taylor back. Okay. Thanks. See you tomorrow.

He responded immediately. I think you need to talk to Oliver. That man is about to lose his mind. Despite what you're going through, he wants to be there for you. Let him, Kinisha. Talk to him. If he still wants to be there, it's his choice. That means he loves you beyond all that bullshit. It's much easier to get over bullshit when you have someone in your corner, helping you fight it. Stop torturing him and yourself. I can tell it's killing you. When you come back, give him air to breathe.

I stared at his message and read it repeatedly. The tears poured from my ducts, and I couldn't stop them. I had an appointment Thursday that I knew he would want to be at. Mr. Taylor was right. I'd shut him out for over a week. As Oliver said, he deserved an explanation. I should have never taken his deal. Jarod had plans to make our lives miserable like his was. I was the only one who should have to battle that bitch, because I put myself in this fucked-up situation.

Oliver was too pure of an individual to deal with this shit. Jarod was spreading lies about me to whomever he could tell. Braylon told me he'd gotten into it with

him when he overheard him and Robert talking at the
gym. I had no idea he and Robert were friends. It made
sense, though. They were both shady-ass niggas. Birds of
a feather flocked together, and those niggas were damn
near twins.

I pulled myself together and messaged him back.
You're right. I'll talk to him when I get back. I have to do a
DNA test before leaving Houston tomorrow, though. Are
you still picking me up?

How do you feel about Oliver picking you up?

I closed my eyes and took a deep breath. After a moment, I texted back one word. Okay.


When my flight landed, I was a ball of nerves. I didn't
know how Oliver would react to seeing me. He hadn't
called or texted me to let me know he would be the one
picking me up, and I hadn't attempted to call or text
either. Walking to baggage claim, it felt like my knees
were knocking. I'd only gotten glimpses of his aggressive
nature. The Oliver I'd gotten to know was tender and
gentle, sweet and caring, considerate and loving.

Just my luck, I didn't have to wait long for my luggage.
There was no time to stall before meeting the inevitable.
I took a deep breath and made my way to the exit. Being
nervous was pointless. Whatever was going to happen
would happen. Nothing would change it. I just had to accept that and respond accordingly. Oliver didn't deserve
my attitude, no matter how he responded to seeing me. I
was the one who created this bullshit.

When I stepped outside, my eyes landed on his. It was
like God had a ray of sunlight shining on him to where I

couldn't overlook him. He looked as sexy as ever, wearing a yellow Polo-style shirt and glasses. I loved those glasses on him. Sometimes, he wore contacts, but I would look forward to when he would give his eyes a break from them. His expression was firm, not a smile in sight. However, he wasn't frowning. There seemed to be a look of desperation in his eyes as he watched me walk to him.

His eyes raked over my body in my summer dress. I wasn't wearing a bra or underwear. The dress was too thin for that. It wasn't see-through, but the print of underwear would be easily noticed. G-strings and thongs were pointless. They didn't hold anything. The sight of them was appealing to men. My coochie ate that shit up, and it was extremely uncomfortable to have wedgies in the front *and* the back. I tried to stick to bikini style or went without.

Even as nervous as I was, my pussy still got wet at the sight of him. He was so damn sexy, and he knew it. His stare was only making me wetter and more nervous at the same time. He didn't try to meet me halfway to get my bag or anything. He just maintained his position and watched me. When I got to him, without saying a word, he took my luggage from me and went to his trunk. I followed him and said, "Hi, Oliver."

He glanced at me, then closed the trunk. Grabbing my hand, he led me to the passenger side, but before opening the door, he went to his knees in front of me and hugged me around my waist, resting his forehead on my stomach. "Damn, Kinisha. Don't ever do this again."

Tears fell down my cheeks as I rubbed my hands over his bald head. He stood and stared at me again, then lowered his lips to mine and gave me the most tender kiss he'd ever given me. That only caused more tears to fall. I didn't expect this response. I was expecting him to be angry. It seemed he didn't give a shit about why I distanced myself from him. He was just happy to see me again.

He opened my door, and I got into the car. He immediately drove off after walking around to get in the driver's seat. It was as if he knew exactly where I needed to go.

"Oliver, I'm sorry."

He slowly shook his head. "We'll talk later, okay?"

I nodded as I swallowed hard. His tone wasn't harsh, but it was definitely stern. I remained quiet as he drove, and I glanced at him when he turned into the DNA testing center. When he killed the engine, I lowered my face to my hands. I was overwhelmed with the love and care he was showing me despite what I'd done to him. He exited the car and walked to my side, gently pulling me out.

"Kinisha, I love you. That shit ain't changed just because you were tripping. Relax, baby."

I wrapped my arms around him and cried into his chest while he caressed my back. He kissed my forehead and pulled away from me. "Let's get this over with."

I nodded, then headed to the building. When I approached the window, I gave the lady sitting there my name, and she gave me paperwork to fill out. This shit was pointless, but if Jarod's ass wanted to waste his money on shit he already knew, I would let him. I had nothing to hide. He was just a ho-ass nigga who tried to make shit complicated.

When I sat to fill out my paperwork, my hand was trembling so much I could barely write. I didn't know why because I knew what the outcome would be. Maybe it was still leftover nerves about how the conversation with Oliver would go. He took the pen from my hand and the clipboard from my lap. "Just tell me what to write."

I gave him the needed information, then took the clipboard to the front desk. Once I sat, he grabbed my hand to soothe my nerves. I turned to him. "Just so you know, I'm not nervous about this test. I know that Jarod is the biological father of my baby, without a doubt. He was the only man I was sleeping with before you."

Oliver gave me a soft smile and rubbed his hand across my cheek but didn't say a word. When the technician/nurse called me to the back, I glanced at Oliver.

"Go ahead. I'll be right here when you're done."

I nodded and followed the woman to the back.

"Hello, Ms. Jordan. Mr. Speights has already given his sample and requested that we expedite the results."

"Good."

She took me to a room where all her supplies were, and I sat in the chair designated for her to do her job. She was done within minutes, and I was headed back to Oliver. Strangely, I felt a sense of relief. I assumed that was because I knew Jarod would have to stop telling fucking lies about me. This blood test would prove that he was the father. I truly hoped he suffered from the results as much as he was trying to make me suffer.

Oliver slid his hand to mine and led me out to the car. Once inside, he turned to me and said, "I scheduled you an appointment. I want you to relax before we talk about things. We will hash this shit out like adults and move on from it, okay?"

I didn't bother asking what type of appointment. I just wanted to talk and get this shit over with, but I was at his mercy if I still wanted him to be in my life. "Okay."

When he turned in the spa parking lot, my eyes widened slightly. I turned to him, and as soon as he put the car in park, he pulled me to him and kissed me with a desire unfathomable. After pulling away, I damn near wanted to straddle him in this car. "Just tell them your name, and they will take it from there. Try to relax. We need to talk, but I promise, you have nothing to worry about. I told you that you were mine and that I was yours. That shit ain't changed . . . unless you want it to."

I quickly shook my head. "I love you, Oliver. I'm just so embarrassed about my behavior."

"There's no reason to be embarrassed. You expect what you've experienced. I'm trying to broaden your horizons and prove to you that not all men move like the ones you've experienced. My word is bond. I know that statement is cliché, but it's factual. I don't say shit I don't mean, and I ain't gon' renege on shit I done said unless it's absolutely necessary. However, it won't be because I've changed. It'll be because the situation has changed."

"You're so perfect. I was a fool to overlook that."

"I'm not perfect, baby, but I *am* a man who will always admit to his errors. My error this time was that I didn't make you feel secure in my position concerning Jarod. But we'll talk more about that after your massage. I plan to make things crystal clear to you, and I want you to make things crystal clear to me in return. Now, go on in there."

He kissed my lips once again, and I got out of the car and wanted to skip all the way to the entrance. I felt so happy inside. I questioned all the time whether I even deserved Oliver. I didn't care what he said. He *was* perfect, and he was perfect for me.

When I walked inside, the lady at the front desk smiled at me. "Good afternoon. You must be Ms. Jordan."

I smiled back. "Yes, ma'am, I am."

"You're a lucky woman," she said, then winked at me.

I smiled and closed my eyes as I nodded. "Not lucky. Blessed. Immensely blessed."

She smiled even brighter and said, "You are absolutely right. Follow me."

She led me to a dimly lit room with wallflowers producing a pleasant scent throughout. A robe hung on the wall. "Go ahead and get undressed and put that robe on. Someone will come and get you shortly."

I nodded, and as soon as she closed the door, I came out of my dress and sandals and quickly put on the robe and the slippers on the floor right beneath it. Shortly after, someone knocked on the door. I opened it, and another lady stood there. "Hello, Ms. Jordan. Follow me."

I wasn't sure where we were going, but I anxiously awaited to dive on that massage table in the room where I disrobed. I was more than sure I would be back. I couldn't help but notice the relaxing music being played. The fact that everyone I saw was Black made the spa more appealing. When we got to the other side, I realized Oliver had paid for the works, from exfoliation and a facial to a mani/pedi and body waxing. I even sat in a sauna for thirty minutes.

After all that, I was taken back to where I disrobed and indulged in a relaxation massage. I fell asleep while getting rubbed on and listened to GIVĒON. When the masseuse finished, she gently shook me. I was so damn relaxed I felt like I could conquer the world. I was slick as shit, but my skin felt so good. I even felt good mentally, and I believed that was what Oliver was aiming for. After dressing, I made my way out. When I got to the front, I received a care package with oils, lotions, and body butter to keep my skin radiant. This would *not* be my last time coming here.

When I exited the building, Oliver stood outside, leaning against the car. He'd changed into shorts and a T-shirt, revealing every bulge his muscles created. My eyes automatically rolled to the back of my head, threatening to have my ass taking a tumble on this concrete. He licked his lips and smiled at me as he opened the door to his car. I put my hand on his cheek and tiptoed to kiss his lips before getting in.

After he got in, he said, "You're probably hungry now, right? The baby is probably kicking your ass too."

I chuckled. "Yeah. Thank you, Oliver. That was amazing. I enjoyed every minute of it."

"I can tell. You look relaxed."

He pulled out of the parking lot, and once he got on the road, he grabbed my hand and kissed the top of it. "Now, tell me. What was keeping you away from me, baby?"

I lowered my head for a moment. "Well, that Sunday when I left your cousin's house, although I said I would wait for you, I expected you to come after me. When you didn't, I thought you were angry and embarrassed. That was the second time I'd done that to you because I couldn't control my temper. So, I asked Ki to pick me up to give you space. It killed me inside to do that, but I assumed that was what you wanted."

"I don't care how angry or embarrassed we think we make each other. I need you to promise me that you won't assume things. I don't have a problem expressing how I feel, and I know you usually don't either . . . until now. For the record, I wasn't embarrassed or angry at you. I felt that way toward my cousin because I always felt like that nigga was up to no good. I didn't come right out because I was explaining how I felt about the situation to my cousin. Then that nigga came in all hostile and shit. I had to make sure he knew that he would get fucked up. When I came outside, you were leaving. I went to your house to see you, but you weren't there."

"Yeah. I went to my parents' house because my mom called requesting that I go over there. I'm sorry for assuming. That won't happen again. I'll be sure to communicate better."

He kissed my hand. "Okay. That issue is squashed. Now, why did your mom need you to go over there?"

I closed my eyes and slowly shook my head. I felt he already knew but wanted to hear it from me. "Jarod was there, telling them all kinds of bullshit about me. Most of it lies. The only truth he spoke was that we'd slept together. That shit broke me because I hated seeing my parents' disappointment in me. I've done my shit over the years, but I was always discreet about things I did. Jarod and Robert are friends, and they are trying to destroy my reputation, life, and relationship with you. I hate it. That's why I haven't been to church. I'm so embarrassed about what he said that people believe about me."

"What people? Besides your parents and Kiana, where do those people even stand in your life?"

I shrugged.

He continued. "Exactly. Fuck those people. Why do you give a damn what they think? If they aren't adding anything to your life, why would you allow them to take from it? That shit has taken your confidence, peace, and overall joy. That includes Jarod. Fuck that nigga. The biggest flex is to show him you are unfazed by his antics. He's a grown-ass man throwing a fucking temper tantrum. Let that nigga look stupid and miserable by himself."

He kissed my hand again. "So, tell me what all this shit has to do with me."

I stared at our hands. The way he was handling this entire situation was so foreign to me. He didn't raise his voice, and neither did I. Oliver was a level of grown I had never experienced. I knew I hit the damn jackpot with this man. As I fidgeted, I felt the car slow down. I looked up to see we were at a traffic light. "Look at me, Kinisha."

I hesitantly looked up at him, and he caressed my cheek. "You don't ever have to be hesitant about telling me what's on your mind or your thought process. Just tell me."

"I didn't want you to have to deal with the bullshit Jarod was putting me through. You agreed to be a father to my baby, but that was because he didn't want to be. Now that he's showing interest, for all the wrong reasons, I'm sure, I didn't want you to feel like he'd taken something from you."

"Let me stop you for a moment. I didn't agree to be a father to your unborn child simply because he didn't want to be. I want you. Since I want you, I want everything and everyone that comes with having you. Your baby is an extension of you, no matter who the father is. I want to be a father to your baby because I want to be your husband. That's it."

He gently slid his hand over my stomach as if bonding with the baby. When the light changed to green, he eased into the intersection.

"My thoughts seem so stupid now. I just didn't want you to be in the middle of the shit I played a part in. I didn't want Jarod to push you to places you didn't normally operate in. You don't deserve that."

"Despite what you may think about yourself, you don't deserve that shit either. You deserve a nigga like me, and I deserve a beautiful queen like you."

I tried hard to stifle my smile, but it was for naught. It shined through anyway. "Oliver, damn. I put us through unnecessary shit. I'm so sorry."

"It wasn't unnecessary. It helped us understand each other better and made us talk to each other. I want you to see that I'm ten toes down for yo' ass no matter what happens. You my baby, Kinisha. Whatever somebody trying to do to you, they trying to do that shit to me too. I'll go to war for you, baby. You my everything, and I'll do whatever I have to do to protect and defend you."

"So we're good?" I asked.

"Better than good."

I smiled, and this time, I lifted his hand and kissed it. He slowly shook his head as I held his hand to my chest. Satan wouldn't have his way this time. Nothing would destroy the bond between Oliver and me, and anyone who tried to do that was wasting their time. *Fuck 'em.*

# Chapter 20

## *Oliver*

When I got to my house, Kinisha looked confused as hell. I told her we would get something to eat, but she didn't know I'd had a meal catered for us at my house. I was so fucking happy to be reconnected with her. At first, I was angry at her, but then I had to realize that there was something I hadn't made clear. Even if Jarod decided he wanted to be a father, I would be there because I loved her. Her baby would always be a part of me because I was fully invested.

Going to appointments with her made me feel like that was my baby. That baby would be mine as long as she and I were together. Her explanation didn't surprise me. She was so selfless. She thought she was preventing me from enduring the bullshit with Jarod, but she was killing me by taking her love away. I didn't give a fuck about Jarod. Although he was the biological father, he was a nonfactor.

I got out of the car and walked around to help her out. As badly as I knew she wanted to ask questions, she remained quiet. She trusted the fuck out of me, but if she wanted to know something, I wanted her to ask. "It's okay to question me, baby."

She smiled. "I was just wondering why we're here."

I bit my bottom lip as I stared at her. "You about to see in just a minute. You trust me?"

"With my fucking life."

"Mm. That's good to know."

I turned back to the door and unlocked it. After opening it, I let her walk in first. I could hear her gasp before I even stepped inside. After closing the door behind me, I wrapped my arms around her waist and rested my hands on her belly as she looked around the room. I placed flowers strategically throughout the room while she was at the spa. She was there for nearly three hours, so I had plenty of time.

"Oliver, this is beautiful."

"You're worth every petal and more."

Her cheeks reddened as I kissed one. "And something smells amazing."

"I hired a chef to cater us a meal. I just wanna spend as much alone time with you as possible. I missed you so much, Kinisha. Damn. I thought I'd lost you, baby."

I kissed her neck, then gently bit her earlobe. She turned around in my arms and put her hands on my cheeks, sliding her fingers through my beard. She gripped the hair there and pulled my face to hers. My hands traveled to her ass, and I squeezed. I missed this shit, and my dick was saying so. That nigga felt like he was about to bust before sliding into her.

I pulled my mouth away and sank my teeth into her bare shoulder. She knew exactly what she was doing by wearing this summer dress. It was evident that she wasn't wearing a bra, and after sliding my hands over her hips and grabbing her ass, I knew she wasn't wearing panties either.

"Oliver, shit. I'm about to feed you your appetizer."

"Hell naw. That shit ain't an appetizer. That's the main course, baby."

I picked her up and cradled her in my arms as I headed to my bedroom. As we passed through the kitchen, I gave the chef a head nod. He smiled and gave me the same. Kinisha started licking and sucking my neck the minute we reached the stairs, making my heart beat erratically. I was dying to feel her insides.

I walked through my bedroom door, kicked it closed with my foot, and went straight to the bed to lay her beautiful body on it. After going back and locking the door, I turned to find her with her dress lifted to her waist and her fingers deep in her wet pussy. I quickly rid myself of my clothing and made my way to her. I licked my lips and slid between her legs. Pulling her fingers from her fondue, I licked and sucked them clean while staring into her eyes.

I glanced down to see her creaming. Removing her fingers from my mouth, I asked, "Is that for me, baby?"

"Yeeees, Oliver. Eat your lunch. We're already late. It's almost dinnertime."

I smiled slightly and dove into her freshly waxed pussy. Feeling her thighs tremble against my ears always motivated me to give her the best I could offer. After indulging in her flavor and digesting as much as possible, I went to her clit and sucked it, making love to it. I groaned as I sucked, wishing I could stay here all fucking day. My dick wouldn't allow that, though. Her taste was magnificent. There was no way I would ever get enough.

She slid her nails over my head, and I knew I had leaked precum on my sheets. However, when she spread her legs more, placed her hands against my ears, and pulled me deeper into her, I fired off onto the sheets. My entire body trembled as I relaxed, knowing that her sexy ass controlled me. She had me by the balls, and there wasn't shit I could do about it. Her body trembled, and I could hear it in her voice when she asked, "Did you nut, baby? Fuck. I'm about to cum."

I didn't dare stop to answer her question. I continued to suck steadily, wanting her to feel every twitch her pussy made before she nutted on my tongue. When she screamed out her release, I slurped up what I could, then went to my knees and pushed my dick inside her. I let out a growl that surprised even me. "Fuck, Nisha . . ."

I lowered my head to the pillow near her ear and stroked her pussy. "Oliver, oh my God, I missed you so much."

She wrapped her legs around my waist and threw that pussy back at me. Lifting my head, I stared into her eyes as my pace quickened. This was the most powerful shit I'd ever experienced. I needed her, and I refused to ever let her leave me again. Although I could have tracked her at any moment, I chose not to. I didn't want to be that way and override her wishes at any point, no matter how ridiculous I thought they were. I wanted her to make a conscious decision to be with me without me manipulating the situation.

The way she rolled her hips against me had me stroking her stronger and faster. She always managed to get what she wanted out of me when she wanted it. I wanted to make love to her, but I quickly realized that she wanted to be fucked. I had her on that front too. She was about to get some shit she wasn't ready for.

I pulled out of her and rolled her over on her stomach, then reentered her as I gripped her ass cheeks, giving her every centimeter of dick I possessed. She buried her face in the pillow and screamed as she creamed all over my dick. Watching that white shit coat me was going to be my undoing. I leaned over her and plummeted her shit until she said, "Let me suck my dick, baby. Let me taste my excitement."

I lifted my eyebrows but immediately withdrew from her. There was nothing sexier than a woman that wasn't afraid to taste herself, and I loved watching Kinisha do that shit. Every time she did it, it felt like the first time. I went back on my haunches, and she turned around and lay in front of me. She stared up at me and said, "Fuck my face, baby. That rough shit like the first time."

Oh, she was really trying to make me crazy as fuck. "Kinisha, you really trying to get fucked up, huh?"

"Yes, baby. Punish me for all the time you went without me. Tell me what will happen to me if I ever do it again. Mm . . . I need you too, Oliver."

I roughly grabbed her by her hair and shoved my dick in her mouth. She was bringing out the savage in me, and she knew that shit. I began stroking her mouth until the spit fell from it, then began rough riding it. She was gagging a lot but wouldn't let me pull out. Pausing briefly to let her get her bearings, I resumed my attack on her throat. She was gonna need a damn tonsillectomy fooling around with me.

The streamers coming from her mouth to my dick had me on one. My nut was about to be strong enough to tear down strongholds in her life. It was about to be powerful enough to burst through a brick wall. I gripped her hair tighter as she scratched the fuck out of my legs, taking my dick like she was literally trying to digest it. "Kinisha, you ever fucking leave me again, I'm gon' fuck you all the way up. I'm gon' shove this shit so far down your throat, that muthafucka gon' come out yo' ass."

She stared up at me, and I swore I saw the smile in her eyes. I bit my bottom lip, then closed my eyes. "Real shit, baby. I was angry and hurt. Don't ever do that shit again. I love you too much for you just to let me go like that. Ahh fuck! Suck your dick."

My dick should have been raw with the suction she was putting on him. The skin should have been a thing of the past. She opened her mouth wider, urging me to do as I pleased. I hit her tonsils with a one-two punch as I listened to that fucking gawk-gawk sound coming from her voice box. That was the end-all for me. I shoved my dick down her throat as far as it would go and gave her all my badass kids. She quickly pulled off my dick and let me finish firing off in her face. "Oh shit."

I swore I started nutting all over again as I painted her face like a fresh canvas. She stuck out her tongue, and it was filled with my nut. I was hard as a hammer all over again. I pushed her backward, stood, and picked her up from the bed. She wrapped her legs around me as I slammed her against the wall. My dick sniffed out her opening and slid through there like a bulldozer. My nut was falling on me from her face, but that wasn't going to stop me from fucking up the way she walked.

Her body slid up and down the wall as I fed her my dick until her pussy was full and throwing up. Her orgasms were so sexy. The way her body arched and her nipples seemed to grow in size excited me beyond belief. She scratched my back as she clawed at me for dear life, but I refused to let up because she was the one who got me to this point. I'd nearly forgotten she was pregnant. "Kinisha, I'm about to nut, baby."

She slid her arms under mine and held me tighter as I emptied into her paradise. For the first time in a while, I was panting uncontrollably. This woman had drained me of everything I was worth. Her legs slid down my body until her feet hit the floor. She nearly collapsed. After scooping her up, I brought her to the bed, then went to the bathroom to get a wet towel to clean her up.

When I came back, her ass was out cold . . . like snoring and everything. I'd never heard her snore. I chuckled as I wiped my nut from her face and cleaned her pussy. Slowly shaking my head, I grabbed the comforter and covered her up. I couldn't help but smile at my work. It was my personal best. After entering the bathroom, I cleaned up and stared at myself in the mirror. Although I felt somewhat awkward acknowledging God after all the nasty shit we'd just done, I still said, "Thank you for bringing her back to me."

"So what are you expecting to happen once Jarod gets the results from the paternity test?"

"Honestly, Oliver, I don't know. He made it clear he didn't want a kid, nor did he want one with me. Whether or not he decides to be there, it's on him. All he did by ordering this test is make it easier for me to file for child support, especially if he won't sign the papers I'm having drawn up for him to surrender his parental rights."

"That's smart, baby."

We were sitting at the bistro-style table in my kitchen instead of going to the dining room table. This was where I often sat to eat when it was just me. Sitting in the dining area was unnecessary when I was dining alone. Today, Kinisha wanted to sit here just because she loved the table. She said it made her feel like she was on vacation somewhere. I could only chuckle. Whatever floated her boat.

We'd taken an hour-long nap, then woke up and took a shower, inciting another round of lovemaking. It was slow and steady, with a lot of kissing. I loved every minute of that. It seemed we connected spiritually whenever we took things slow. It was more passionate and intentional, especially when we made eye contact. Whenever I slowly made love to her, I always asked her to look at me. There was no better feeling than having the woman you loved reciprocate that through every movement of her body.

While eating my pot roast and savoring the taste, Kinisha said, "I just wish I didn't have to deal with him

at all. I know I can't do anything about it now, but damn."
She paused and took a deep breath, then turned to me.
"He's not fucking up anything but his own life. Not ours.
Thank you for helping me see that. I will do my best to
remember that when he gets my feathers ruffled."

Setting my fork down on the plate, I brought my hands
to either side of her face. "Whenever you feel down,
discouraged, or in despair, find me. Whether that's by
phone or in person, I'm here to encourage, uplift, and
love you through it. Lean on me, and you won't go wrong.
I can bear all that shit for you. If he wanna act crazy, I can
stoop to his level and be a crazy muthafucka too. I work
for myself, and my contracts are well established. I'm set,
so I have plenty of freedom to fuck him up."

She gave me a one-sided smile. "I don't want you
fucking up nobody but me."

Just that fast, she had my mind shifting to other things.
The anger I felt had dissipated before it could fully
manifest, and I was feeling soft as shit. "You mean to tell
me you didn't get enough earlier?"

"Get enough of you? Impossible."

I bit my bottom lip as my eyes scanned her body,
noticing how hard her nipples were through the T-shirt
that she wore. "Touché, baby. I'm a bottomless pit when
it comes to you. A nigga never get full."

Her face reddened slightly as she turned back to her
food. I could see her glancing at me from the corner of
her eyes. After putting some food into her mouth, she
stood from her seat and made her way to the bathroom.
I figured she had to throw up, so I followed behind her
to make sure she was okay. When she opened the door, I
asked, "You okay, baby?"

She didn't look sick, so that was throwing me off. She
gave me a slight smile, then went to her knees in front
of me, pulling my shorts down and taking just what she
wanted. "Oooh fuck."

I couldn't even contain that shit because she caught me all the way off guard. Although we were talking about sex and satisfying each other, when she returned to eating, I thought the conversation was over. I grabbed her shoulder-length dreads and slow fucked her mouth. My dick wasn't even ready, but as soon as her lips touched him, he woke the hell up like *Damn, who summoned me?*

As she sucked, she stared at me and began massaging a spot right beneath my balls. My dick sputtered and got choked, then spewed his excitement without warning right down her throat. "Fuck."

Kinisha had me just where she wanted me. I couldn't leave her ass even if I tried. She sucked all the residuals while I shivered and trembled like a damn female. Once finished, she stood and kissed my lips. She walked off and returned to her food like nothing had happened. I was standing here with my dick still out, trying to get my life together, and she had done moved on with hers.

She glanced back at me and chuckled. Finally gathering the energy, I pulled my drawers and shorts up, then joined her at the table. "What did you even go to the bathroom for?"

"To rinse the food particles out of my mouth. Can't have that shit getting in my pussy. I was pretty sure you would take me right here in this kitchen."

I didn't know where this nasty-ass woman came from, but I was here for that shit. She could be nasty like Lil Duval described in that song with Tank and Jacquees. I'd make sure I was ready at all times. I snatched her from her chair and pulled my T-shirt over her head, then immediately pulled her nipple into my mouth. My fingers found her pussy, and I began stroking it, ready to feel her walls wrapped around my dick . . . until the doorbell rang.

I frowned instantly. No one popped up here. My mind automatically went to Mya. She'd been quiet as hell for the past two weeks or so, but I knew she would be back. After taking a deep breath, I sucked Kinisha's juices from my fingers as the doorbell rang again. "Are you expecting someone?" Kinisha asked as she pulled my T-shirt back over her head.

"No. Hopefully, it's not who I think it is."

Kinisha frowned but followed me as I went to the washroom to get a T-shirt to put on. She grabbed a pair of basketball shorts from the top of the dryer and slid them on. She was right on my damn heels on the way to the door. When I opened it, Mya stood there just as I thought she would be. However, I didn't expect her mother to be with her.

She cowered in my presence. Technically, she was violating the restraining order, but I would see what she had to say as long as she wasn't on any bullshit. "Hello, Mr. Andrews. Mya and I wanted to come by to say something to you."

I nodded as she gently nudged Mya. She looked up at me, and I could see the tears in her eyes. The woman I hired was standing before me, trembling in what I presumed to be fear. She looked nervous as hell with the way she was fidgeting.

"Mr. Andrews, I owe you an apology. When I don't take my medicine, I become someone else. Although I wasn't in control of my actions, I remember mostly everything that happened between us. I'm embarrassed. I also should have made you aware of my diagnosis. These manic episodes, depending on what triggers them, can be hell on me and anyone else involved. It wasn't fair or right to leave you in the dark."

I nodded as she turned her attention to Kinisha. "I owe you an apology as well. I got you in so much trouble. It was never my intent to get you caught up in my foolishness. I knew Oliver didn't see in me what I saw in him.

I'd long gotten past that . . . or at least I thought I had. My manic moments proved that I hadn't. I hope you will forgive me."

She lowered her head as I glanced over at Kinisha. She was still frowning. My baby was on probation for that shit she pulled and would be for the next month or two. Kinisha took a step in her direction. "I forgive you."

Mya looked up at her with a soft smile and hugged her. "If I could drop the charges, I would. I'm so sorry."

"Mya, while I hate being on probation, that situation has made me better. I've learned to control myself. The old me would have hit you again when Oliver opened the door simply because I know he has a restraining order against you. I would have gotten away with it too. You helped me to realize that I was quick-tempered and hostile. I want better for myself and my baby. There was no way I should have done that, *especially* since I was pregnant. You could have chosen to attack me, and I could have lost my baby. That wouldn't have been your fault. It would have been mine. So thank *you*."

Mya hugged her again, then turned to me. "Mr. Andrews, I know I can't take back everything I put you through and the bind I put the company in, but I hope you can find it in your heart to forgive me."

I watched her fidget more as I stared at her. This was the Mya I was familiar with. She was somewhat reserved and shy. I glanced at Kinisha as she slid her hand into mine. "I forgive you."

Kinisha squeezed my hand, and oddly, I knew what she wanted me to do. "And if you still want it, you can have your job back. However, that's on one condition. You do what you're supposed to do regarding your health and mental well-being. This can't happen again. I get that sometimes, even with medication, it can be out of your control, but intentionally not taking your meds won't be good. At least I know now. I may be able to handle it better if it happens again."

Mya glanced at Kinisha as if seeking approval, then fell into me. She was crying so hard. I gently rubbed her back, not to comfort her but more to coax her to let me go. She pulled away, and her mother smiled at me. "Thank you so much for forgiving Mya. She's such a good person. It's this disease that turns her into someone else. She loved working for you, and she loves computers. I remember when she first got hired and had worked a couple of months. She was so excited because you were so laid-back and trusted your employees to handle their responsibilities without micromanaging them."

I smiled back at her mother. "Well, things may not be that way for a while. It will feel like I'm micromanaging you because I want to ensure everything's good. So, you will be on probation for at least ninety days. If there are any issues, the probationary period could be extended. You will have to prove to me that I can trust you again. You were a good employee, Mya. That's the only reason I'm hiring you back. You know your stuff. Kinisha could have squeezed my hand until it turned white, but I wouldn't have given you your job back if I didn't value your work."

Mya smiled and slowly shook her head. "I can't thank you enough . . . you or Kinisha. I was so disrespectful, and again, I'm ashamed of my behavior. I'm going to do my best to stay as healthy as possible. Congratulations on your baby."

I nodded as Kinisha said, "Thank you."

"You can report back on Monday. We could sure use you. I have two new hires starting Monday."

She smiled at me as her mom shook my hand. "Thank you again. See you on Monday."

I nodded as they walked away, and Kinisha wrapped her arms around my waist. I turned to her and said, "I didn't think you had it in you."

Her brows furrowed. "What?"

"To be forgiving instead of petty."

She playfully shoved me and walked back to the kitchen. I chuckled as I closed the door and followed her. Before she could sit, I pulled her to me and asked, "Now, where were we?"

"Back to me being petty and choosing to finish my food instead."

My lips parted as she laughed and sat in her chair to finish her food. *Ain't that 'bout a bitch.*

# Chapter 21

## *Kinisha*

"So everything worked out. You're all smiles."

I smiled even bigger at Mr. Taylor. I'd just gotten to work and put my things on my desk. Yesterday with Oliver was amazing. Things were beyond "worked out." They were better than before. Oliver had me so soft and vulnerable that I couldn't help but express that to Mya. Having a legitimate excuse for her behavior made it easier to forgive her.

With Oliver, I was able to feel like a woman. Like Aretha said, *a natural woman*. I could be soft and vulnerable. I didn't have a thing to worry about as long as he was around. We weren't married, but knowing I could depend on him in *every* area of life was overwhelming. I didn't have to be on my grind or worry about not having enough money to do whatever I wanted. He'd already scheduled a trip for us to the Maldives next month.

"Everything went extremely well, Mr. Taylor. Thank you so much for your advice. Oliver was even able to make things right with Mya. He hired her back."

"Oh, that's good. She has a mental illness, right?"

"Yes. Bipolar disorder."

"Aww shit. I have plenty of experience with that."

"Who's bipolar in your family?"

"My sister-in-law, Sonya. Shannon, Serita, and even Sidney have mental disorders they deal with, from sexual addiction to depression. Their family was in turmoil for the longest. Thank God the last ten years or so things have been pleasant but before that . . . They couldn't be around one another for more than a couple of hours—or at all. Sonya stayed into it with Serita and Sidney. It was a mess. Shannon was the only one that stayed pretty neutral and got along with everyone."

"Oh wow. Does Oliver know? Maybe you can be of assistance if he ever needs it concerning Mya."

"No, he doesn't know, but I'll tell him. My sister-in-law, Serita, is a family counselor and has her own practice. She can be of assistance as well. She counsels more than just families."

I nodded as I heard the door open. I glanced out to see it was Mr. Taylor's brother, Shawn. They slapped hands, and Mr. Taylor asked, "What are you doing out here?"

"I had to come check on a few things. Everything good on your end?"

They continued to talk as I sat at my desk to get settled. Shawn knocked on the door frame after I put my purse in the file cabinet and booted up my computer. "How are you, Ms. Kinisha?"

"I'm good. Thank you. How about you?"

"I'm good. Enjoy your day."

"You too."

He winked, then left. He was friendly, just like Mr. Taylor, but somewhat flirty. Those blue eyes of his had to be the charmers that got him whatever he wanted. Mrs. Sonya was a blessed woman because he was fine as hell. From what I gathered just by being around Mr. Taylor and Mr. Sheffield, they were all well off. I was amazed that none of them were involved in politics. I was shocked when I heard Mr. Taylor say something about Mr. Sheffield's private jet. They were all so down to earth, and I was happy to be connected to people of their character and caliber.

Today, I would be going to my parents' house. I had to make things right with them. I'd been pushing them away. Kiana had been blowing up my phone. I only responded to her occasionally. I knew that was wearing her thin. I just didn't know how to deal with their disappointment because it mirrored mine. Maybe I was dealing with how I saw myself, and I couldn't take being around people who agreed with me.

I had a doctor's appointment at one, so I would be going to their house whenever I left the doctor's office. Oliver would be going with me, and I couldn't wait to see him. He had a few errands to run this morning, so he would have to meet me at the doctor's office. I was excited to get there and see how the baby was progressing. Although I didn't know the sex yet, knowing everything was on the right track eased my mind.

Oliver's cousin had even invited us back to her house. Oliver said she'd called him last night to set a date. She'd broken up with Robert and wanted to have a do over. I was shocked as hell. She seemed pretty firm in her decision not to get to know me. Apparently, Robert had convinced her that I was ratchet and undesirable. Since I was there with Oliver, she had to know something wasn't right about that analysis. Oliver wouldn't date someone like that. That proved to her that he was hiding something.

He didn't like me because I saw him for what he was. Not to mention, his hatred of me had only gotten worse after I stole off on him at the club. I had a hell of a right hook. Letting him catch that fade was one of my proudest moments. I didn't know where the fight in me came from, but Kiana didn't have it. My mother didn't seem to have it either.

Then tomorrow, I had to report to my probation officer. They were enrolling me in anger management classes. I wasn't upset about it because I knew it could benefit me. Besides the situation with Jarod, things looked to be heading in the right direction. I was tired of the bullshit, and as soon as this shit was wrapped up with Jarod, I could concentrate on the joys of being pregnant and my new love with Oliver.

When I arrived at the doctor's office, Oliver was already there and standing outside waiting for me. I hadn't seen him all day, so to say I was excited was an understatement. Although I'd briefly seen him this morning before going to work, that wasn't nearly enough time to count. After grabbing my bag, I practically hopped out of the car and ran to his arms.

"Well, damn. I guess you missed me as much as I missed you, baby."

"Yeah. I've gotten spoiled. I wish you could be at the office every day, all day. I never get tired or feel smothered being around you. That's new for me."

That was the God's honest truth. It didn't take much for me to get tired of a clingy nigga. I needed my space and time to myself. Now, here I was, the clingy one, but I didn't think it bothered him. Oliver would give me my heart's desires, and if that was only his time and attention, I knew he'd give it in a heartbeat.

Oliver leaned over and kissed my lips. "It's new for me too, but I wouldn't trade the feeling for the world."

I smiled at him as he grabbed my hand and led us to the entrance. Once he opened the door, I walked through it and immediately wanted to throw up. Jarod was seated in the waiting area, staring right at us with a smirk on his lips. *How in the fuck did he know I had an appointment today?*

I turned to Oliver, and the look on his face sent a chill up my spine. However, he leaned over and said, "Go check in."

I swallowed hard and did as he said. My legs were trembling, and I suddenly wanted to piss. This nigga was determined to be a nuisance in my life. After signing the clipboard, I took steady, deep breaths, then knocked on the glass. When the receptionist slid it open, she smiled big. After scanning my face, her smile faded. "Are you okay?"

I shook my head. "There's a man here . . . the biological father of my child. I don't want him here. I'm going to ask him to leave, but I need reinforcement. My blood pressure has to be high now because I feel like I have to throw up and feel slightly dizzy."

"Okay. We'll observe from here. If he doesn't leave—"

"I'll get him out of here," the lady standing behind her said.

She frowned deeply as she pulled her cell phone from her pocket. I walked away and saw that Oliver had stayed on the other side of the waiting area, but his eyes were trained on Jarod. I walked right over to Jarod. "Why are you here? And how did you know I would be here?"

"Because I want to see how my baby is doing. How I found out doesn't matter."

"Oh, now the baby is yours?"

He shrugged. "I don't know for sure yet, but I thought it might help if I at least tried to be a part of the journey."

"Help what?"

"If we have to go to court for child support or custody. If the DNA test proves it's my baby, I will want joint custody."

I rolled my eyes. "Please leave. This is *my* appointment and an invasion of *my* privacy."

He stood, and Oliver walked right over and joined me.

"Kinisha, I have a right to know how the baby is doing. You said it's mine, right? If it's mine, I want to be in the picture."

"This is still my body. You no longer have access to that. I'm going to ask you one more time to leave."

Just as he was about to respond, his phone rang. His eyes didn't leave mine as he pulled it from his pocket. He frowned when he answered. "Hello . . .? How do you know where I am . . .? I'll talk to you when I get home. . . . Oh yes, you *will* be there waiting for me. If you aren't, you'll be sorry."

He ended the call and glanced at the front desk. "This isn't over, Kinisha. When I get those results next week, I will proceed as necessary. If I'm not the father, it will prove that you're the ho I thought you were."

Before I could blink, Oliver knocked his ass out cold. After jumping out of the way, I looked over at him, and he was staring at Jarod while breathing deeply. He glanced over at me. "I guess he didn't learn his lesson after Lazarus fucked him up."

Oliver grabbed him by the arms and dragged him to the other side of the room while everyone looked on in shock. Thankfully, it was only staff. We were the first to arrive in the office after their lunch hour. Oliver slapped him a couple of times to wake him up. When Jarod opened his eyes, he scanned the room, clearly stunned.

"My lady asked you to leave. I'm not asking. Next time, you won't be conscious when you're dragged out of here. Learn some respect so you can stop suffering this fate. I'll do hard time for that woman. Don't fuck with her if you wanna keep walking away with your life. I hope we have an understanding."

This was a serious moment, but seeing Oliver this way was sexy as hell. Jarod only stared at him with a frown, then stood and slowly walked out of the office. The office staff stood there watching as Oliver pulled me in his arms. "You okay, baby? I can feel your heartbeat. Take deep breaths for me."

He seemed calm as hell, but I knew he had to be worked up a little. *Damn*. His heart rate didn't even appear elevated when I laid my head against him. I didn't know how he did that shit, but I was now aware that this side of him had made appearances before. He seemed pretty acquainted with it.

I did as he said until the nurse called me to the back. They immediately checked my blood pressure, and, as I thought, it was extremely elevated. "Since the situation has been deescalated, we'll wait and see if your blood pressure will come down on its own. We'll recheck it before you leave. Are you having any other problems?"

"No, ma'am. The morning sickness is just about gone, and the cramping from the uterus stretching is minimal now."

"Okay. Good. Let's get a urine sample, and the doctor will be in to talk to you soon."

"Thank you."

I took the cup from her and went to the restroom. My legs trembled as I sat on the toilet. I couldn't believe the shit that Jarod had pulled. I still needed to know how he knew about my appointment. I wouldn't dare give him any information. Seeing him pissed me off, so I surely wouldn't want him in my space. I was grateful the doctor's office didn't call the police. I just knew they would have. I had Sidney Taylor on speed dial these days, but I still wouldn't want to see Oliver handcuffed.

After setting my sample in the compartment in the wall behind the toilet, I washed my hands and returned to the room. Oliver was seated but resting his elbows on his knees. He stood when I entered and helped me to the examination table. "Oliver, you okay?"

"Yeah, I'm good. What about you?"

"I'm okay."

"I'm sorry about earlier."

"Sorry for what? Defending me? I appreciate you more than you know. Had you not been here, they probably would have had to call the authorities to get him out of here. You don't owe me an apology for that. Actually, I thought it was sexy."

His eyebrows lifted, and a slight smile reached his lips. "Sexy, huh? How sexy?"

"Sexy enough to fuck you in this examination room. If I felt like we had time before the doctor came in, I would straddle you in that chair."

He pulled me into his embrace and chuckled. "You so nasty. I got yo' sexy ass tonight, though."

I kissed his lips. Then he went to his seat. Shortly after the doctor came in, he checked the baby's heart rate. Everything was good. He pressed my stomach in various places and asked me a few questions about how I felt. Since everything was great, he sent the nurse in to recheck my blood pressure. It was still slightly elevated, but it had come down from what it was earlier. They were sure it would continue dropping until it was normal again.

Oliver helped me off the table and to the front to schedule my next appointment. He was quiet, and I knew it had a lot to do with what happened earlier. It was sad that he even had to go there with a grown-ass man. I still couldn't understand why Jarod wanted to be involved suddenly. His being jealous wasn't even worth all this bullshit.

As we left the building, Oliver placed his hand on the small of my back. "I'm gonna stay with you tonight if that's cool, baby."

I glanced up at him. "Why wouldn't it be? You know I always want you close to me."

"I don't ever want to assume, though. There may come a time when you just not feeling it for whatever reason. I always wanna respect how you're feeling."

"Thank you."

He opened my door, and I kissed his lips, then got in. Now to my parents' house.

# Chapter 22

## *Oliver*

"I can't believe that nigga did that shit," Lazarus said.

"Shit, me either. I was stunned when I saw him. I never expected him to pull up on her at the doctor's office, especially for a baby he said wasn't his."

"Right. I just know he a bold muthafucka," Devin added.

I agreed by nodding. It was Saturday night, and Kinisha, Kiana, and Ramsey were together, so I decided to hang with the fellas tonight. I introduced Lazarus to Devin, WJ, and Corey, and they seemed to hit it off. I appreciated my circle of friends. I knew these guys had my back no matter what. I never really had that, but I was grateful for it. If Shawn didn't live in Dallas, I knew he would be here too. They were all old enough to be my father, except for Lazarus, but that was what made this special. They all offered great advice, and I needed that shit more than a little bit for my new relationship and drama.

Being a loner wasn't the most appealing thing. Everyone needed some human interaction. When my mom was here, she was my go-to person. After she died, I never filled that position. She was irreplaceable, and no one could fill her shoes. However, I could still enjoy the camaraderie and brotherhood of these brothers, making room for them in my life and the wisdom they offered when I needed it.

"So, where is Kinisha now?" Corey asked.

"She's with her sister and best friend. They needed a ladies' night to catch up on everything going on in each other's lives. Something about a nigga named Blaze that Ramsey was seeing."

"Blaze? From the club?" Lazarus asked.

I shrugged. "I don't know."

"It's about time. It has to be him. He's been feeling her for a while, but she was too busy playing with Robert's ass to notice."

"You sound like Nisha, bruh."

He chuckled, and I did too as the waitress set a beer before me. We'd come out to a sports bar called Walk-On's Sports Bistreaux in Nederland. They sold Cajun cuisine, and the shit was good as hell. I had the crawfish étouffée. As we talked about random stuff, my phone chimed with a text message. I saw Kinisha's name, so I opened it. I miss you.

I smiled slightly and responded. I miss you more.

When I looked up, everyone was staring at me. Then they all began laughing. "He got those googly eyes and shit," Corey said.

I rolled my eyes as they kept laughing and cracking jokes at my expense. I held up my middle finger and circled it around the table for all of them. When they calmed down, WJ said, "Well, I have a question. What did that nigga look like after you fucked him up in the doctor's office?"

I chuckled. "Just a li'l blood coming from his mouth and a red mark on his face. He probably bruised up later. Hopefully, he won't be at church tomorrow, so I don't have to see him."

"Well, hopefully, he's bruised up enough to not bother going to church," Lazarus added.

"Hopefully."

As I took a swig of my beer, my phone chimed again. I opened the message from Kinisha. Jarod and Robert are here. Ugh. This muthafucka just won't go away.

Where are you?

Tia Juanita's.

"Fellas, I need to go."

"What's up? Everything okay?" Devin asked.

"Naw. Jarod and Robert are at the same restaurant as the ladies. I need to be there so he won't try shit. I don't know if he's following her to fuck with her or if it's just a coincidence, but either way, I don't trust neither of their asses."

Devin dropped $300 on the table and said, "Looks like we're all going then."

"Absolutely. My wife is there, and she will definitely try to protect Kinisha, although she's almost seven months pregnant," Lazarus added.

We all left the table and headed to our vehicles. Devin, WJ, and Corey had ridden together, and Lazarus had ridden with me. When we got in my car, he asked, "What is his deal?"

"He can't have his way, and that shit is driving him crazy. He's doing everything he can to break her. When he sees that shit ain't working, it pisses him off more and makes him try something else. He gon' fuck up, though, and go too far, and he won't be able to come back from the consequences."

Lazarus glanced at me as I drove like a bat out of hell. "I don't like the look on your face, man. That nigga ain't worth you losing your life. I'm not talking about you dying. I'm talking about you getting locked up and leaving your family out here alone. As far as I'm concerned, that's your son or daughter that Kinisha is carrying. Is he worth you not being here when that baby is born? Is he worth your child not knowing who you are?"

I sat with his words as I drove, not offering him a response right away. When we reached Tia Juanita's and parked, I turned to him. "You right, bruh. But keep that nigga out my fucking face, and we won't have any problems."

He slowly shook his head as I called Kinisha.

"Hello?"

"Hey, baby. Y'all got room for five niggas to sit by y'all?"

"Huh?"

"We're here. Is there somewhere for us to sit?"

"Umm . . . yeah. Why are you here?"

"Why wouldn't I be after that text you sent? I don't trust that dude. My boys wouldn't let me go alone, so we're all here."

"That's so sweet, Oliver. I'll tell our waitress."

I ended the call as Devin, Corey, and WJ approached, and then we walked inside. When we did, I immediately saw Robert and Jarod off to my right. Neither of them saw us because they were too busy ogling Kinisha, Kiana, and Ramsey. We continued to their table, and my baby stood and greeted me. I kissed her lips, subtly sliding my tongue to hers. I did that shit because I knew he was watching. He needed to see that he would never have her again. I couldn't believe he was still trying to pursue her after what he got at the doctor's office last Thursday.

When she pulled away from me, she smirked. After speaking to the fellas, she gave her attention back to me. "Was that show for me or Jarod?"

"Both. I have more in store for you, though. That was just a warmup."

"Come on now. You know I never need to be warmed up when you're around. Your presence alone does that. Shit, just the thought of you already has me hot and ready."

"Mm. That's good to know. Don't make me take you to that restroom. I'm not beneath fucking in a restaurant restroom."

"Neither am I, so make sure you mean what you say, Oliver Andrews."

"Mm-hmm. Let me show and prove then."

"After I finish my bisque because your baby is tripping."

I laughed and glanced behind me to see Jarod and Robert were gone.


When we walked into church, it seemed all eyes were on us. We were a little late, so we drew attention when we walked all the way to the front where Kinisha usually sat. Had she not wanted to fuck this morning, we would have been on time. After we left Tia Juanita's last night, she came home with me and stayed the night. We woke up early so I could take her home to get ready for church, but she incited a whole freak nasty love session. That shit lasted for almost an hour.

She plopped next to Kiana, and they hugged and kissed each other's cheeks as I scanned the crowd. I wanted to be sure I saw where Jarod was seated so I could keep tabs on him. When my eyes landed on him, he stared at us despite the woman on his arm. This nigga was crazy as hell.

Just as I was getting comfortable in my seat and had put my arm around Kiana, Brooklyn appeared at my side. She handled the Ambassador TV show, a church news segment she was an anchor of. "Oliver, I hate to bother you in church, but there's been some kind of glitch in the computer. Can you come take a look at it for me?"

"Yeah, sure."

I leaned over to Kinisha and told her where I was going, then followed Brooklyn to the balcony from the lower-level part of the sanctuary. I could see Jarod and his lady talking as we headed to the stairs. They looked to be arguing. I didn't even know why she was still with his ass. He seemed to be a narcissist. If she was the one he'd talked to on the phone at the doctor's office, she clearly needed someone to help her understand how a man should speak to a woman.

There wasn't an ounce of respect in his tone or his words. That didn't surprise me, but it did surprise me that some women allowed that shit. She seemed educated from how Reverend Speights introduced her to the congregation when he announced their engagement. He said she was an alumna of Xavier University in Louisiana. He didn't say what her degree was, but surely she didn't need a degree in trifling niggas to recognize one.

When I got to the balcony and went to where the media team had the main computer located, she showed me what it was doing, and I realized it would be an easy fix.

"Are you and Kinisha dating?"

I glanced up at her and smiled slightly. "Yes, ma'am."

"Congratulations. You've been here for a while, and I've never seen you with anybody."

Deciding to mess with her, I asked, "You keeping tabs on me, Brooklyn?"

I glanced up at her to see her face was red as hell. "No . . . nooo. I was just observing. I mean . . . I noticed y'all together, and you usually sit alone . . . Ugh. I'm not making this any better."

I chuckled as she pushed my shoulder, realizing I was picking with her. After clearing the program error, I handed it back to her by standing from the seat. "It's all yours."

"Thank you so much, Oliver. Right on time," she said as Pastor Adolph made his way to the podium.

She always put his text, sermon title, and key points on the big screens. Knowing that I could keep all that functioning properly filled me with a sense of pride. As I descended the stairs, I saw Jarod walk by like he was leaving. The nigga in me wouldn't just let him go without knowing what he was up to. I secretly followed him down the hallway to the room where the security team congregated.

I wasn't sure who he was talking to, but someone said, "If this is your baby, it won't be good. Your salary and bonus depend upon your having good moral character. This woman isn't even your girlfriend. Had you not announced an engagement to someone else, it may have been something you could have fixed. Now, I don't see you getting out of this unscathed."

"She has a boyfriend now. I don't have to be involved. I thought it would be honorable to admit I had a lapse in judgment but was still handling my responsibilities. I need that $10,000 bonus from Eastern Progressive. I'm almost a shoo-in for the position."

"Naw. That's a mess. It wasn't a lapse in judgment. You wanted what you wanted, messed around, and got caught up. Is that engagement even real?"

"No. It's so my dad can get off my back. Plus, Mila's family is loaded. I marry her, and I won't have to worry about a stipend from the church."

I walked away. I'd heard enough. As usual, people's fuckups and evil tendencies practically always involved money. I should have known that was what it had to do with. Hopefully, judging by this conversation, he would let the shit go and move around like before.

I returned to my seat with Kinisha to enjoy the rest of the service. When I sat next to her, she had a deep frown on her face. I wasn't sure what had made her so angry until I nudged her, and she dropped her phone on my lap. There was a text on the screen from a number not saved in her contacts, but I could clearly see the message was from Jarod once I started reading it. I filed for full custody. The DNA results were emailed to me. I'm the baby's father. I want to raise and take care of him in the same home as me. Get lawyered up and unblock my fucking number.

This was the total opposite of the conversation I'd just heard. Whoever said church people weren't shit ain't never lied. I had to find a way to get his ass off my baby. The Taylors and Corey Sheffield had experience with this level of drama, and I would be hitting them up as soon as we got out of church.

# Chapter 23

## *Kinisha*

It had been a week since that fucking text message from Jarod, and I was beyond stressed. Between Jarod's bullshit, meetings with Sidney Taylor, and work, I was overdue for a vacation. Last Sunday, we'd gone to dinner at Oliver's cousin's house. She and I exchanged pleasant-ries, and she apologized for her behavior the last time regarding the situation with Robert. She was more naïve than Ramsey to believe his bullshit.

The Taylors had shown up, and I later found out that Oliver had called them to consult about the situation with Jarod. He was being proactive, and I appreciated that. I also talked to Sidney, and she gladly took on my case. She said she had a family lawyer in her firm and would be the second chair. She was a criminal defense attorney, so family law wasn't her specialty, but she was extremely knowledgeable about it.

I was confident about having her on board. There wasn't much information I could give her other than how everything went down and proof of his text message saying he wanted no part in raising a baby that may not be his anyway. She was all worked up from what I told her, which made me confident in her abilities. She was passionate, and I loved that.

Jarod had sent more text messages throughout the week, trying to make me believe that he just wanted what was best for his child and that the baby being with his ho ass was best. I could only roll my eyes. He was crazy as hell if he thought he could raise a child better than I could. Although I had no experience in child rearing, being the mother had to count for something. He would have to prove me unfit, and I was extremely interested to see what he would come up with besides that fucking assault charge.

So today, Oliver said he would be sure I had a day I would never forget, just like I did when he picked me up from the airport that day. I couldn't wait. I needed some serious relaxation. The extra weight of the baby growing had me drained. I often rubbed the little pouch that was forming and talked to my baby as much as possible. Although I knew he or she couldn't hear me at first, I wasn't quite sure when the baby would be able to hear. So, to be safe, I started talking at twelve weeks. My baby needed to know who would always be there for them—*Mommy*.

My brain was definitely in need of a break as well. I just needed peace. Talking to my mother about the situation was more helpful than I anticipated. I was just happy that she and my dad were there for me despite not agreeing with how I did things. What remained to be true was that a baby was coming that would need love and care. How it got here was no longer important.

After getting dressed in a T-shirt and leggings, I pulled my dreads into a ball at the top of my head. I was so happy I'd gotten them. The maintenance was minimal, and I didn't realize how much of a difference that would make in my day. It saved me more time than I expected. I put on some lip gloss, then sat on my couch, waiting for Oliver to arrive. I went to my Hulu app and watched *Law & Order: Special Victims Unit* until he came.

About fifteen minutes into the second episode, my doorbell rang. I smiled and went to the door, opening it without checking to see who it was. When I saw Jarod, I had to have lost all the color in my face. I was speechless. He wore a stupid grin, and when I tried to close the door, he pushed it open, nearly knocking me to the floor.

He glanced at my belly. "How far along are you?"

I rolled my eyes. "What do you want before I call the police? You have no right to barge into my place."

"You haven't been responding to my text messages. Did you unblock me?"

"Unfortunately, yes. You may actually say something that I need to know. Everything you've sent so far has been bullshit, and you know it."

I grabbed my phone to prepare to call the police, but I also began recording.

"All right, don't call. Just listen."

I shifted my weight as I felt slight flutters in my belly. A little smile made its way to my lips, and I instantly rubbed my belly.

"I'm sorry. Can we sit?" he asked.

"You have five minutes, Jarod. That's it."

I sat in the chair to make sure he didn't try to sit close to me. I didn't want him touching me or being too close. Just my luck, Oliver would walk in and think something was happening between us. He sat on the couch and stared at me like he was trying to intimidate me or something. "You can stare for your entire five minutes if you want. The clock is ticking."

"That baby is my seed. It deserves the best life can offer. You can't provide that on your little-ass salary as a CPA. Plus, your history says you aren't even fit to be a mother."

"History? Let's talk about history, fuckboy."

He chuckled. "What proof do you have?"

"How about your child, and we're not a couple. You texted about not wanting the baby because you didn't want me. Announcing your engagement, knowing you'd been fucking around with me."

"None of that is illegal, Sugar Ray. Yeah, I know you're on probation. You think I want that influence in my child's life?"

"You're a jackass. It is very possible to provide for your child without contesting custody. Second, your moral compass is so fucked up it *should* be illegal. You're only doing this to save face. You're afraid people will discover that the minister's son isn't all he's cracked up to be. Now, get the hell out of my place."

I stood from my seat and went to the door with my phone in hand while he quietly seethed. Finally, he stood from his seat and approached me. "You gon' regret this. I would have let you see your baby. Now, I'm finna get your rights revoked. Watch me."

"Nigga, get the fuck outta here."

He walked out of my place with a smirk on his lips. That man was beyond stupid. No judge in their right mind would take my baby from me and give it to him. Whatever Oliver had in store, I needed it more than ever.


Although I'd just gotten a pregnancy massage, Oliver rubbed my feet as we enjoyed time together at home.

He had soft music playing and candles lit, creating an ambiance that would surely have me facedown, ass up in a little while. I was already sitting here stewing in my juices as he applied pressure to the balls of my feet.

My eyes rolled to the back of my head. "Oh, Oliver. That feels so good."

It came out so passionately. It sounded like something I would say as he was stroking my insides. I was ready —*beyond* ready. When I felt his lips on my foot, I opened my eyes to watch him. His eyes met mine as he said, "You have some pretty-ass feet."

"So you've told me. Thank you."

He smiled at me and rubbed my feet again, kissing them periodically until he got to my toes and decided to lick one. I almost came on myself when he did that. My clit was tingling something serious, and I wanted his tongue to be there instead. However, he continued pleasuring my toes with the presence of his tongue. When he sucked my middle toe, I came unglued. My body stiffened, and I came in my panties.

His eyes lifted to mine, and it was like I could see his savage emerging. He slid his hand between my legs. "Damn, baby. I can feel the moisture through these pants."

He grabbed the waistband of my leggings and pulled them off, along with my underwear. "These panties wet as hell."

After throwing them on the floor, he spread my legs and brought his lips to my southern ones, taking his time to please me. He slowly licked and sucked my pussy like it was a delicacy he was trying to savor. I slid my freshly done nails over his slick head and pushed him in farther as he moaned. *God, his moans are intoxicating.*

"Oliver . . . shit . . ."

I detonated all over his face, but he didn't dare stop. He liked me to have multiple orgasms. He'd once said that he wasn't doing his job if I didn't have multiples. He wanted me to be completely satisfied. When finished, the only thing I should be fit to do was sleep. My entire body trembled and tingled as my eyes fluttered shut. I swore I was about to go into convulsions.

"Oliver, I'm about to cum again. . . . Ooooh."

He pulled away from me as if he knew what would happen. I squirted everywhere. He sat there watching for a second, then patted my pussy, making it squirt even more. I swore I blacked out for a minute because I never saw him get undressed. When I opened my eyes, his dick was inside me, and my knee was damn near to my head. However, he was winding slowly into me while biting his bottom lip with his eyes closed.

I lifted my head and stared down at the action, which proved to be an aphrodisiac like no other. I saw my elongated clit as his dick rubbed against it with every stroke. I'd never seen it that long. This man turned me on even more during every encounter. He gently caressed my nipple and slowly filled me repeatedly while stroking my G-spot. My eyes involuntarily rolled back, and my body practically lifted from the couch as another orgasm surfaced.

He put his hand around my throat as I came hard. My other leg was wrapped around his waist, but I tightened my grip on him, forcing him to lower himself to me. He licked my lips, and his saliva rolled down my chin to my neck. He sucked my skin, taking the same path his saliva did. The man never increased his pace . . . just remained steady as he refueled my drained body.

"Kinisha, I love you, baby."

"I . . . love you . . . toooo."

I came again. He was right. Today was a day I would never forget. After getting my hair and nails done, having a body exfoliation and massage, this was the icing on the cinnamon roll, the main fucking attraction. "Open your eyes, baby," he said softly.

I did as he requested, staring into his. He slowly shook his head. "I never thought I would be making love to you this way. I didn't feel worthy of your attention at first. However, after I reevaluated myself, I knew I deserved everything you had to offer, but I still doubted that everything I offered would be enough. Then I exploited you, knowing the situation you were in. I'm sorry for that, but I'm not sorry about the outcome."

I wasn't sure why he was saying all this as he stroked me, but he had tears falling down my cheeks. I could feel his love for me through his words and how his dick caressed my insides. As my eyes fluttered shut, he said, "Naw, Kinisha. Look at me."

Struggling to reopen my eyes, I did as he requested. I could feel another orgasm building, threatening to detonate and take me out. He'd better get his nut before I completely tapped out. "You everything I need, baby. I knew it before I even experienced your conversation, before I saw your pettiness, before I even stroked this juicy-ass pussy. You're the woman I wanna do life with, beautiful. I can only hope that I'm the man you wanna spend your forever with . . . that I'm enough for you . . . that I satisfy you."

"Oliver," I said, succumbing to the cries in my throat. "You are so much more, baby. So much more than what I felt I deserved. You thought I was too good for you? No. It's you who are too good for me," I said through my cries.

He gently wiped away my tears with his thumb, then dug into the couch cushions, allowing his dick to rest inside me. Pulling out a small box, he said, "I told your parents I wanted to be a permanent fixture in your life. I know it's soon, but that's how sure I am about us. You it for me."

He began stroking me again, painfully slow while staring into my eyes. When he opened that box, it felt like I was hyperventilating. I was already crying uncontrollably. That diamond was shining so brightly I could barely stare at it. The recessed lighting was hitting it just right. Oliver pulled it from the box and stroked me a few times. He closed his eyes and moaned, then said, "I wanna be permanent, Kinisha. Tell me you'll marry me, baby. I need you to be Mrs. Andrews ASAP."

I wrapped one arm around him and held my other hand to his face. "Yes, I want to marry you. No one else is more deserving of my love, devotion, loyalty, and affection. Yes, Oliver."

He slid the ring on my finger, then slid his hands beneath me and gripped my ass, giving me all he had. I held him tightly to me as he wore me out like he was a demolition team. He tore down walls and made his way through the rubble. Our love manifested into this. Despite the issues with Jarod, this easily had to be the best time of my life simply because Oliver was a part of it.

As he reached his orgasm, I expressed another one. My body was so drained. I'd lost count of how many times I'd exploded on Oliver tonight, but I was thoroughly satisfied. He rested his forehead on mine and closed his eyes.

"Thank you, Lord, for giving me something so precious . . . someone so valuable. I promise to cherish the gift you gave me and protect her and our baby with my life."

Submission was hard for me, but not with a man like Oliver. I thought about it constantly, knowing that this was what God intended: for the man he created to be so loving that his wife wouldn't have an issue with submission. I'd fallen for the right man and was so grateful that I tripped and fell into him that day. However, I was certain that God had orchestrated even that.

# Chapter 24

## *Oliver*

We'd just gotten to the lawyer's office. I was beyond ready for this shit to be over. Kinisha was now my fiancée, and I just wanted her to bask in that without worrying about this nigga. He was irritating and annoying, like a fly or gnat flying around your food while you were trying to eat. He wasn't a threat, but he was definitely a nuisance.

After our lovemaking session, we couldn't do anything but sleep. Although I was excited about our future, I was exhausted. I knew the same was true for her. She was already relaxed from the long day at the spa. I'd had her favorite Chinese dish delivered to the spa. She loved egg rolls and beef and broccoli. By the time I'd gotten to her, she was beyond relaxed.

As I searched for a parking spot, I glanced over at Kinisha. She was staring out the window, and I could tell she was nervous. We'd gone to her parents' house before coming here, and they prayed for her. Kiana and Lazarus met us there as well. Of course, the prayer didn't begin until her mom and Kiana gushed over her ring again. We'd gone there the day after I proposed to make the announcement and for Kinisha to show them the ring. Today, it was like they hadn't seen it before by the excitement on their faces.

However, last night, I'd met with the fellas, and we'd already discussed an alternate plan if this didn't go well. We had a private investigator on speed dial at Watchful Eyes here in Beaumont who would find plenty of dirt on Jarod. A nigga like him had to have shit he was hiding that they would dig out. We wanted to try legal means to handle him, but I wasn't beneath doing something illegal to assure my babies would be good.

When I parked, Kinisha turned to me. "I didn't tell you he came to my apartment a week ago before you arrived to pick me up."

I frowned hard. "What?"

"I told Sidney because I recorded him threatening me, but I didn't tell you because I didn't want you to go looking for him. I opened the door for him, thinking it was you. When I saw it was him, I tried to close the door on him, but he barged his way in. He pretty much threatened to take my baby from me if I didn't give him primary custody. He said he would drag me through the mud and brought up me being on probation."

I lowered my head for a moment, trying to subdue my irritation. She'd seen my angry side in the doctor's office. I had to see things from her perspective before responding. I had to study who she was and why she reacted the way she did. She was a critical thinker and incredibly selfless. She didn't do that with malicious intent. She just didn't want me to get in trouble.

I lifted my eyes to hers and slowly nodded. "I understand why you didn't tell me. However, for future reference, I won't jeopardize my freedom or livelihood if it can be helped. You can trust me to put your well-being and that of our baby at the forefront. Just like I asked you to do with that situation with Mya, I will do the same. I can't expect something from you that I'm unwilling to do. I got'chu always, baby."

I grabbed her hand and kissed it as she smiled softly. "Thank you, Oliver. I didn't want Sidney to say something about it that would stun you. I'm sorry for not telling you."

"You don't have to apologize. Let's go and get this over with."

This was to be an arbitration of sorts to try to reach some agreement and avoid going to court. I could only pray that Sidney had enough shit up her sleeve to where Jarod would back the fuck off. I got out of the car and walked around to help Kinisha out. Once I listened for the doors to lock automatically, we headed inside to the elevator.

Once inside, Kinisha held my hand between her cold, trembling ones. "Everything will be fine, baby. I need you to exercise that faith and claim that too."

She nodded. "You're right. Everything will be fine."

As we exited the elevator, Sidney and another lady exited the elevator next to us. "Hey, y'all. I had another meeting on the second floor. I'm so ready to get this over with," she said as she rolled her eyes.

Kinisha let out a nervous giggle as we proceeded down the hallway to the attorney's suite. Sidney turned to me and said, "I'm sorry, Oliver. This is Amanda Spears, the lead on Kinisha's case."

I nodded and shook her hand as I smiled.

"Nice to meet you, Mr. Oliver."

I chuckled and slowly shook my head at her calling me mister. The moment we walked in, the receptionist said, "Hello. You must be Attorney Sidney Taylor. Please come on in and follow me."

That li'l girl looked so excited to see Sidney in the flesh. If I were into law, I probably would be too. The woman was a beast. She was known nationwide for the high-profile cases she'd won. I learned from Shawn that she'd gotten the commissioner of the Professional Basketball League incarcerated at the beginning of her career while avenging his mother's death. That had catapulted her into stardom, and celebrities sought her services after that.

What I liked about her was that she didn't let that go to her head. She still represented everyday people without turning their pockets inside out. Kinisha said she had yet to give her a price for her services. She didn't charge her for the last case either. There was no way I could allow her to do all this work for free, though.

I opened the door to the conference room for the ladies, and they all thanked me. Sidney and Amanda shook hands with Jarod and his attorney when I stepped in. Before going to the table to sit, I realized that I probably shouldn't be in the meeting since it didn't concern me legally. As I was about to go to the waiting area, Kinisha turned around and asked, "Oliver, where are you going?"

"To the waiting area, baby."

"No. I need you here with me. Please."

Amanda asked the room, "Gentlemen, will that be a problem?"

Jarod's attorney looked over at him, and he shrugged his shoulders like he didn't care, so his attorney responded, "No, ma'am. He can stay."

I sat next to Kinisha, and she grabbed my hand as the proceedings began. Jarod's attorney introduced himself as Alex Spectrum and started by saying, "My client is seeking full custody of the child once he or she is born. He intends to raise the child in what he believes will be a better environment in love and one where he can provide for the child's needs and some of its wants."

"Why does Mr. Speights think that's acceptable, Attorney Spectrum?" Ms. Spears asked.

"Well, after Ms. Jordan's involvement in a fight at a club and her assault charge from a month or so ago, which I might add happened while she was pregnant, he believes Ms. Jordan is incapable of providing the protection and guidance the child will need. He's respected in the community, has an established career as an insurance agent, and has a village to help him raise the child."

"Is that it?" Amanda asked.

My frown was ever present, as was Kinisha's. Jarod had a smirk on his face like they'd dropped a bomb on us. That nigga was clueless. Had to be. What judge was gonna grant him custody of a child before it was even born? The attorney chuckled and asked, "Isn't that enough, Mrs. Spears?"

Amanda looked over at Sidney with a slight smile on her face. Sidney pulled a thick file from her satchel and dropped it on the table. Jarod and Mr. Spectrum's eyes went to the folder. "Mr. Spectrum, in this file are all the questionable things we brought up on your client. So, first, I will point out that he didn't want this baby to begin with."

"I only said that because I wasn't sure it was mine. That was why I had a paternity test done," Jarod said.

Amanda stared at Jarod with narrowed eyes. "Right. Anyway. Also in this file is proof that Mr. Speights is seeking custody to avoid breaking the ethics clause in a religious organization he's a part of. He's currently trying to be the president of said organization. I'm told that will come with a hefty salary and bonus. If they were to find out that he has a baby on the way with a woman who isn't even his girlfriend, let alone wife, he wouldn't be eligible for the position. For the record, that's barely the tip of the iceberg. I *can* go on."

"Jarod, you wanted nothing to do with the baby until you saw I had a man willing to take care of your responsibilities anyway. You're a narcissistic individual who can't handle rejection, although you rejected me first. Your desire to have women chasing your pitiful ass is sickening. You were just fine as long as I was texting you, trying to contact you, while you ignored me. The minute I started ignoring *you,* you couldn't handle it. However, knowing that money is your driving force doesn't surprise me. You and the people involved with your conniving ass give the church a bad rep," Kinisha added as Ms. Spears gently patted her hand.

I assumed she was silently telling Kinisha to let them handle his ass. Jarod leaned over and said something in his attorney's ear. His attorney said, "We are also aware of your client's philandering ways."

"Just as we are aware of your client's tendencies," Sidney said, leaning forward, clearly irritated, as she started pulling pictures from her file of Jarod with different women. "We can do this all day. You're actually making me angry, and I'm two steps away from being unprofessional. What you're gonna do is drop this foolishness. If you want to be a part of your child's life, fine, but if you wanna drag my client through the mud, we're gonna drag you to hell. You don't want this battle. I'm a winner, Mr. Spectrum, Mr. Speights. I *don't* lose."

"Oh, and your *ex*-fiancée is willing to testify against you. She has receipts as well," Amanda added.

These women were efficient as hell. Jarod's eyes had widened at the mention of his ex-fiancée. She finally gathered the nerve to leave his ass. *Good for her.* He leaned over again to consult with his attorney as Kinisha and I looked on. "We'll settle for joint custody."

"What you *will* do is pay one grand a month in child support if you want to be a part of the baby's life. Kinisha Jordan will remain the custodial parent, and you will pay all her legal fees for this bull—See, you almost got me. I'm heated at your audacity. This was an inconvenience for my client. If you don't agree to that, then you can sign this stating that you are giving up your parental rights. Oliver Andrews will gladly be your child's father. You will still be responsible for the legal fees, though."

His face twitched at the mention of my name, but he responded, "I will sign over my rights if the information is sealed."

Kinisha slapped the table. "It would have been sealed had you not gone running your mouth. Everyone who knows is because *you* told them . . . even my family. You were so concerned about making me look bad you contributed to your own downfall. Idiot. Everyone in our circles know, thanks to you. So that stipulation is inadmissible."

Sidney and Amanda smiled at Kinisha, then gave Jarod a "now what" look. Once again, his face twitched.

He snatched the paper and signed it. Sidney slowly shook her head. "You know, it's a sad day when parents will sell their children. That stipend won't get you far. Because of this, the joys of having a kid will elude you for the rest of your life. Have a great day, gentlemen."

We stood from our seats, and when we got outside, Kinisha threw her arms around me. "Oliver, I'm so happy."

"Me too, baby."

I kissed her forehead, and she pulled away from me to hug Sidney. "Thank you so much. You are amazing."

"I didn't want to tell you everything I had up my sleeve. We bluffed him a li'l bit, though. The rest of those papers in that file were all filled with random stuff that had nothing to do with him."

Kinisha's eyes widened as I chuckled. That went to show just how much shit he'd gotten away with. He thought all that shit was stuff he'd done. Jarod joined us at the elevator as we made our way out, talking amongst ourselves. Kinisha tried to go to him, but I pulled her to me. "Let it go. Let him go and be miserable. He deserves that shit for what he put you through."

She rested her head against my chest before pulling away and nodded. "You're right . . . as always. Let's get out of here."

I smiled at her as we walked Sidney and Amanda to the car they came in, then walked to my car. After I helped her in and got in the driver's seat, Kinisha said, "Now that that's over, I can eat. I'm starving. Where are you taking me?"

She couldn't eat breakfast because her stomach was so nervous about how this would go. I had a surprise for her, though. I couldn't tell her where we were going. "You'll see when we get there."

"You know what? I don't even care. As long as there's good food there, I'm cool with whatever."

I laughed, and she did too. When we ended up at her parents' house, she frowned. "My mama cooked for us? Why are all these cars here?"

"She said she was cooking. I'm not sure who the cars are for, though."

I didn't lie. I wasn't sure who the cars were for. I helped her out and led her to the backyard, where her dad was cooking meat. When we walked through the gate, everyone yelled, "Surprise!"

Kinisha jumped into me because they'd scared the hell out of her. She looked around, and when the realization of what this was hit her, she smiled big. "An engagement party?"

She turned back to me and hugged me. "You're good at keeping secrets. I'm gonna have to watch you."

I pulled her in my arms. "I thought that you liked that I could keep secrets. I mean, that was how this started, right?"

She wrapped her arms around my neck. "Mm-hmm. You can keep *my* secrets. You have to tell me everyone else's."

She laughed loudly, then pulled me along to greet everyone. Lots of people were here from church, including Ramsey, her new boyfriend, Blaze, and her brother, Braylon, and his girlfriend. When I continued looking around for the people I invited, I saw them at a table. I'd only invited people from my offices, Anise, and Corey Sheffield. The Taylors were on Kinisha's list. However, I'd invited Shawn and his wife. I was surprised everyone showed up on a weekday. However, the more I thought about it, most of our friends were business owners, so they could come and go as they pleased or even shut down shop if they wanted to, like Devin had done.

I pulled away from Nisha as she talked to Ramsey and walked over to greet them, noticing Mya had a plus one. Thank God her infatuation with me was over.

"You done pulled a fast one on us," Devin said. "I don't recall you asking our permission."

I chuckled. "Well, it's too late now. She sleeps and showers with that ring on."

He laughed, as did everyone else, as I shook hands and gave hugs. Kinisha's parents had the backyard decorated like we were getting married today. When I'd asked their permission to marry her, her mother had practically jumped in my arms. They thought what I'd said to them wasn't real after they learned the truth, but if my words didn't convince them, this surely did.

Since we were having a party, Kinisha and I needed to come up with a date. I was almost sure her parents would want her to have something fancy, so she would probably want to wait until after the baby's birth. As I walked away to find her, she appeared behind me. I knew her touch anywhere, even in a crowded room. I turned to her to see her beautiful smile, and I couldn't help but reciprocate.

"I want to get married next month."

I frowned. "Really?"

"Yeah. Why wait?"

"Shiiiid, you ain't said nothing but a thing. I thought you would want a big fancy wedding that would take months of planning."

"No. We have a baby coming. This backyard will suffice. We can put that money in an account for the baby. I can't wait to go to the doctor to find out what we're having."

"Me either. Well, next month it is. I mean, I'll marry you right now, so next month is fine."

She kissed my lips, then pulled away and shook her head. "And to think, this was supposed to be fake."

"On your end. Nothing about us was ever fake to me. You made me feel things I'd never felt before, and I didn't even know you. So to me, it was always real."

She kissed me again and walked away to talk to someone. I looked around the backyard at everyone who had come to celebrate with us. It couldn't get any better than this, at least until the baby got here. We would be a family, something I'd been missing since my mother died. She would be so proud right now. I was proud. Glancing at the sky, I said, "God, you're good, and you never fail to prove it."

# Epilogue

## *Kinisha*

*Six months later . . .*

"Kinisha, she is gorgeous!" Kiana said as she slid her finger over Kaia's head full of hair.

"I know. I can stare at her all day long. It's gonna kill me to go back to work."

"I know the feeling. I cried the entire week when I had to leave Lawson with Mama. Mama said he even cried a lot. He missed me as much as I missed him because he was spoiled rotten. So I'm pretty sure Mama will give you the speech about not spoiling this gorgeous princess."

I giggled at Kiana. I'd had Kaia two weeks ago and couldn't put her down. When she cried, I held her. When she stared at me too long, I picked her up. When she slept, I held her. I just couldn't get enough. If I wasn't holding her, Oliver was. She had both of us wrapped around her tiny fingers. I was able to have her naturally without medication. It was a little rough, but I made it through. After eight hours of labor, Kaia Nicole came out screaming . . . all seven pounds, two ounces of her.

Thankfully, she looked like me for now. Hopefully, she wouldn't develop any of Jarod's features as she got older. He didn't get the position he was vying for, so he lost his baby *and* the money. God didn't like ugly. On top of that, some other chick had come out saying she was pregnant by him. She blasted it to his parents and everyone she could contact who knew him. A month later, she ended up miscarrying. My mama and his mama talked occasionally at church, so I got all my intel from that. Sidney's words about fatherhood eluding him rang true in my mind.

I stood to put Kaia in her crib, but Oliver intercepted and scooped her right out of my arms. I chuckled as I returned to where Kiana was nursing Lawson. He was four months old and looked just like Lazarus. He was the most adorable baby boy I'd ever seen. He had a head full of hair, big eyes like Kiana's, and thick lips like Laz's. He didn't have a choice about the hair because both his parents had heads full of it.

"Oliver is so good with her," Kiana said as she watched them.

"He really is. He hates leaving to go to work. He's been the perfect father and husband."

We married a little over four months ago in my parents' backyard as I originally planned. However, we waited two months instead of the month I wanted. We only invited a few people. More people were at our engagement party than our wedding, but I didn't care who was there. No one else mattered as long as the preacher and Oliver were there.

Oliver had taken care of me completely. I'd moved into his home with him since I lived in an apartment, and I didn't have to lay a finger on a thing during the transition. Oliver made sure I was always out of the way and comfortable. I never fathomed I would be so blessed. Oliver made me feel blessed—period. I was numb for so long, just going through life without a clear direction regarding my love life. He came along and swept me off my feet. I always thought it was so cliché when people said that, but I now understood exactly what it meant.

He caught me by surprise and showed me what love was supposed to look and feel like. Oliver overwhelmed me with his touch, his gaze, and just how much he cared for me in a short time. Despite his temper, he was perfect. He never let his temper get the best of him when dealing with me, and I could appreciate his effort. It helped me to reciprocate that since I could have a temper at times too.

Besides my beautiful princess, Oliver was the best thing that had ever happened to me, and I was beyond happy to call him mine. He walked over to me and pulled me from my seat next to Ki, into his embrace. "Where's Kaia?"

"Your mother stole her from me. She's like a little magnet that draws people to her. I knew to expect that, though, because her mother is the same way."

I smiled big, then kissed Oliver's lips in awe of his presence and aura. Nothing would ever separate us. As he'd said about Kaia and me, he was also a magnet. We were all stuck together, so he'd better get used to feeling me against him as often as possible because things were precisely as they should be.

# *The End*

## *From the Author . . .*

This story between Oliver and Kinisha was so beautiful. Oliver was my favorite. Although his method of getting Kinisha to commit to him was a little unorthodox, I loved him. He was very expressive and didn't hesitate to tell her exactly where he saw their future going. Kinisha was out there having the time of her life sexually, so she wasn't quite ready for a commitment . . . or so she thought. She was receptive to Oliver's deal because she was already intrigued by him. Together, they made a fantastic couple.

Jarod could have died a horrible death in my eyes. I wanted to kill him badly, but the characters wouldn't allow that. It wasn't in their psyche to have someone killed, although Oliver probably would have given it some thought had Jarod not caved and signed over his parental rights. He was very protective of Kinisha. Jarod probably would have been a dead man walking had he done anything else.

Thankfully, Mya got herself together before Kinisha had to get at her—on probation or not. LOL. Mental illness is real, and people need to take it more seriously. I liked that Oliver gave her another chance within the company even after all the drama she'd caused. Forgiveness is a common theme in my books, and despite Jarod's fate, I knew there was someone in this story I could redeem.

I genuinely hope you enjoyed this drama-filled ride that probably had your feelings all over the place. As always, I gave it my all. Regardless of whether you liked it, please take the time to leave a review on Amazon and/or Goodreads and wherever else this book is sold. If you did not read the author's note at the beginning, please go back and do so before leaving a review.

There's also a wonderful playlist on Apple Music and Spotify for this book under the same title, including some great R&B tracks to tickle your fancy.

Please keep up with me on Facebook, Instagram, TikTok (@authormonicawalters), Twitter (@monlwalters), and Clubhouse (@monicawalters). You can also visit my Amazon author page at www.amazon.com/author/monica.walters to view my releases.

Please subscribe to my webpage for updates and sneak peeks of upcoming releases https://authormonicawalters.com.

For live discussions, giveaways, and inside information on upcoming releases, join my Facebook group, Monica's Romantic Sweet Spot, at https://bit.ly/2P2lo6X.

# *Other Titles by Monica Walters*

## *Standalones*

*Love Like a Nightmare*
*Forbidden Fruit*
(An Erotic Novella)
*Say He's the One*
*Only If You Let Me*
(a spin-off of *Say He's the One*)
*On My Way to You*
(An Urban Romance)
*Any and Everything for Love*
*Savage Heart*
(A KeyWalt Crossover Novel by T. Key)
*I'm in Love with a Savage*
(A KeyWalt Crossover Novel with *Trade It All* by T. Key)
*Don't Tell Me No*
(An Erotic Novella)
*To Say, I Love You: A Short Story Anthology with the*
*Authors of BLP*
*Drive Me to Ecstasy*
*Whatever It Takes: An Erotic Novella*

*When You Touch Me*
*When's the Last Time?*
*Best You Ever Had*
*Deep As It Goes*
(A KeyWalt Crossover Novel with
*Perfect Timing* by T. Key)
*The Shorts: A BLP Anthology with the Authors of BLP*
(*Made to Love You*—Collab with Kay Shanee)
*All I Need Is You*
(A KeyWalt Crossover Novel with
*Divine Love* by T. Key)
*This Love Hit Different*
(A KeyWalt Crossover Novel with
*Something New* by T. Key)
*Until I Met You*
*Marry Me Twice*
*Last First Kiss*
(a spin-off of *Marry Me Twice*)
*Nobody Else Gon' Get My Love*
(A KeyWalt Crossover Novel with
*Better Than Before* by T. Key)
*Love Long Overdue*
(A KeyWalt Crossover Novel with
*Distant Lover* by T. Key)
*Next Lifetime*
*Fall Knee-Deep In It*
*Unwrapping Your Love: The Gift*
*Who Can I Run To*
*You're Always on My Mind*
(a spin-off of *Who Can I Run To*)
*Stuck On You*

*Full Figured 18* with Treasure Hernandez
(*Love Won't Let Me Wait*)
*It's Just a Date: A Billionaire Baby Romance*

## The Sweet Series

*Bitter Sweet*
*Sweet and Sour*
*Sweeter Than Before*
*Sweet Revenge*
*Sweet Surrender*
*Sweet Temptation*
*Sweet Misery*
*Sweet Exhale*
*Never Enough*
(A Sweet Series Update)

## Sweet Series: Next Generation

*Can't Run From Love*
*Access Denied: Luxury Love*
*Still: Your Best*

## Sweet Series: Kai's Reemergence

*Beautiful Mistake*
*Favorite Mistake*

## Motives and Betrayal Series

*Ulterior Motives*
*Ultimate Betrayal*
*Ultimatum: #lovemeorleaveme, Part 1*
*Ultimatum: #lovemeorleaveme, Part 2*

## Written Between the Pages Series

*The Devil Goes to Church Too*
*The Book of Noah*
(A KeyWalt Crossover Novel with
*The Flow of Jah's Heart* by T. Key)
*The Revelations of Ryan Jr.*
(A KeyWalt Crossover Novel with
*All That Jazz* by T. Key)
*The Rebirth of Noah*

## Behind Closed Doors Series

*Be Careful What You Wish For*
*You Just Might Get It*
*Show Me You Still Want It*

## The Country Hood Love Stories

*8 Seconds to Love*
*Breaking Barriers to Your Heart*
*Training My Heart to Love You*

## The Country Hood Love Stories: The Hendersons

*Blindsided by Love*
*Ignite My Soul*
*Come and Get Me*
*In Way Too Deep*
*You Belong to Me*
*Found Love in a Rider*
*Damaged Intentions: The Soul of a Thug*
*Let Me Ride*
*Better the Second Time Around*
*I Wish I Could Be The One*
*I Wish I Could Be The One 2*
*Put That on Everything: A Henderson Family Novella*
*What's It Gonna Be?*
*Someone Like You*
(2nd Generation Story)
*A Country Hood Christmas with the Hendersons*
*Where Is the Love*
(2nd Generation Story)
*Don't Walk Away*
(2nd Generation Story)

## The Berotte Family Series

*Love On Replay*
*Deeper Than Love*
*Something You Won't Forget*